REA

ALLEN COUNTY PUBLIC LIBRARY

P9-AFS-420

Dear Reader,

Wow! My third book. It's hard to believe that I'm doing what I always wanted to do—writing for Harlequin.

Before this, I used to give advice to my university students—all aspiring writers. On the first day of class I would tell them to give me a good Elvis snarl, growl, then say, "I can do that!" Surprisingly, I got a lot of resistance, but after a couple of minutes of good, solid growling I explained how that pit bull attitude is the start of achieving anything they want. It's all about the attitude.

My friend Toni—who was the inspiration for Lilly, the heroine of this story—had that "can do" attitude. An immigrant from Italy, she went after what she wanted. Her dream was to be an attorney and later, a criminal court judge. She snarled, growled and she did it! Just like Lilly does. And you can do that, too. So let me see that snarl, hear that growl and say, "I can do that!"

I'd like to thank my editor, Wanda Ottewell, for letting me do that.

Wishing you love, laughter and a pit bull attitude!

Dianne Drake

P.S. There was only one time Toni didn't succeed in her "can do" attitude and, sadly, that was in her battle with breast cancer. So, about those monthly breast exams and mammograms—let me hear you say, "I will do that!"

ROMANCE

Disorder in the court!

"Do I get to speak candidly here, or are my rights forfeited the minute I step into your courtroom?" Mike Collier glanced around, shook his head in disdain, then added, "Such as it is."

"By all means, be candid, Mr. Collier. I certainly wouldn't want you leaving my courtroom—*such as it is*—feeling like you didn't receive every opportunity to tell your side of the story before I make my judgment and tack on an extra hundred bucks for that little insult."

Lilly dropped her gaze to the file containing copies of all nineteen tickets, not to peruse it so much as to stop herself from glaring at him.

Of course, she already knew what he looked like—in vivid detail, right down to the lips tattooed on his derriere. Right side, midcheek. A drunken college escapade. And of course she could conjure up that eye candy in minute detail—along with every other Collier detail—even when she wasn't looking at him, which she was trying not to do, especially in court.

Jeez, where was an iceberg when you needed one?

Lilly's Law

Dianne Drake

TORONTO • NEW YORK • LONDON
AMSTERDAM • PARIS • SYDNEY • HAMBURG
STOCKHOLM • ATHENS • TOKYO • MILAN • MADRID
PRAGUE • WARSAW • BUDAPEST • AUCKLAND

If you purchased this book without a cover you should be aware
that this book is stolen property. It was reported as "unsold and
destroyed" to the publisher, and neither the author nor the
publisher has received any payment for this "stripped book."

ISBN 0-373-44190-8

LILLY'S LAW

Copyright © 2004 by JJ Despain.

All rights reserved. Except for use in any review, the reproduction or
utilization of this work in whole or in part in any form by any electronic,
mechanical or other means, now known or hereafter invented, including
xerography, photocopying and recording, or in any information storage
or retrieval system, is forbidden without the written permission of the
publisher, Harlequin Enterprises Limited, 225 Duncan Mill Road,
Don Mills, Ontario, Canada M3B 3K9.

All characters in this book have no existence outside the imagination of
the author and have no relation whatsoever to anyone bearing the same
name or names. They are not even distantly inspired by any individual
known or unknown to the author, and all incidents are pure invention.

This edition published by arrangement with Harlequin Books S.A.

® and TM are trademarks of the publisher. Trademarks indicated with
® are registered in the United States Patent and Trademark Office, the
Canadian Trade Marks Office and in other countries.

Visit us at www.eHarlequin.com

Printed in U.S.A.

ABOUT THE AUTHOR

What's life without a few pets? Dianne Drake and her hubby Joel have seven—four dogs and three cats, all rescued strays. In the few spare minutes her animals grant her, Dianne goes to the Indianapolis Symphony, Indianapolis Colts games and the Indiana Pacers games—can you tell she lives in Indianapolis? And occasionally, she and Joel sneak away and do something really special, like take in a hockey game.

Books by Dianne Drake

HARLEQUIN DUETS
58—THE DOCTOR DILEMMA
106—ISN'T IT ROMANTIC?

Don't miss any of our special offers. Write to us at the following address for information on our newest releases.

Harlequin Reader Service
U.S.: 3010 Walden Ave., P.O. Box 1325, Buffalo, NY 14269
Canadian: P.O. Box 609, Fort Erie, Ont. L2A 5X3

To Toni—an extraordinary judge, an extraordinary woman. The world is a little less bright without you.

And as always, to Joel.

1

Friday morning, and what a way to end the week!

"OH, NO!"

Lilly moaned the words louder than she intended, and his speedy response to what she'd meant to keep under her breath was, "Oh, yes! And I want a change of venue, Your Honor."

"Change of venue, Mr. Collier? You're telling me you want a change of venue?" She was struggling to preserve what was left of her judgely comportment. "This is traffic court, sir. We don't do change of venue here." Even though she'd like to have changed his venue to an iceberg somewhere way up in the Arctic, and personally paid for his one-way ticket to ride.

"But don't I have the right to be tried in an impartial court?"

Big iceberg, she decided. Huge, with lots of freezing-his-butt-off jagged edges. "And you're suggesting, *sir*, that my court isn't impartial?" An iceberg at least as cold as her voice.

Mike Collier stepped away from the rickety wooden podium, which was scarred by fifty years' worth of fist-pounding, pencil-gouging defendants, but he didn't cross the yellow tape on the floor—the tape designating the one thin line separating the Honorable Judge Lilly Malloy from the accumulation of humanity on trial in her courtroom. The warning sign, posted clearly on the wall directly above her head, read Stay Behind the Yellow Line at All Times. Those Who Cross over the Line My Be Subject to a Fine and/or Arrest.

Someone had doodled a happy face with devil horns on it. "What I'm suggesting, *Your Honor*, is that under the circumstances, I don't think you're the right person to hear my case. Wouldn't you agree?"

"Your case, Mr. Collier, is nineteen unpaid parking tickets, pure and simple. And my impartial decision is that you'll pay them to the tune of fifty dollars apiece, plus throw in an extra couple hundred dollars for the use of this courtroom and all of its fine amenities—you know, the paper we used for your subpoena, the expense of having our diligent sheriff hand-deliver it to your office. All according to the statute, by the way. It seems pretty simple to me, *under the circumstances*, since you've already admitted your guilt." She scowled across at him. "You did admit your guilt, didn't you? The statement to the effect that you willfully parked in a posted no-parking zone...that would be a straightforward guilty plea, wouldn't it, Mr. Collier?"

"Straightforward? You call turning my parking space into a no-parking zone straightforward? I call it extenuating circumstances," Mike grumbled. "And I don't believe you're going to set aside your personal feelings to listen to my version."

"Your version," Lilly muttered, shaking her head. She already knew that version—she'd been on the receiving end of one of Mike's *versions* a time or two. "Well, I have a version, too, Mr. Collier. You've stated for the record that you don't believe I'm able to be unbiased here—that I'd allow my personal feelings to interfere with the law." She shot him a caustic smile across her desk—an old, gray, metal office desk hunkering down into the sixty-year-old grooves in the unpolished linoleum floor. Unlike the judges upstairs, who towered above their domains at fine, hand-carved mahogany desks designed for looking down—desks that *belonged* in a courtroom—Lilly sat level with everyone else. Her official judge desk was plainly a castoff appropriate for her castoff court that convened in a damp, dim corner room in the city hall basement. "So let me tack a little something onto *my* version for you. Your first insult to the court is a freebie. My gift to you." Leaning back in her seat, folding her arms across her chest, she continued, "But the next one will cost you, I'm thinking about a hundred bucks an insult, by the book, by the way. Sounds fair, doesn't it?" She glanced over at her court clerk, Tisha Freeman, an early twenty-something who spent more time in the courtroom making eyes at the men than observing the proceedings. Tisha nodded her approval, not that she knew what she was nodding at, then smiled at the biker type seated in the second row who, with ripped-out shirt-sleeves, was flexing his muscles and tattoos for her.

Give me strength, Lilly thought, looking back at Mike. "And as far as your version, Mr. Collier? Other than the fact that you've admitted to parking in the same no-parking zone nineteen times in the past two months, what else is there to say but 'I'm guilty, Your Honor, and I'll be happy to pay the fine'?"

"Do I get to speak candidly here or are my rights forfeited the minute I step into your courtroom?" Mike Collier glanced around, shook his head in distinct disdain, then added, "Such as it is."

"By all means, be candid, Mr. Collier. I certainly wouldn't want you leaving my courtroom—*such as it is*—feeling like you didn't receive every opportunity to tell your side of the story before I make my judgment and tack on an extra hundred bucks for that little insult." She dropped her gaze to the file containing copies of all nineteen tickets, not to peruse what was in it so much as to stop herself from glaring at him. Of course, she already knew what he looked like—in every vivid detail, right down to the lips tattooed on his derriere. Right side, midcheek. A drunken college escapade—he'd passed out at a frat party and his frat brothers had hauled him to the nearest tattoo parlor. Then voilà! Big red lips, half the size of her fist. And of course, she could conjure up that eye candy in minute detail—along with every other Collier detail—even when she wasn't looking at him, which she was trying not to do, especially in court. *Geez, where's an iceberg when you need one?* And if she could have found a judge pro tem for the morning session, she would have gladly relinquished the helm.

She was the judge pro tem in traffic court, though. A perpetual temporary, because she hadn't lived in Whittier long enough to qualify for the permanent job. But she would be crowned the regular queen of traffic court after a year there. And she wanted that to happen. Nobody liked the job, nobody wanted it and hardly anybody outside the janitor and a few assorted court employees ever wandered down into the judicial netherworld she called her work space, even though her department brought in a big chunk of the city budget, or so she'd been told when she'd dotted her i's and crossed her t's on the contract.

So unless she had two broken legs and amnesia, nobody *but nobody* would be sitting in for her, not even for a few minutes. But that was okay because she actually liked her job.

Speeding tickets, parking tickets—everyone had an excuse for doing something wrong.

"Didn't see the sign, Your Honor."

"I had to go to the bathroom, Your Honor."

"Thirty? I thought that was eighty, Your Honor."

"I only left my car there for two minutes, Your Honor."

"I wasn't parked that far up on the sidewalk, Your Honor."

Which was why Lilly got the traffic court job in the first place—nobody else wanted to hear the same ol', same ol' excuses. Low status, low regard, low pay. And literally the lowest room in the courthouse. But it was *her* low status, *her* low regard, *her* low pay and *her* lowest room in the courthouse. *All hers!*

So when she'd found out that the Mike Collier on her

docket for the day was *her* Mike Collier—the one man in the whole wide world she never, ever wanted to see again—she'd elected to tough it out instead of going upstairs and panhandling in the halls for another judge since, short of judicial hijacking, no one would do it anyway. Meaning, it was up to her to try Mike, convict him if he was guilty—she hoped he was, *boy, did she hope he was*—and then sentence him, the fun part! Too bad iceberg exile wasn't an option. But on the bright side, the law book she was going to throw at him was a big one.

"Like I said, the city put a no-parking zone almost directly in front of my office, Your Honor, and the next closest place for me to park is a block away—in the paid public parking. I'm always coming and going, chasing down stories and whatever, and parking so far away is damn inconvenient. Wastes a lot of my time. Then in any bad weather, rain, snow... No way I'm going to walk that. Plus sixty bucks a month for a parking permit is ridiculous, especially when I had *free* parking right outside my door until two months ago, when the mayor's cousin set up a flower shop right next to me and complained, *apparently to the right people—or person—as it turned out*, that my parking spot obstructed a clear view of her shop. In my opinion, we're talking conspiracy here, especially since I ran an editorial against the mayor just a couple of weeks before that and I'm sure this no-parking thing is his way of repaying me, since my paper isn't backing him in the next election. Good old-fashioned political harassment for choosing to exercise my right of free speech, that's what it is." Mike took a deep breath and grinned at Lilly. "I rest my case, Your Honor." Then he winked.

Or did he? She wasn't sure. She looked up at the ceiling tile, noting the pattern of yellow staining on it, then silently begged, *Please don't let* that *start again*. But it already had—little voices, little gestures, more little voices—all things that happened, or didn't happen, only when she was around Mike.

Twelve yellowed ceiling tiles later, without a solution to the thing she grudgingly called *the thing*, Lilly wrenched her attention back to Mike's case. He was sooo cool...sooo calculated...sooo relaxed about it. Working her. That's what he was doing. Working her, and she had to give credit where it was due. He did it brilliantly. The way he shoved his hands into his khakis—as though this was a casual meeting between two friends, not a court of law...*her* court of law. Smiling, grinning, winking...or not. It irritated her. *He* irritated her, and the only transient panacea was an effigy of Mike swinging a pickax on a rock pile. Good image; she liked it a lot. Suddenly he was shirtless and glistening with sweat—like she needed that distraction. So she made a hasty retreat back to Mike's iceberg, since in a parka he wasn't nearly so dangerous. Then...oh, no, not that! The parka was slipping off. Zipper sliding down, sleeve slithering off, and underneath...

Mike cleared his throat. "I said I rest my case, Your Honor."

He didn't have anything on under that parka, but thank the gods of the Northern ice cap that his voice dragged her back into the courtroom. "Good old-fashioned political harassment, is that what you said, Mr. Collier? A parking conspiracy? Are you sure you want that particular accusation to go down on the record with your name attached to it? I mean, I know you've spent your career chasing down so-called conspiracies, but this seems rather melodramatic even for you, don't you think?"

"For the record, *Your Honor*, I shouldn't have to suffer the unfair, and I might add unjust, consequences of the mayor's cousin's inability to attract customers. Nor should I be forced to pay the penalty you're imposing on me for using one lousy parking space that's rightfully mine to begin with."

"Then I'd suggest you take it up with the city, Mr. Collier.

My only job is to hear your case—the one about nineteen un-paid parking tickets—and render a guilty verdict...if you're guilty," she added hastily. "Which apparently you are, since you've admitted to your crime."

"Crime?" Forgetting the yellow line, Mike crossed over it and started to amble toward her desk. One step, two steps. Taunting...taunting. "Come on, Lilly. Give me a break here." Three steps, four. Taunting...taunting. "Don't let a couple of tickets..." Five steps, six steps. Taunting...tempting, er, taunt-ing.

Lilly banged the gavel so hard on its wooden block it woke the old man snoozing in the back corner of the room, who jolted up out of his seat bug-eyed and sputtering, "I didn't do it!" Then, seeing that it wasn't his turn in front of the judge, he sank back into his chair and shut his eyes to try and catch the remains of his nap.

"Get back, Mr. Collier," Lilly ordered, pointing to the line. She watched him take a good, hard look at his thirty-six-inch encroachment into the wrong side of "authorized" turf, then dig his heels in, so to speak. That little act of Michael Collier defiance made her want to dig a little something into him—maybe her heels, maybe a nice sharp jail sentence. "And add another two hundred dollars to the court's tab while you're at it," she stated, raising her eyebrows in distinct nonchalance even though they didn't show above the black rims of her oversize glasses.

But Mike didn't budge. Didn't blink, didn't flinch. None of that. He simply reached deep into his bag of play-acting pre-texts, the ones she'd seen him use so many times before, and came up with a colorful palette of supplication and woe. "Fair's fair, Your Honor, and what the city's doing to me isn't fair. I'm just a hardworking businessman trying to run my business. I'm not asking for special favors or unjustified con-sideration here—just what's mine...my right to park in my parking spot. That's all." He twisted around, playing to the crowd. "How would these good folk like to go to work one day and find a No Parking sign at their place of employment? Or better yet, in their driveway when they get home? It's the same thing, Your Honor. I work there, I live there. I just can't park there."

As if on cue, a low rumble of agreement ran through the crowd. Solidarity with the masses. He'd claimed the public support, something he was so good at, Lilly recalled. Then he turned back to her, still supplicating and woeful, but with a smidge of martyred-for-the-cause now plastered on his face, and continued, "I'm a busy man, Judge. Making me run half way through town to get my car is a travesty of justice." Then the cool, calculated grin sneaked back as a nod of agreement rippled through the crowd like the wave at a football game. "It's the principle of the thing."

Was he baiting her? she wondered. If anyone knew how to bait, it was Mike Collier. Or maybe he thought she'd simply throw this case out on account of their sleeping together a time or two or ten had earned him the special privileges he claimed he didn't want. But boy, was he wrong about that one. If anything, her big ol' blunder in judgment way back when earned him the judge's fullest contempt. "I said get back, Mr. Collier," she repeated, still trying to sound professional, not reactionary—which she was, right down to her phalanges, when it came to all matters with Mike Collier. Had been for years, and nothing, not even having him in her courtroom, was going to change that. But he wasn't going to see it. Neither was the crowd. Amazing what the black robe hid. And didn't hide, she thought, glaring at him.

"You know it isn't fair, Your Honor," Mike continued, unfazed by her warning. "And I'm betting you'd be pretty angry if they took away your parking spot and you had to walk a block to get to work."

Actually, she *did* walk a block to work because there were no parking spots left in the municipal lot. The janitors had spots, the cafeteria attendants had spots, but not the traffic court judge, and she was obliged to pay that sixty bucks a month Mike didn't want to pay, and park in the very same public parking lot Mike was complaining about. "Get back," she exclaimed, banging her gavel again. "This is the last time I'm warning you, sir. Stand back or face the consequences." Well, maybe not a cold, hard iceberg, but a big chunk of cold, hard cash.

Mike did quit speaking in that instant, but he held his ground. Folding his arms resolutely across his chest, he stayed on Lilly's side of the yellow line, still smiling at her. And she knew that smile. *Oh, how she knew that smile.* It was a cross between something downright pigheaded and a testy I double-dare you. And she'd been on the receiving end of it more than once—never emerging a victor from the war, though. Of course, that was then, and this was today. And today was beginning to feel *so good* all of a sudden. In fact, this might just turn out to be the best day she'd had in any Mike Collier dealings outside the bedroom...the garage...that one time on the roof....

Suddenly, the smile was all Lilly's. "And as of right now, your tally comes to $1,350, Mr. Collier. Payable by cash, check or money order to the court clerk on your way out the door."

Mike leveled his sparkling blue eyes on Lilly's jade-greens and shook his head. "Like I said before, it's a matter of principle, Your Honor. I'm the one who's been wronged here. Besides, I'm broke. Couldn't pay the fine even if I wanted to, which I don't." To prove his point, he turned his front pants pockets inside out, then shrugged. "See? Nothing there. Not even enough money to plug the meter outside, which means you'll probably be adding another parking ticket to the official complaint, and I can't afford to pay that one, either."

And you think this is a game. Well, Mike, Lilly's not the same old Lilly you used to know and she's not backing down. "I'm only the judge here, Mr. Collier. Sworn to do my duty and uphold the law. And I find that you're guilty of breaking the no-parking law—nineteen times. If you want to challenge that law, then be my guest. Challenge away. But this isn't the time or place, and you don't get a free pass out of my court because you think your matter of principle exempts you from anything. It doesn't, sir. Neither does being broke. The fact remains that the area in front of your office is designated as a no-parking zone and you have continued to park there regardless. You chose to take the risk and you got caught, so you pay. That's the law as it stands, and my verdict, accordingly. Now, step back or the bailiff will *assist* you over to the defendant's podium. Then, as I said before, see the clerk about settling your account with the court. And we do accept weekly payments because—" she cast him a victorious smile "—we aim to please."

For an instant Mike looked stricken—well, almost. For him it was stricken, and that was the biggest victory. Overall, Lilly was satisfied with the patience she was exercising in his case. God knows, he didn't deserve it, but she wasn't about to let him see how much she wanted to just hurl the gavel at him and do some good old cathartic screaming. But that's what he expected from her, wanted from her, was trying to goad her into. And actually, that's what she'd done on account of him a time or two, pretty much without reaction from him. But now, that little flinch of chagrin she evoked, the one she saw for just that split second...it was all the reaction she needed. Lilly—one. Mike—zero.

Mike hadn't changed, she thought, waiting for him to actually step back, which he wasn't doing with any great haste. Hadn't changed in attitude, or in physical appearance, either. Tall, nice muscles, over-the-collar sandy-brown hair, a little shaggy and mussed... Her mind drifted to the tattoo and she shook her head to clear away the image. How long had it been? A year since the last time they'd met? Five years since the first time? *And look at him now. Just standing there, holding his ground as if he owns the court, as if there hasn't been a lot of water under our bridge. A positive deluge!* Stifling an impatient sigh, Lilly toughened her stare. She didn't need another go-round with Mike Collier. The first time should have been enough to teach her to stay away, and the second time absolutely did. And now, today—right here—she wasn't going to be affected by him, not in the least. Cold, leery, impervious...she was counting the ways she'd promised herself she'd greet Mike should they ever cross paths again. In addition, every single one of those resolutions bottom lined at *no way, no how,* and the sooner she got him out of her courtroom, the sooner *no way, no how* could get back on track, because it sure as hell was fighting to slip.

So keeping with her own personal decree, Lilly lowered her glasses, then frowned over the top of them at him. No mistaking her frown, she thought. Even Mike wouldn't misconstrue the meaning. "Get out of here now, Mr. Collier. Last warning. You're wasting the court's time." Her time, too. But it was so good to hide behind the power of the court.

"Like I said, I won't pay it," he said, shrugging indifferently. "And I want to appeal your decision."

"Appeal a parking ticket? Nobody appeals parking tickets, especially after they've already admitted guilt," she remarked, tilting her head down just a little farther so her stare over the top of her glasses was even more pronounced. She didn't need them, not even for reading. Clear glass all the way. She sure liked their effect, though. Thought they gave her a bit of an austere look—black glasses, black robe, black gavel...red hair. And that was the problem. Hair red and wild—barely tameable even when pulled into a knot at the back of her neck—plus that splash of freckles across her nose... Definitely not the image of a judge, at least not the image *she* had of one, so she did what she could to achieve the stern judicial look, including the monster-size glasses.

"So let's get this straight, Your Honor. You're denying me

my legal rights?" Mike raised his head and looked down his nose at her. "Is that what you're doing? Taking away my inalienable rights?"

"Inalienable rights, Mr. Collier, have nothing to do with your parking tickets." Lilly took her eyes off Mike long enough to nod at her bailiff, Pete Walker, a small, near-retirement-age man who was simply serving out his last year of employment in an easy, low-profile job. Leaning on the wall under the exit sign, Pete moved his hand immediately to his gun holster, unsnapping it. Seeing that he was ready, Lilly continued her ocular duel with Mike, her over-the-rim glare meeting his down-the-nose stare. "There are other people here, waiting their turn to be heard, you know. Plus, you're getting on my nerves. So I'm giving you thirty seconds to comply." She raised her arm, looked at her wristwatch and started counting down the seconds. "Which I believe is generous, under the circumstances." *Better than you deserve.*

"Thirty seconds, then what, Your Honor?"

She smiled at him—a practiced, patient smile that gave away nothing. Then she glanced at her watch again. "Twenty seconds."

Mike merely stared back.

"Ten seconds, Mr. Collier."

And he kept on staring.

"Five."

Then he started to tap his right foot...a slow, meticulous rhythm that didn't break its meter by a fraction.

Finally, bingo! "Pete..." Lilly said, waving him over.

Lilly's call to her bailiff hushed the crowd, and Pete Walker snapped to attention, pulling the handcuffs from his belt. He studied them for a second since, in his nine months as bailiff, this was the first time they'd ever been off his belt. When he was satisfied that he remembered how to use them, he marched straight to Mike, each and every one of his footsteps clicking in sharp military precision on the floor. "You have the right to remain silent," he said on approach.

"Lilly, you've got to be kidding," Mike exclaimed, seeming genuinely surprised. "You're not really going to do this to me, are you?"

"This is Friday, Mr. Collier. Consider yourself a guest of the city jail until Monday morning at nine, at which time we'll resume this conversation. And maybe by then you'll be persuaded to see it my way. Not that you really have a choice, because *it is* my way in my courtroom—such as it is. And that fine...let's say we make it an even two thousand just on account of—" Lilly removed her glasses and looked directly at him "—I can." Then she put them back on.

"Honest to God, I really think you'd do it, wouldn't you?" Mike exclaimed. "You'd really throw me in jail. Over parking tickets. Come on, Lilly, give me a break here."

"Please turn around and hold your hands behind your back, Mr. Collier," Pete instructed, his voice on the verge of quivering, since this was, after all, the first time he'd ever arrested anyone. "Anything you say can and will be used against you in a court of law. You have the right to an attorney and if you can't afford one..." Mike, at six foot three inches, towered over Pete by a head and a half as he submitted to the man's cuffs. And Pete, whose hands were shaking, fumbled with the latch until the cuffs slipped from his grip and hit the floor. A congenial-looking seventyish woman, decked in floral capri pants and a white straw hat, picked up the cuffs and winked when she handed them back to Pete.

"You do know that I own the newspaper, don't you?" Mike asked, spinning back around to face Lilly. His hands still behind him, he inched forward to allow Pete sufficient room to continue the protracted cuffing ordeal.

"Boy, do I know," she snapped. "And I certainly hope that's not intended as a threat, because if it is...if you intend to use the power of the press to—"

"A news item, Your Honor," Mike interrupted, a thin edge of anger finally sounding in his voice. "Not a threat."

It never was a threat, she recalled. Her last year of law school, she had been at the top of her class with some great career prospects lining up for her future. Mike was working on his postgraduate degree at the time, teaching at the university and overseeing the campus paper. And she'd made that ominous mistake of kicking their relationship up a few notches. A whopper, in retrospect, and she really had liked him back then. Maybe even a little more than like...and after one great week of their relationship kicking into even newer and better notches every single day, he'd gone and written an article proclaiming a campus plagiarism epidemic. Names were named. Hers was at the top of the list—Mike's list.

Sure, she *had* purchased a plagiarized paper, but she was writing a thesis on how easy the process was, with an emphasis on the legal implications. But Mike Collier, superjournalist in his own bent estimation, hadn't asked her any questions about it. He'd simply snooped for his scoop in her research notes because, of all the dumb things, *she'd trusted him!* Meaning she didn't bother hiding her research from him before they adjourned to the boudoir, silly Lilly. And that on the day they'd achieved the most unbelievable notch ever. Of course, Mike's discovery netted him a front page splash, not only in the school paper, but the *real* newspaper as well. The result—she was expelled from law school. One tidy, speedy, out the door and don't come back.

But she did go back, a full semester later, after a whole string of appeals and some utterly pitiful begging. To his credit, Mike did make an appearance on her behalf, thankfully leaving out the part that he'd done his snooping on his way to the kitchen to satisfy some after-sex munchies while she was still in bed basking in the afterglow. No matter, because the damage to her reputation was already done, leaving her in the bottom slot of her class ranking instead of the top, where she'd been before Mike. Years to build a reputation, minutes to destroy it—Lilly was placed on probation until she graduated, constantly the object of watchful, if not distrustful, speculation by the powers that were. Not an auspicious ending to her school days, even though she *was* absolved of the charges. But after that, the jobs weren't forthcoming. The ones already offered backed out. No more pick and choose. Instead, she was forced to take whatever she could get, and pickings were slim. All because of Mike Collier's little snoop after sex.

Consequentially, Lilly was uniquely aware of what one of Mike's "news items" could do, and had done to her. And she was also aware of how he procured those news items. "Monday morning, Mr. Collier. Have a nice weekend."

Lilly banged her gavel and Pete led Mike out of the room. At the edge of the door though, Mike turned back around to face her briefly and he...

Lilly blinked. Was that another wink?

2

No Friday afternoon get-out-of-jail-free cards allowed

MIKE DUMPED HIS wristwatch and car keys into the plastic box bearing his official prisoner number, then absently searched his empty pockets for change. "I don't suppose you'll let me keep my cell phone, will you?" he asked, pulling it off his belt, which he was also forced to surrender.

Juanita Lane, a humorless, sixty-something jail matron who had to look up to see a full five feet tall, didn't even glance over from the property list she was dutifully recording when she boomed, "No cell phone, no personal property. Hand over your shoelaces, please." Dripping wet she might have weighed ninety pounds, and with spiked, champagne-colored hair and big purple-rimmed glasses clashing with her khaki-colored uniform blouse, she wasn't the typical image of cop that came to Mike's mind. But when she glared at him through those glasses, patted the pistol on her hip and barked, "Do it now, please!" he knew that the weapon was there for more than show. So he promptly gave up the phone and bent to unlace his rip-off Nikes. When he'd complied with every item on Juanita's official confiscation list, he automatically put his hands behind his back to be recuffed for the fifty-foot walk into the next room, where he would be uncuffed again, stripped, disinfected, showered and garbed in the very trendy, bright orange jail jumpsuit.

"So when do I get a phone call?" he asked, as Juanita handed him off to Cal Gekas, a Humpty-Dumpty-ish burly man with abundant hair growing in thick patches every-where except on his head.

"You're the one who's here from traffic court, aren't you?" Cal asked, handing Mike a plastic bag for his clothing. "That's a new one. Parking tickets." He chuckled. "And I thought I'd about seen it all. Just goes to show ya, doesn't it?"

Mike was waiting to hear what it was that went to show him, but when Cal didn't continue, he simply nodded. "Cal, old buddy. Think you could you do me a favor here and turn around while I undress?"

Cal shook his head. "Gotta watch. Department policy."

"Then I'm hoping you're a married man, Cal."

"Twenty years, three kids." He grinned. "And if you're un-comfortable, *you* can turn around so you don't have to watch me watching you."

"Good idea." Mike shook his head, spun around and dropped his khakis. "Can I keep the shorts?"

"After the shower."

"This isn't negotiable? I mean, it's a damn parking ticket, Cal. I didn't rob a convenience store or mug a little old lady for her social security check."

Cal shrugged. "Hey, I'm giving you the benefit of the doubt on the cavity search, but that's all I can do for you." He paused, then chuckled again. "Damn. A parking ticket. Not even speeding. I heard that new judge was a tough one, but don't this just beat all."

Mike nodded. "It sure does." And he stepped out of his briefs and into the footbath of disinfectant, then on into the shower. "You don't happen to have any soap-on-a-rope handy, do you?"

Ten minutes later, showered and dressed, Mike was es-corted through fingerprinting, then lined up in front of a cam-era to have that very stylish rendition of him captured for posterity—orange clothes, washed-out face, glazed eyes, black numbers on a strip of cardboard held up to midchest for proud display. "Think I could get a copy of that for my Christmas cards?" he asked, following Cal through a long gray hall filled, predominantly, with empty cells. At the end they met up with the jailer du jour, Roger Jackson, who, as it turned out, also worked as a crime-beat stringer on Mike's very own *Journal*. He'd taken pity on Mike and assigned him to a cell for one, far, far away from the madding jail population, which today was poor old Bert Ford, who'd had one too many drinks the night before and selected Mrs. Clooney's prize-winning rose garden as the place to relieve his bladder on his stagger home from the pub, and made the mistake of losing his balance in the process, pants down. Which was where Mrs. Clooney had found him this morning. The rest was a matter of public record, including a few thorny scratches in all the wrong places. And poor Bert was still sleeping it off, Mike noted as he walked by him. Sleeping, and probably oblivious to the fact that his brief encounter with the great red American Beauty would be his last dalliance with public intoxication, or Mrs. Clooney's roses, for quite a while.

And so at two in the afternoon, on a hot, humid August Friday, Mike rolled the thin mattress issued to him onto the creaky metal coils of his cot, tossed his single pillow on top and plopped down in his cell for the weekend. "I still didn't get to make my call," he shouted to Roger, who was busy writing up the story of Mike's arrest for the morning edition.

"Okay, as soon as I finish this. I'm on deadline." His hearty laugh clanged through the empty jail. Roger was a friendly cop, always ready with a smile. With a great marriage, great family, Roger had stability, something Mike had never found a place for in his life, but something he was beginning to envy. And he could almost see himself having that with Lilly.... Well, almost, since Lilly would have a say in that and he knew exactly what her "say" would be—*I'd rather be staked to an anthill.*

"Got a tough boss," Roger continued. "But fair. So fair, in

fact, that after he reads this headliner he won't demote me to obituaries. Might even give me a raise." Half an hour later, after Roger hit the Send button and his first-ever front-page piece was winging its way through cyberspace to the newspaper office two blocks away, he finally took Mike down the hall to the public phone. "Use your call wisely. We're pretty strict on jail regulations around here and you might not get another one." He laughed, heading into the break room, leaving Mike uncuffed and unattended. "And don't escape," he called back. "Care for some coffee?"

The number Mike meant to call was burned into his brain, even though he'd never used it before. As he waited for the first ring, he wondered why he was even bothering. She'd hang up when she heard his voice. Or tack another couple of days on to his sentence for some kind of trumped-up harassment. But he owed her this one. Make the call, then be done with it, and her.

Yeah, like he could ever be done with Lilly Malloy.

"Hello," a voice said from the other end.

"Lilly?" Mike asked.

"You've reached the voice mail of Judge Lillianne Malloy. Please leave your name, phone number and a brief message, and I'll return the call as soon as I can. Have a nice day." *Beep*.

"Have a nice day like hell.... Look, Lilly. I need to see you. I can't go into it on the phone...you know where I am, where I'll be until Monday morning. And it's important. Hell, this was a stupid idea. I should have called my attorney instead of you. Lilly, I know that the situation between us isn't the best, but—"

Beep.

"Hell."

"Arms behind your back, Mike," Roger said, setting the coffee on the desk, then taking his handcuffs off his belt. "Sorry, but it's the rules. You like it black, no sugar, right?"

"You're not going to make me strip again, are you?" Mike

growled, turning around and gritting his teeth when the cuffs went on. They didn't hurt, but he sure didn't like the thought of what they signified. Tried, convicted, sentenced. Prisoner. As a journalist, going to jail on principle such as not revealing a source or being in the wrong place at the wrong time to get the right story, now, *that* was honorable. It made a statement about ethics and principles and high moral integrity. But being nabbed for parking in the wrong place? The only statement coming from that was dud, flop, washout, bomb, a big bust. "No sugar, but some whiskey would be good. In fact, skip the coffee. Just bring on the whiskey."

"Sure wish I could Mike, but..."

"I know. You've got rules." When he'd learned he was going to Lilly's court, he'd hoped that after all this time she was over the bad history between them. *Bad, bad history!* Forgive and forget, or just forget. Yeah, and wasn't that just being pointless and optimistic after what he'd done to her? Thank God parking tickets weren't a hanging offense.

First time with Lilly he'd been canned over the mix-up, and sure, he'd deserved it. One slight error in judgment and his job was out the door along with his postgrad degree. But she *did* have that damned bought-and-paid-for paper sitting right out on her desk for anybody to see who cared to look.

Second time...well, he shook his head over that one. What were the odds she'd turn up on the receiving end of another of his investigations? She'd been innocent that time, too. In fact, he'd never even connected her to that story—probably because she *wasn't* connected, not directly, anyway. But her law firm epitomized that notoriously fictitious Dewey, Cheatham and Howe. They'd done some book cooking, trust-fund skimming, creative billing, so on and so on. And even though Lilly was only a contract employee, not a real member of the firm—meaning she'd never gotten near the trusts, never did any billing, hardly ever got out of the research library—she'd been swept into the sting along with everybody else. Swept, cuffed and locked up tight.

And he'd never forget the look on her face that day when they shoved her, handcuffed and horrified, through the lobby, in front of friends and co-workers. On her way out of the building she still hadn't known who was responsible for the bust, but as the police hustled her past him and their eyes met briefly, she'd realized who'd done that to her. That look of betrayal in her eyes had punched him in the gut, and the heart, because he knew she'd trusted him—she'd put everything else behind her and trusted him.

If ever there was a defining moment in a life, that was his.

Lilly had been released hours later, thanks to one of the partners, who'd mustered enough integrity to un-implicate her. Afterward, Mike had sent her flowers, written a dozen contrite e-apologies and printed the damned retraction she'd demanded in place of suing him. Granted, it ran on page seven, when the picture of her being arrested was a first-page classic. But apparently that make-good hadn't done the trick. Problem was, he wasn't sure even sending him up the river now, if only for a weekend, would be enough to satisfy her yet. Lilly was clearly holding on to some surplus rage after all this time. And she deserved to. But he'd sure been hoping it wouldn't trickle into this little matter. "So should I drop my drawers again, Mike?" he asked, his voice on the verge of acceptance, since there was no other choice but to accept his fate for the next three days. If there was one thing he knew for sure about Lilly, she wouldn't give in. Once she'd made up her mind, nothing changed it.

Smiling, Roger shook his head. "Nope, not another strip search, unless you insist. But if you want, I'll call Jimmy and let him know where you are. Maybe he can figure out what to do—how to get you out of here or something." Roger chuckled as he led Mike down the gray hall to his home-away-from-home for the next few days. "Or at least he can bring you a pizza for supper. He's good for that much, I'll bet." Jimmy Farrell, the *Journal*'s lawyer on retainer, had finally passed his bar exam six months earlier, after four tries. And he was really cheap to hire, which was the cardinal circumstance surrounding Jimmy's status at the newspaper. No one in Whittier particularly embraced Jimmy for their legal affairs, since he'd grown up there and had a reputation for off-centered intelligence and out-on-a-limb common sense. But he'd muddled through law school somehow, surprised everyone when he finally passed the bar exam, and optimistically hung out his shingle to practice. So far, his clients were only court-appointed, those who couldn't afford their own attorney, and he represented them adequately. No one complained too much, because no one had great expectations of Jimmy.

The day he'd approached Mike to represent the *Journal*, the offer had been so ridiculous Mike didn't have the heart to turn him down. "Fifty dollars a month, Mike, will keep me on retainer for the paper." Mike knew it would also pay the electric bill in Jimmy's office slash apartment. "Most reputable papers keep a lawyer on retainer, and this is your chance."

More out of charity than anything else, Mike had agreed, and from that day on, three months now, the *Journal* had been duly, if not well, represented. And today's pizza delivery would mark Jimmy's first official appearance on the paper's behalf. "Lilly's not letting me out of here, Roger. No way in hell. So tell Jimmy I like pepperoni and sausage. Hold the onions."

"Lilly?" Roger interrupted. "You mean Judge Malloy? That Lilly?"

Mike cringed. Her Honor Judge Lillianne Malloy wasn't the image of the Lilly Malloy that was in his mind when he'd discovered she'd been hired for traffic court in Whittier. That Lilly was still the one he'd...well, suffice it to say there had been some nice dreams of her from time to time. Gorgeous, responsive, just a little unsure. Always eager. But when he'd sneaked into the back of the courtroom a couple of times to watch her work, the Lilly he observed was so much more than he ever expected from her. Still gorgeous beyond reason, tall, round in all the right places, soft—even though her sexier-than-hell hair was pulled severely back and half of her face was covered by ridiculously large glasses—she now possessed confidence—self-assurance like he'd never before seen in her. And it showed in her movements, in her voice, and especially in that tangy smile she'd used on him earlier—the one meant to castigate him, but which had the opposite effect. All in all, Lilly wore her judicial robe well, and in spite of everything, he was happy for her. But she should have done so much better than that moldering little traffic court in a dark basement corner, and Mike knew he owned a big part of the responsibility for that lesser destiny—lesser than she deserved. "Yeah, Judge Lillianne Malloy. We go back a ways and she's not going to go easy on me for old times' sake. Not in this lifetime, anyway."

"Bad history, I'm guessing?"

Mike winced. "Defining it as *bad* is pretty damn optimistic. The list of how I've done that lady wrong...well, it fills up both sides of the page in small print, that's how bad it is."

Roger let out a low whistle while closing the cell door behind Mike. "Well, with your current run of parking tickets, I'd say you're in for some real big trouble, my friend. And that judge—your friend Lilly—she has a tough reputation, if you know what I mean. She's strictly by the book and nobody gets the soft end of her gavel. I understand she's sentencing them right and left in her court." He slipped a copy of his Mike Gets Busted story through the bars to his boss, then stepped back. "I really hate leaving you here like this, but, well..." He shrugged. "Anything I can get you before I go home?"

Mike shook his head, dropped down on his cot and re-signed himself to the lumps and bumps. The only good thing that could be said for the long weekend ahead was that he'd be able to catch up on some much-needed sleep. Tight money at the *Journal* these days meant he had a staff too small to run the paper, which meant he wore lots of hats, which meant he worked lots of hours. And all that meant he never got away from his job, not even here, in jail. So maybe this imposed furlough was a good thing. Sleep, perchance to...to what? Dream of Lilly? Not a chance in hell.

Not a chance in hell on the sleep, either, he discovered almost immediately. Sure, he shut his eyes and tried to clear his head, but his to-do list replaced the mental void he'd hoped to achieve, with all the to-dos that wouldn't be getting done for the next two days trying to pound their way to the forefront of his mind lest he might forget about them. Which he never did. Edit the piece about the new thrill ride inspection regulations at the county fair; cover the high school preseason football game and get a statement from the coach; interview Mayor Lowell Tannenbaum for whatever Mayor Tannentwit wanted to be interviewed about this week. Certainly not the type-A assignments Mike had gone after in Indianapolis, not even close. But he'd been a different kind of journalist back then. And not the kind he'd set out to be at the beginning. That realization had hit him the day he'd watched the cops handcuff Lilly and cart her off to jail.

Two weeks after that awful day he'd given up journalism as he'd come to know and practice it, and had bought his struggling hometown newspaper. And after that, life was good...poorer than dirt, but good. Sure, he missed some of the big-city excitement. Missed a lot of it, actually. There was no substitute for the adrenaline buzz that came when he broke a huge story or saw his byline tacked on to a red-letter article. But that was then, and now he owned a small daily paper where the biggest story this week would be about its owner sitting in jail over a few stupid unpaid parking tickets.

Them's the breaks, he thought, resigning himself to his short-term fate. Mike shut his eyes once again and tried to tackle that mental to-do list, but thoughts of Lilly crowded it out. Lilly in her robe, out of her robe, hair up, hair down, with glasses, without glasses, with clothes, without clothes...without clothes... without clothes....

Dear God, what was he going to do about Lilly, anyway?

What a miserable way to end a perfectly bad Friday!

"No, I DIDN'T KNOW he owned the newspaper here. Do you think I would have accepted the job if I'd known there was a chance I'd run into him?" Lilly paced barefooted across the black-and-white-checkered linoleum floor in the circa 1935 kitchen, scrunching her cell phone to her ear and shaking a bottle of apple juice. "Sure, I saw the name on my docket, but it's a pretty common name, you'll have to admit, so I didn't think much about it. I mean, who would have ever guessed that Mike Collier—*the* Mike Collier...*my* Mike Collier— would end up at a newspaper here in Whittier? The town's what? Fifty thousand people, tops? The Mike I've known and despised would have never settled in a place like this. Not enough people here to railroad, not enough action or sensationalism, which is what he thrives on."

"So are you gonna stay?" Rachel Perkins asked. "Even with Mike there?" Rachel was Lilly's best friend, the one she'd met on the first day of first grade and spent some part of almost every day with, in one way or another, ever since. "And if you do stay, am I gonna have to come to Whittier to make sure you don't you-know-what again with Mike? Because you know how you are about him." She laughed. "And I know how you are about him even if you won't admit it, which you won't. And I'm betting doing you-know-what with you-know-who has been on your mind a time or two already. Hasn't it?"

"No," Lilly snapped. She opened the fridge and pulled out a bowl of last night's leftover tuna noodle casserole and sniffed it just to be sure. "How I used to be isn't how I am now. The first time between Mike and me was, well..." She popped the casserole in the microwave oven and set the timer for a minute. "Lust," she admitted. "I was twenty-two and stupid, and he was twenty-four and *convincing*."

"Convincing, Lil? You mean drop-dead, don't you? 'Cause he was, and you almost did drop dead every time he looked at you. Remember? And I'm betting he still is drop-dead, maybe even more than he used to be. Is he?"

"Well, he *was* pretty cute, and I suppose you could say he still is, in an older sort of way," Lilly admitted grudgingly. Pretty cute, pretty sexy—actually the sexiest thing she'd ever met in her life. Then and now. And back then all he'd had to do was crook his finger and she'd gone running. Good thing she'd taken off those track shoes the second time they'd... Yeah, yeah. Another big mistake, second time around. But the shoes were off now for sure.

"Pretty cute?" Rachel asked. "It's pheromones, Lil. He emits them and you can't control yourself. You just sniff them right in, you know that. And if you ask me, you always liked sniffing them in," she said. "And yeah, I know it wasn't love, at least that's what you told me a billion times. But if it wasn't love, it was certainly something like it, and I voted for love back then. Still do."

The microwave dinged and Lilly popped open the door. Her leftovers were steamy, so she let them sit while she trudged over to the fridge for... She opened the door, looked for and found the rest of a salad left over from the night before. If it wasn't wilted beyond recognition, it would suffice as the remainder of her dinner. If it was wilted, she'd eat crackers. "It was a mistake, okay? A mistake and I learned my lesson, especially the second time. I mean, we had a couple of drinks and yes, I suppose I was still attracted to him—*then, not now*. But that was a long time ago."

"And you've gone out with how many men since a long time ago?"

Lilly plunked the salad down on the kitchen table and returned to the microwave for her tuna noodle. "Dozens," she lied. "I just forgot to tell you."

"Well, girlfriend, you don't lie about that any better than you lie to yourself about Mike. And I'm betting you're already getting that same old tingly *thing* for him like you used to."

"Am not."

"Sweetie, tell yourself anything you want. But I know the truth and I say go for it. Most people don't get a third chance."

"The only thing I'm going for is my tuna casserole, which is getting cold."

Rachel issued a deliberate huff of futility into the phone, one meant to be heard across the fifty miles between them, and one Lilly knew well. Then she did it a second time for effect.

"Knock it off, Rach," Lilly grumbled. "I'm fine, dandy. Impervious."

"School doesn't start for a couple weeks, Lil. I've got all my lesson plans together for the first semester, so I'm free to come chaperon you two, or nag or keep you out of the line of his pheromones, if that's what you intend on doing."

"I don't need you to chaperon, *or nag*," Lilly stated flatly. "I'm fine."

"I'd give you my opinion of what you really are, but you'd hang up. So I'm going to shut up and let you go eat. Just watch out for the pheromones, if that's what you really want, and those are my last words on the subject of Mike Collier. Now I'm going to sit in a dark corner and wonder why I don't have somebody in my life who's as crazy about me as he is about you." Before Lilly had a chance at a comeback, Rachel had clicked off.

Lilly's casserole was barely warm by the time she got around to it, and as she speared a chunk of celery, she punched into her voice mail. "This is your mother—" as if she didn't recognize her mother's voice "—calling to remind you not to forget to send something for Aunt Mary's birthday next week. Kisses, sweetie." *Beep.* "If you're in the market for replacement windows, call—" *Beep.* "Lilly, how about stopping by Saturday evening for drinks and hors d'oeuvres. I'm having a few people over around seven." That from Ezra Kessler, her former law school professor and the person who'd recommended her for the pro tem job. *Beep.* Then a message from...no, not Mike! "Look, Lilly. I need to see you...need to see you...need to see you...." She listened to it, then listened again. And the third time she listened her appetite quit, so she sat the bowl of casserole down on the floor for Sherlock, her basset hound.

In spite of the doughy lump of dread shaping in her stomach, Lilly's heart skipped a beat. Headache time...need an aspirin and... She hit the redial button on her phone. "Rach, help!

3

Just when she was finally dozing off from Friday night—Saturday morning!

IT WAS BRIGHT AND EARLY Saturday morning, just a little after seven, when Lilly, still bleary-eyed and fuzzy-brained, stumbled to the front door and threw it open, only to be greeted by Mayor Lowell Tannenbaum waving a newspaper at her. He was tapping his left size-thirteen frantically on the concrete, holding the headlines straight out in front of him so she couldn't see his face. But she knew it was him from the overall testy disposition circling around him like a swarm of hungry mosquitoes. "I think we could have a real problem here, Judge Malloy," he screeched from behind the newspaper.

He could have started off with a friendly little hello, Lilly thought, or "Excuse me for barging in at this ungodly hour." Or "I've brought you a cup of Starbucks to drink as we go over a serious problem." That one would have been her choice. But no. He was straight to the point, snarling and snapping like a churlish Chihuahua. On the bright side, that did clear the fuzz right out of her brain.

"Just look at the headlines about—" his whole body shook in rumbling fury "—about what you've done."

Lilly did look, not surprised about what she saw. Journalist Jailed For Illegal Parking. "So I made the headlines." She yawned. She'd expected to. She was dealing with Mike Collier, after all. This was his norm. *Not* making headlines would have been the unexpected. "What's the problem?" Other than the fact that she wasn't ardently engaged in her every Saturday morning Starbucks fix.

"Read on," the mayor snapped, shaking the paper.

Lilly snatched it out of his hand, pushed her hair out of her eyes and glanced at the first paragraph.

In a turn of events that shocked the entire city to its very core, *Journal* owner and investigative reporter, Mike Collier, was jailed Friday for failure to pay the fine for several parking tickets.

"Several?" she exclaimed. "Hello...try nineteen."

"Just read," Mayor Tannenbaum hissed.

"'It's a travesty of justice all the way around,' Collier stated in an exclusive interview."

Lilly shook her head. "The only travesty here is that it took nineteen tickets to get him into court. He should have been hauled in at five or six."

"Keep reading."

"According to Collier, 'It's a political move. I was robbed of my rightful parking space, then jailed because I had the courage to stand up for my convictions as well as my place to park.'"

"Poor baby," Lilly laughed. "The courage to stand up for his convictions? I threw him in jail because he *and his convictions* were in contempt of court." He'd refused to pay *and* he'd stepped over her yellow line.

"Keep going."

In pair of green Grinch boxers and a gray T-shirt, covered up by a decade-old pink chenille bathrobe her mother had fashioned from an old bedspread, Lilly wasn't in the attire, *or the mood*, for the mayor, or anything else this early. And she didn't want to keep going. "Couldn't this wait until later?" she asked. "Say, till I'm up and dressed? After I've had my coffee?" Caramel *macchiato*—drink of the gods.

"You threw him in jail for parking tickets," he shrieked. "Parking tickets! And all hell's going to break loose over this, mark my words!"

All hell? Not hardly. Just a ninny mayor going over the top. "Contempt, Mayor Tannenbaum, not tickets," she corrected, keeping her eyes glued to the ground—not to the size thirteens that were way bigger than a man of his meager stature needed—but to the cement, because if she looked him in the face, her eyes automatically went to the oversize, way-off-color cap he sported on his front tooth...the cap he'd gotten from the local dentist who proudly boasted the slogan More Teeth, Less Money. And the mayor's front one was a bright and shiny testimony to that! "Had he paid his fine he wouldn't be in jail, but he refused. That's contempt and I didn't have a choice. And what I do in my courtroom isn't any of your business, by the way."

Tannenbaum yanked the newspaper out of her hand and waved it in her face again. "Just read it."

"According to witnesses, Collier breached the yellow line separating Judge Lillianne Malloy from spectators in her courtroom, a move that cost Collier an additional two hundred dollars plus three nights in jail. This is the first time in the history of Whittier that anyone has been jailed for a failure to pay parking tickets."

"Which is exactly what happened," she said. "Actually, that's pretty good reporting. Bet Mike Collier didn't write it."

The mayor merely sniffed at the comment, then took over the reading.

"When asked why he believes such a sentence was handed to him, Collier declined to comment other than to say he believes it's a conspiracy. 'First my parking place, then jail. What else could it be?'"

"Maybe just his disagreeable personality," Lilly retorted. "That, and...oh, let's see...nineteen unpaid tickets, tickets he has no intention of paying even after this publicity."

Tannenbaum continued.

"Asked if Collier has any details on the conspiracy he claims to be the center of, he says the matter bears further investigation, which he vows to do. But he did warn, 'Judge Malloy may have been within her legal right to sentence me to jail, but all I can say to the good citizens of Whittier is, better not cross over her line or you may end up here, too.'"

"Traffic court doesn't make headlines, Miss Malloy," Mayor Tannenbaum barked. "It's there to make money and keep quiet. No controversies, no attention."

"Make money and keep quiet," she repeated. "Nothing about upholding the law? Funny, I always thought that part was incumbent upon a judge. Silly me."

The mayor folded the paper and tucked it under his arm. "You've got to go down to the jail right now and spring him before he says something else, and I don't care how you do it. Just get him out of there no matter what it takes."

"Spring him?" Lilly finally let her fiery greens make contact with Lowell's watery hazels, but not before they paused ever-so-briefly on *the tooth*. "I'm going to do you a favor here, Mayor, and shut the door and pretend we never had this conversation. Okay? Because if we did have it, and if you happened to tell me to release Mr. Collier in the course of that conversation, *to get him out of there no matter what it takes*, I might be forced to lock you up *with him* for trying to influence a judge, because as the town mayor, you don't have the right to interfere with my court, which is what you'd be doing if you were here. Which you aren't."

Mayor Lowell Tannenbaum, a twitchy man, average height, mostly bald on top with a few mousy-brown strands arranged in a sparse comb-over, always concealed a sneer in his smile, if not in actuality, then in implication. And as soon as Lilly quit speaking, the smile, and the sneer, appeared. "I wasn't trying to interfere with your court, Miss Malloy…just looking out for the best interests of Whittier, since Mike Collier can be pretty mean in print. And if you thought I was doing anything other than that, I'd suppose you were mistaken."

"Maybe I am." Not a chance! "But in any case he stays until Monday unless he pays up," she said firmly. "And if you don't want to provoke his wrath in print any further, I'd suggest giving him back his parking space and telling your cousin to find another way to advertise her flower shop." *That way Mike won't be back in my court with another pile of tickets.* "A few feet of pavement in exchange for the *Journal's* goodwill. That seems like a fair trade-off to me, especially with the election coming up." Before Lowell Tannenbaum could sputter out an answer or excuse, Lilly shut the door on him. He was way out of line, and apart from that, she *never* conducted judicial business in the remains of her childhood bedspread.

With the mayor gone now, and the house to herself once again, going back to bed for another couple hours was an option, but not one Lilly took seriously because in her normal day, when she was up she was up. No going back to bed, back to sleep. That wasn't the way her body worked. *So thank you very much, Lowell Tannenbaum, for robbing me of two more hours of sleep,* two hours she needed and deserved. And she groused about it all the way through her morning rituals.

Tame the hair, brush the teeth so she didn't end up with a
More Teeth, Less Money special, then head down to Starbucks and grab that caramel *macchiato*, the only thing that
would set the rest of her day straight.

Once there, the impulse to buy Mike a regular coffee,
black—he wouldn't try anything else—overcame her and she
did it, regretting the impetuous deed before she was even out
of the shop. Was she getting soft? Absolutely no way. Not
about Mike, anyhow. Making nice with him was the last thing
she wanted to do. So the plain black coffee went down the
plain chrome drain in the ladies' room, and minutes later,
when Lilly entered city hall carrying her caramel ambrosia—
something that good really couldn't be called coffee—she
was signed in by the guard, who was drinking his coffee in a
white cup, poured from a plain red-and-silver thermos.

"What brings you in on a weekend, Your Honor?" he
asked, taking Lilly's purse and coffee as she walked through
the metal detector. "Don't recall you coming in here on Saturday too often, especially this early in the day." He chuckled. "I read the paper this morning. I'm betting things are
shook up around here pretty good and your being here has
something to do with sending Mike Collier to jail."

"Understatement," she muttered. "Big time."

"Well, good for you anyway, Your Honor, for doing what
you had to do regardless of who you had to do it to. Folks
may talk for a while—they always do around here when
something different happens—but I admire a person who
takes her job seriously." He scanned the contents of her purse
and paper cup, then handed them back to her, laughing.
"Tossing someone in jail for parking tickets...glad I'm taking
the bus these days." Howard McCray shook his head in
friendly disbelief. "Well, we do what we gotta do, don't we?"

Lilly nodded, smiling. At least he wasn't a critic.

"You go on and have a good day now," Howard said, sig-
naling her through.

Heading to the basement, to her office, Lilly told herself her only purpose for being there was to shuffle through the top layer of her ever-growing mountain of paperwork. At least that's what she kept telling herself on her way down the escalator and through the usually dim hall, which was even dimmer—almost to the point of dark—on the weekend. Tannenbaum pinching a few pennies, she guessed. But as she passed by the connecting tunnel that veered off from her dank hole in the ground and ran under the street straight to the jail—the jail where she had no intention of looking in on Mike Collier—she veered off, too, following the enamel gray walls until they emerged into a dull green room with a decades-old black-and-white sign directing her up to the first floor...that is, if her intention was to visit the jail. Which it was not! She was merely...merely... Nope, nothing came to mind. No explanation, no excuse. So she simply wandered onto an elevator, sang along with Barry Manilow on the Muzak and eventually came to the jail entrance, then the cell block. Flashing her credentials to the guard on duty, one who wasn't as friendly as Howard McCray, she found the wave of police blue parting for her as she entered, still with no intention of actually hunting down anyone in particular, and still with no particular reason for being there, either. Which was what she kept telling herself while she followed a cop named Roger, who, of all things, actually led her straight to Mike's cell without even asking her where she wanted to go or who she wanted to see.

When she got there, pretty much the whole cell block was empty except for a couple of Friday night overindulgers up at the front. And Mike, of course, who was all the way in the back, isolated from everything and everyone...everyone except a delicate looking, well made-up, bleached-white-blond man with tight, black leather pants and a white silk shirt opened halfway down to his belly button revealing...well, nothing particularly interesting. He was endeavoring some painfully slow, click by click typing on a laptop computer and humming a tune from *Cats*. The bronze nameplate on his desk read Fritz.

She envied Fritz his fashion flair if not his actual outfit. "Excuse me," Lilly said. "I'd like to speak to Mr. Collier...alone."

"Do you have an appointment, sweetie?" he asked, barely looking up at her.

"An appointment?" Glancing sideways into the cell, Lilly noticed that Mike had his Starbucks, all right, plus a plate of steamy hot breakfast muffins—blueberry, she guessed. He always liked blueberry the best.

"Yep, sweetie. An appointment. Mike's a pretty busy boy right now, and he's not seeing anybody today unless they have an appointment." His attention was sidetracked when Roger Jackson walked down the hall, his eyes taking in Roger's every movement and flex until Roger was out of sight. Then his attention snapped back to Lilly. "So do you?" he asked.

"Mike..." Lilly grumbled.

"Should I have someone kick her out, Mikey?" Fritz asked.

"She's okay," Mike said, grinning at Lilly through the bars.

"Well, okeydokey, then." With no further interest in Mike's guest, Fritz, the pseudosecretary, went back to work, switching his repertoire to *Phantom of the Opera*.

"Why am I not surprised?" Lilly snapped, stepping up to the bars. "Why am I not surprised that even in jail you find a way to take advantage of the system?"

"I'm not taking advantage," he protested. "Just trying to get by the best I can."

"When I went to jail I sure wasn't offered anything like this *just to get by*." Lilly said.

Fritz gasped. "Oh my God! Did they make you wear orange with your red hair?"

Ignoring Fritz, Lilly continued, "Remember *that* jail cell, Mike—the one I shared with a prostitute, a shoplifter and an ax murderer? One toilet, one sink, two bunk beds and no blueberry muffins."

Mike grinned, holding out a muffin through the bars. "She was a husband beater, not an ax murderer. And if I recall, you were there...what? Two hours?"

"Three. Three hours longer than I should have been. And get that muffin out of my face before I add the charge of bribing a judge."

Pulling it back, Mike took a bite, then strolled casually over to his cot and sat. "So what brings you to my neck of the cell block, Lilly? Feeling guilty about something...like throwing an innocent man in jail?"

"Yeah," Fritz said. "You bully!"

She glanced over at Fritz and gave him her best bully frown, which browbeat him back to his work. "Shouldn't that be your department, Mike? Feeling guilty? Especially after what you did to me?"

"You too, sweetie?" Fritz chimed in again. "Want to know what he did to me? He dragged me out of the middle of the best date I've had since 1997, and just when we were..." He stopped in the nick of time, biting his quivering lower lip.

Trying to force a little bit of sweetness into her smile, Lilly gestured to Juanita Lane, who was stationed down the hall at a desk, her feet propped up on a plastic step. She was reading the morning paper, drinking a Starbucks, munching on a fresh blueberry muffin. "Could you get someone to remove this stuff from the hallway, please?" she asked, pointing first to the desk, then Fritz.

"And you would be who?" Juanita asked in a blasé tone, in between bites.

"I would be the judge who put Mr. Collier here, and I would be the judge who prefers to see my prisoners treated like prisoners, not houseguests."

Juanita gave her a lackadaisical once-over. "Most of the judges who come in here are dressed like judges," she said.

"Guess I didn't take you to be one, not in..." She didn't finish the sentence. It was implied. Not in jeans, a T-shirt and all that untethered red hair. "Give me a couple of minutes, *Your Honor*. I'll see what I can do." Grumbling, Juanita picked up her coffee instead of the phone.

"You're taking away my secretary, Lilly?" Mike said, shaking his head, sighing even though the sparkle in his eyes betrayed the tease. "You would rob me of my only tie to civilization? My only means of making a living?"

"Should I take a break, Mike?" Fritz asked, glaring at Lilly. "Come back later, when *she's* gone?"

"You do that, *sweetie*," Lilly said, spinning around to shut the lid of the laptop. "Take a break, but don't come back. Mike's office is closed for the weekend."

"Is that okay, Mike? Can she do that?"

"She's the law in these parts, Fritz. Guess she can do pretty much what she wants."

"What I want?" Lilly sputtered, watching Mike fall back into a pile of pillows on his cot. One pillow was issued per jail cot, but he had at least ten. "Looks to me like you're the one who's getting to do pretty much what *you* want."

"What I wanted was to spend today getting out the Sunday edition," he commented, kicking off his shoes. "So far we have two stories—one about a trash fire over on Elm Street that spread to a pile of tires. Probably my lead, since the story about the scanner at Gilroy's Market going wacky and charging Mrs. Patterson $790 for a can of cling peaches doesn't have quite as much edge to it...unless you're Mrs. Patterson."

Waiting until Fritz had gathered his belongings—nameplate, picture of his poodle and a bud vase with a single rosebud—and trotted away, Lilly finally pulled Fritz's office chair up to the bars and sat. "I'm not even going to ask what happened to you, Mike—why you ended up doing stories on cling peaches—because frankly, I don't care. And I don't care that you can't park your car outside your office, or that your

Sunday edition won't get out. But what I do care about is the way you're mocking not only me, but the whole judicial system here in Whittier. And that's so like you... 'Judge Malloy may have been within her legal right to sentence me to jail, but all I can say to the good citizens of Whittier is, better not cross over her line or you may end up here, too.'"

"That's why I'm here, isn't it? For crossing your line?"

"You crossed over my line years ago, Mike. Problem was I couldn't do anything about it back then." She grinned wickedly. "Times sure have changed, haven't they?"

"And you're really liking the feel of all that power, aren't you?" He gave her a lazy grin. "Didn't expect it from you, Lilly. *But all that power sure makes you hot and sexy.*"

"What?" she sputtered, caught off guard until she realized *the voice* was back. Like she really needed that *and* Mike Collier at the same time—those disobedient little innuendos, naughty little suggestions, popping in and out in all the wrong places. Another one of those Mike Collier consequences.

"I said I didn't expect it from you."

Shutting her eyes, taking in a deep breath, she opened them again slowly, then said, "You may not have expected it from me, Mike, but that's the way I am now. Older and a whole lot wiser."

"With perky breasts."

She gulped. "Huh?"

"I didn't say anything."

Drawing in another deep breath, she continued. "The thing with you, Mike, is that you take advantage because you can. Just look at this place—the desk, Bambi the boy secretary—"

"Fritz," he corrected.

"Fritz and blueberry muffins. You always get away with it. Always have and you expect that you always will. Well, it's my turf this time, and no more getting away with it."

"So what you're giving me here is the this-town-ain't-big-enough-for-the-both-of-us speech?" Mike crossed one leg over the other and cupped his hands behind his head. "Get outta town or else...."

"Indianapolis has three-quarters of a million people and *it's* not big enough for the both of us," she quipped. "I've got a good start here and you're already messing it up. I own a nice little house, have a good job, and I'm trying to find some roots."

"At least you have a house. I'm sleeping underneath my printing press. And I have a boy secretary named Bambi—"

"Fritz."

"Think they'll mind if I take some of these pillows home with me?"

"See how you are?" She huffed out an impatient sigh. "Always trying to avoid the subject."

"You were talking about your house... I just asked about pillows. Thought it sort of fit into the flow of conversation...."

A challenge flickered into his eyes and she saw it. Didn't want to see it, but it was there, glimmering right at her, beckoning her, like a manly Siren, to come crash on the rocks...one more time. "Shut up, Mike! Just shut up. I came here to have a serious talk with you, but if you don't want to talk—"

"Want to talk? I called you, Lilly. Told you I wanted to talk, *after*, I might add, you threw me in jail over a couple of lousy parking tickets. And you know that was overreacting. Admit it. You blew a gasket and threw me in the dungeon. Payback, right? And you've just been waiting for your chance."

Lowering her voice so that Juanita, at the other end of the hall struggling to hear, couldn't, Lilly whispered, "And it feels so good to be on the giving end for a change. Better than I could have ever imagined."

"I knew it!" Mike exclaimed, jumping up. Moving closer to the cell bars, just inches away from Lilly, he smiled down at her—an irascibly patient smile, an imperious smile. "So Lilly's got some fangs now."

Standing to meet him eye-to-eye, but still a respectful distance from the bars, Lilly gave him that same smile right back. "No, not fangs. Just the law on my side." She wrinkled her nose at him. "And the knowledge of how to use it."

"And you really do intend to keep me here until Monday, don't you?"

She nodded. "But I did leave instructions that if you pay the fine in full they can let you out."

"So want to loan me a couple of grand?" he asked.

"Sell the Porsche."

"Did that."

"And the stock portfolio."

"Ditto."

She shrugged. "Well, I suppose it looks like we'll be keeping you here for a while longer, doesn't it? And I should think that a man with your, shall we say, paltry pecuniary resources would appreciate a few days of free upkeep."

"Cruel, Lilly. Really cruel." He laughed, then lowered his voice as Juanita scooted her chair even closer so she could hear more. "But on you cruel is good. So do you ever let your hair down, figuratively speaking, or are you all judge, all the time now?"

Instinctively, Lilly reached to her hair and finger-brushed the wild strands around her face. "All judge, Mr. Collier. A judge who came to give you fair warning that she won't be messed with. You mess with me or my court again, you go to jail again. And that's the way it's going to be. And no, this town ain't big enough for the two of us, but unless you intend to get out, seems like we're going to have to coexist."

"It's my town, Lilly. Born and raised here and the people know me."

She smiled. "If they know you, that makes it all the easier for me."

"You really do hate me, don't you?"

Stepping aside for the maintenance man to take away the

chair, Lilly walked over to the bars, raised her hands and took hold, then pressed her face to the cold metal. "Hate is such a strong word, Mike. The first time I hated you, then I forgave you. Stupid move, I know. But I did forgive you. Then the second time I hated you again, but that time I didn't forgive you. And now...it's not hate, really. Just a need to see you in your proper place."

Moving to the bars also, Mike pressed himself to them so their faces were almost touching. She could feel his breath, his heat—smell the scent of him mingling with the oxygen she took into her lungs. And for a moment she lost everything—her senses, her bearings—and the only thing that occupied the scant space between them was the memory of how good they'd been together back then. God, they'd been so good...so perfect...their fit, their touch, their rhythm...his hands...his lips...his lips on her breasts...

Pheromones, Lilly! Look out it's the pheromones.

"What?" Lilly yelped, jumping back from the bars as if they'd taken a bite out of her.

"I said I need a phone...to call my office. Let them know I won't be getting out, since you intend to keep me in my proper place until Monday, and I used my one call yesterday to call you."

Flushed, a bit shaken by the encounter, and looking over her shoulder to see who had shouted pheromones—or was that the pheromones themselves shouting a warning?—Lilly breathed in a deep breath, reached into her purse and handed him her cell phone. Easier to do that than argue with him, since her knees were shaking, which meant her voice was probably shaking, too, and no way was she going to let him hear that.

"Hi, Jimmy..." Mike looked at Lilly, then said, "Jimmy's my lawyer." He spoke into the phone again. "I've been thinking it over and I've decided to go with Chinese for lunch."

Chinese? Lilly heard the word, but she wasn't recovered

enough from her close encounter—thank heaven for the bars—to let it sink in all the way.

"Wong's—a number three, with two egg rolls, spicy mustard, and have him throw in an order of fried rice, too. Shrimp fried." To Lilly he added, "Want anything? The chow mein's great. So's the sweet and sour pork."

That snapped her out of it—lifted her right up and out of his spell and dropped her back down into the jailhouse. "Hang up," she demanded, holding out her hand for her phone.

"Would you rather have Italian?" he asked, backing far enough away from her that she couldn't reach through the bars and snatch it away from him. "Or Mexican? Jimmy can go anyplace you want. You'll pay for your own, won't you? 'Cause lately I've been of paltry pecuniary resources."

"Hand me the phone, Mike."

"I guess she doesn't want anything, Jimmy. So get me an almond cookie with that and tell Wong we'll do a make good—another ad." To Lilly he quipped, "I'm the guy you see on the street corner with the cardboard sign—Will Trade Ad Space for Food."

"The phone, right now!" It wasn't funny. Not him, not her reaction to him, and geez, she knew he'd felt it. How could he not, with the heat they were giving off together—a real blast furnace of lust or pheromones or whatever it was called.

Want to go to bed with me, Lilly?

"What?" she shrieked.

"I said what happens Monday morning when I'm back in court?" He handed the phone through the bars and she took it being careful not to come into contact with his skin.

She was sweating now. No hiding, no denying. "I, uh..." She didn't know. Didn't know the question, didn't know the answer. "I've got to go," she whispered, her voice infused with the hoarseness that comes in the aftermath of good sex. Oh no! Not that voice. He knew that voice.

"And was it good for you, Lilly?"

She didn't hear that! He didn't say it; she didn't hear it.

"Lilly? Don't you want to know?"

"Know what?" she choked out.

"What I just asked."

"No," she panted, having no clue what that was.

"You don't want to know why I called you last night?"

She ventured a look into the cell to see if he was smoking a cigarette—the relaxing smoke that capped off awesome sex—but he was finishing the last of his blueberry muffin. "So tell me and make it fast," she snapped.

He shrugged. "In the last couple of weeks I've been involved in this little investigation and..."

That she heard loud and clear, and it was *all* she wanted to hear. "Another investigation? Fool me three times, Mike? Is that it? Well, not a chance." And she spun around and left.

Then just before she reached the guard desk... *"Hey, Lilly. Are you wearing underwear?"*

4

Empty shopping bags; a Saturday afternoon horror story

WHO WOULD HAVE BELIEVED there wasn't a simple black dress in her size in town? Lilly didn't after the first store, and even after the second. But at store number three and counting, the trend was becoming pretty clear. No dress for the judge who'd done that terrible thing to poor Mike Collier. No shoes either, unless the size fives Mrs. Milhouse tried to force onto Lilly's size sevens counted. "Wasn't that a bit harsh, throwing Mikey in jail?" Mrs. Milhouse asked, practically bending back Lilly's big toe to wedge a pair of black pumps on her foot. "Oh dear, did I pinch your toes?"

Then there was the ice cream cone, plain vanilla, something that should have been a nice treat in the middle of a futile shopping spree. The scoops right before hers were generous, overflowing the cone. Her scoops, though, were so dinky she thought about asking for a magnifying glass to find them in the *cracked* cone, one that dripped out the bottom.

In spite of the clogs in her shopping expedition and the ice cream stains down the front of her shirt, Lilly did find her dress and shoes—thank you, Big Bob's Discount Mart. It was a clearance special, where everything must go: heaps and heaps of clothes on tables, more heaps of shoes in piles of boxes. After some elbow-to-elbow excavating among a bunch of frantic shoppers who were whipped into a dress-tugging, shoe-flying frenzy, Lilly managed to escape without bruises, carrying a dress that was a little too slinky and short for

Ezra's party, and a pair of shoes way too platform and clunky for anything other than a high school dance. But they were black, and that's all that mattered.

On her way home from Big Bob's, Lilly detoured over to the jail. It was only a couple of blocks out of the way, and she'd overhead some Big Bob's chitchat about the protestors at the jail. Professional curiosity, she told herself, regretting her decision the instant she turned the corner. The first sign she saw read Loony Judge Lilly. People were actually marching in a circle with them. And along with Loony Judge Lilly, there was an abundance of Free Mike Collier signs. The group was shouting at cars passing by, telling them to honk if they were in favor of freeing Mike Collier. Naturally, everybody was honking...everybody, that is, except Lilly, who, stalled in a Mike Collier traffic jam, couldn't take her eyes off a steadily growing line of compassionate and, most likely, husband-hunting women lining up at the jailhouse door, armed with home-baked cakes probably concealing metal files for sawing through iron bars, and notes of hopeful marriage proposals. Something about a man behind bars that got the ol' hormones flowing, she guessed, putting on a pair of sunglasses as though people wouldn't recognize her in them.

And they did recognize her. Halfway through the traffic snarl, and just when she thought she just might make it all the way past, one fervent Mike fan recognized her and shouted the war cry to the rest of the protestors. "It's the judge," he yelled, and everybody ran to the curb. Lilly expected rotten tomatoes or something similar to the riot she'd survived in Big Bob's, but the group of people merely frowned at her. One old lady did shake a mean index finger at her, and one brave vigilante held his Loony Judge Lilly sign a little higher than the rest of them.

It took Lilly five whole minutes to inch her way through the gauntlet, one scowl at a time. And by the time she turned off the block, she'd decided she'd take a good wrestling match at

Big Bob's over this any day. At least at Big Bob's she'd walked away with a battle trophy. Here at the jail, she *was* the battle trophy.

Saturday night and the perfect potted palm

LILLY MANAGED TO GET out of town, though not looking quite as polished as she would have preferred, and an hour later than she wanted. Consequentially, when she arrived at Ezra's she was frazzled, her hair frizzled, and overall she wasn't in tip-top form. Then she discovered that Ezra's "few people" turned out to be a veritable jackpot of notoriety in the judicial world—her first time invited into such hallowed ranks and she was looking like a dowdy interloper in her Big Bob's special, while they were looking austere and accomplished in their distinguished, well-cut grays and charcoals. A federal judge, several superior court judges, a supreme court judge, dean of the law school... Lilly almost turned around and ran before she was all the way inside. "Don't you think I'm a bit out of my league here?" she whispered at Ezra as she exchanged her Big Bob's five-dollar mark-down shawl for a manhattan, the ingredients of which probably cost more than her entire outfit.

Ezra, now retired from teaching at the law school, hobnobbed with all the big judicial names. He could have been one of those names, and probably should have been, but his love was in the classroom, where he could teach the pure elegance of the law. Over the years he'd had offers from prestigious firms and yes, even a judgeship. But he was a permanent fixture in the classroom, and now, after his retirement, he still taught from time to time, just not as much. "You're out of your league only if you want to be, my dear," he replied. "And if you don't dazzle them with your legal repartee tonight, that dress will go a long ways." Soft and round, with abundant white hair not a whole lot less wild than her own,

and sagacious thick eyebrows over bright brown eyes, Ezra
Kessler was her mentor, her friend, her substitute grandfa-
ther. So many important roles in her life all wrapped up in
one person, and she loved him dearly, in spite of the fact that
since he'd retired from teaching, he'd been spending a little of
that free time meddling. Like tonight, tossing her in the mix
with all the heavy hitters—for her own good, he'd tell her. It
was and he was right. That was Ezra, who, no matter what,
had always been in her corner. "And your little exploits
down in Whittier made the paper here, by the way, so I'm
guessing a few of my friends will be eager to hear the particulars. It's not every day a judge gets to send a member of the
press to jail, you know. Even though I think that's every
judge's secret fantasy." He chuckled. "And for parking tickets. I've got to hand it to you, Lilly, what you did takes courage. Makes an old teacher proud."

"It made the paper here in Indy?" she choked out. "No
way."

Ezra nodded. "On television, too. Good picture of you, I
might add. The robe looks a little big though, but it suits
you."

"A judicial hand-me-down. The guy before me was a line-
backer in college or something, and a robe in my size isn't in
the city budget until next year. Tight money or something.
The mayor's always harping on city funds." Shaking her
head, she tossed back the manhattan in a couple of gulps to
brace herself for the onslaught, ridicule...whatever her esteemed colleagues might throw at her. "You might have had
the decency to warn me about this, Ezra," she said, sidestep-
ping her way over to his hulking potted palm in the corner.
Sanctuary in any form...an evening communing behind na-
ture. Better than an evening communing with critics. "And I
didn't throw him in jail because he's a member of the press.
He broke the law."

Ezra nodded. "Parking tickets," he chuckled. "The pretty

judge packs a pretty big punch. I always knew you would be good." Snagging a shrimp puff off a passing tray, Ezra handed it to her. "And I'm assuming you had legal ground to do what you did...." He frowned, then lowered his voice. "You did, didn't you? I mean, it *was* Mike Collier, after all. With the history between you two..."

Lilly choked on her shrimp. Ezra knew about the plagiarism incident, and he was the one who'd championed her back into law school. He was also the one who came to her rescue when she was arrested, but he didn't know that she and Mike...that they had... No, he didn't, couldn't, know that. That was a little piece of history she wished even *she* didn't know about.

"Are you okay, dear?" Ezra asked, handing her a napkin.

She arched her eyebrows as she grabbed a glass of sparkling water from a passing waiter to wash down the rest of the puff, which seemed to be sticking in the back of her throat, sticking there like Mike Collier seemed to be sticking in her life. "Fine," she finally sputtered, picking up her pace to the palm. "Just fine.

"Well, as I was saying, with the history between you two I certainly hope you're on good legal footing with this." He followed her, stopping just short of his plant. "Especially since it's drawing some attention now."

"Got you a little worried, do I, Ezra? Suddenly not feeling so good about getting me appointed to the bench in Whittier?" Taking another sip of water, she continued, "You knew Mike was there, didn't you? When you recommended me for the position, you knew he was in Whittier. And you didn't warn me."

"Coincidence, my dear," he insisted. "There was an opening to fill and you needed the job. And Mike's being there..." He shrugged. "What can I say, Your Honor? Circumstantial evidence at best, so I'm pleading innocent."

"Liar," she laughed.

"Would it have made a difference, knowing he lived in Whittier?"

"Probably not."

"Liar," he accused. "You would have turned it down, Lilly. And you needed to get back on sound footing in the legal community."

She shrugged. "What can I say? I'm pleading innocent."

A tight-faced man joined into the conversation just before Lilly stepped between plant and wall. "Well, if it isn't Lilly Malloy. Judge Lilly Malloy these days, I hear." His expression noncommittal, his movements crisp, he kept his distance, didn't even offer to shake her hand, which she didn't offer to extend. Of course, both her hands were full—one with her water and the other with another shrimp puff. Good defensive maneuver, one she used in iffy situations, and this was, indeed, one of those iffy situations.

"Dean Blount, imagine running into you here." She cast Ezra a quick evil eye, then turned a polite smile to her former law school dean, the one who'd kicked her out, then complained when he was forced to let her back in.

"Just what I was saying to Judge Lindstrom when you arrived. Imagine seeing Lilly Malloy here. Traffic court, isn't it, Lilly? Parking tickets and the like?"

"Funny how that worked out, isn't it? You kicked me out of law school and now I'm a judge, parking tickets and the like." She gave him a malicious wink. "Better watch where you park in my town, George. I hear the judge there is none too friendly when it comes to handing out parking sentences." When Lilly walked away from him, George Blount was grappling for a comeback, but still too stunned to find one. Smiling, she sidled up to Ezra and gave him a kiss on the cheek. "I think I'm going to like this party, after all." In spite of her Big Bob attire.

"Apparently," he replied, glancing over at the muddled dean, who was double-fisting a couple of drinks at the bar.

"So, Judge Malloy, tell me about your little brouhaha down in Whittier, if you don't mind." It was a request from an Indiana Supreme Court judge, *and he'd addressed her as "judge."* Equal ranking, equal respect. If she hadn't been standing in the middle of a circle of her peers, all who wanted to hear about her now-famed parking ticket case, she just might have cried, she was so happy.

Saturday night, much later, and no perfect potted palm this time

WELL AFTER MIDNIGHT and Lilly was finally rolling back into Whittier, stone-cold sober, of course, and feeling much better than she'd felt in quite a while. They'd complimented her on her decision—the other judges. They'd accepted her as one of them. Lilly Malloy, the legal outcast, had been told "job well done" by people whose opinions mattered. Big Bob notwithstanding, it was a spectacular night. And Ezra, the old dear, simply had stood on the sidelines and watched every bit of it, priding himself on her acceptance. It was her night, one he'd brought together only for her, and she wasn't over it yet. She wasn't ready to go home alone, or go to sleep, because when she awoke tomorrow morning tonight would be but a memory. The evening—her evening—was still too fresh and vital to pass into past tense.

Driving past the jail, a couple of blocks off the beaten path to home, Lilly told herself she was doing it just to see if the picketers had gone yet, which they had, since Whittier's sidewalks rolled up at ten. But after that little drive-by, she circled back, and circled back again, refusing to let the whys of what she was doing emerge. Three times around the block, refusing to look up at the floor where he was…the corner where he was…the light from the corner where he was before she finally stopped. No use kidding herself about it, she decided. She was on her way to see Mike, although she wasn't sure why. She'd carved her place in a little niche earlier—a place really important to her, a place where she really wanted to be. So maybe it was time to set Mike straight about her position here in Whittier—another place really important to her. And maybe her place with him, too.

"You're still awake," she said, keeping a good distance back from the cell bars.

Lounging on the cot, writing on a yellow legal pad, Mike sat up, took off his glasses—the ones he wore in the wee hours when eyestrain set in—and stood. "Got lots of work to do. More now that you took away my secretary."

He looked shaggy, tired, she thought. But that challenging little glint was still in his eyes. "You don't give up, do you?" she asked. "You're wrong about this and you know it, but I'm the one who will end up looking like the bad guy here. I'm the one who got shortchanged on the ice cream cone because you did something wrong and my job requires me to deal with it. And that's not fair, Mike. I just wanted you to know that. It's not fair, and if I didn't know that when I accepted that ice cream cone, I know it now."

"You've changed, Lilly."

"I had to. Every time I was around you, you did something that forced me to change, like it or not. But I landed on my feet, Mike. I always land on my feet and tonight, for the first time, I finally began to realize that. My peers recognized me. They validated me. And I just came by to tell you that come Monday morning you can apologize to the court and set up a payment schedule for the fine, then you'll be free to go. After that, if we're lucky, we won't have to run into each other more than is absolutely necessary."

"And what if I don't believe that I owe the court an apology, Lilly? That I really was railroaded?"

Lilly smiled. "Then I'd suggest you call your attorney and see if he's good for something other than a Wong's number three with a couple of egg rolls because, since you intend on staying, you might like some culinary variety. Maybe a Wong's number four?''

Sunday morning's erupting, and that's putting it mildly

SEVEN A.M. AND SOMEONE was at her door. Two days in a row now, no sleeping in. Lilly looked at her alarm clock just to make sure, then she flopped over onto her belly and put her head under the pillow to muffle the pounding. Mayor Lowell Tannenbaum, or whoever was knocking, would just have to wait this time. This was Sunday, her lazy day. No exception. She wasn't getting out of bed until nine or ten, or noon if she wanted, even if the mayor himself climbed up her trellis and banged on her bedroom window.

But as it turned out, he didn't have to. The noise outside in her yard by seven-thirty finally aroused Lilly's curiosity enough that she climbed out of bed and lumbered over to the window to have a look. And...oh no! There were picketers out on her front lawn. Dozens of them. Plus a vendor wagon on the street in front of her house selling coffee and dough-nuts.

By seven forty-five the media started pulling up. A couple of news cruisers from Indy and was that...no, not a satellite truck! Was she making national news? Eight o'clock brought the curious onlookers, the ones the police cordoned back from her lawn with yellow tape that acted just like the tape in her courtroom. Then the pounding on her front door started again, and didn't let up for almost an hour. Nine o'clock, and her wake-up alarm went off, but Lilly was long since wide-eyed, sitting on the floor under her bedroom window, peek-ing out at all the commotion. And muttering the "Damn you, Mike Collier" mantra.

At ten, Lilly finally rounded up the nerve to take a quickie shower, fearing that any second a wandering paparazzo would stray into her bedroom and snag a few *Judge Gone Wild*

shower shots for whichever rag or late night TV video huckster would mete out the biggest bucks. Then she dressed in
the first thing she could grab from her closet—mid-thigh
shorts, middy T-shirt—and raced back to the window on the
off chance everybody had gone away. Which they hadn't. In
fact, the individual entities down below had morphed into
one big blob.

Was that another news cruiser out there? And...oh no! Free
Mike Collier T-shirts with his picture on them!

Free Mike Collier, her fanny. Free Lilly Malloy! She was being held prisoner in her own home, while the Mikey-loving
masses were getting bigger by the minute. And of course,
Mayor Lowell Tannenbaum was right there in the middle of
it all, his face toward the camera, *the tooth* no doubt twinkling
in the floodlights as he repudiated all responsibility for his
debatable part in this mismanagement of parking ticket injustice. "We're a friendly town," he shouted into a bullhorn.
"Friendly and fiscally responsible."

Leave it to Tannenbaum to find a campaign moment, she
thought.

Plodding to the television, Lilly plopped down on the floor
in front of it, turned it on and flipped through the stations until she found one that was broadcasting live from her pussy
willow bush in the front yard. "Inside sources have told us
that Mike Collier, who, if you recall, was jailed for unpaid
parking tickets—not speeding tickets, folks, parking tickets—
may not be released even tomorrow, as Judge Malloy first
ruled last Friday. Our inside sources have revealed that Judge
Lillianne Malloy, in an unprecedented late night visit to Collier's cell, hinted that a longer jail sentence might be handed
out as early as Monday morning if Collier fails to meet his
conditions for release. Collier declined commenting."

"Good thing," she muttered, wondering if a traffic court
judge could, or ever had, called up a gag order.

"Now, let's switch back to the studio, where our very own

Brandy Bartlett has an update on just who Judge Lillianne Malloy is. Brandy?"

"Thank you, Preston," Brandy began. And Lilly closed her eyes, bracing herself for it.

"It seems that Judge Lillianne Malloy has a very interesting past."

Interesting past, my foot. "Don't you mean victim of circumstances?" she asked the screen, opening her eyes to glare at Brandy, as if that would do any good.

"Starting with her expulsion from law school..."

"Actually, Brandy, in the interest of accuracy, it started the day I met Mike Collier."

"Buying a term paper..." Brandy continued.

"Then slept with him, and don't you wish you had *that* little news flash."

"Journalism instructor Mike Collier discovered..."

"He stole it, Brandy. Rifled through my property and stole it."

"Expelled from law school..."

"Well, Brandy, at least you got that one right. So let's hear about my getting arrested, now."

Then the rest of it came out, with the emphasis on the bad, and the resolution in each instance almost an afterthought in Brandy's lopsided report. "She was later reinstated in law school after charges were dropped...."

"One sentence exonerating me. That's all I get, Brandy?"

"Later released from jail after charges were dropped...."

"That's it? Another lousy sentence?"

"She has a very interesting past, and not one you'd expect from a judge," Brandy Bartlett concluded. "Even a traffic court judge. Now, let's take you back to Preston Powell, who's standing by with George Blount, former dean of the law school Judge Malloy attended. Preston?"

"Thank you, Brandy. And yes, I'm here with Dean Blount...."

The red crawler under Dean Blount read The Man Who Expelled Lilly. "Yes, I had the occasion to expel her from law school several years ago, but she was cleared of the charges and later reinstated." Then a picture of Lilly went up—in her big robe, big glasses, gavel in hand—under which the red crawler read The Judge Who Jailed Mike, while George Blount droned on. "Yes, she did blame Mr. Collier for the incident, even though he did speak on her behalf at the hearing. And I understand she blamed him later, when his exposé resulted in her arrest." Blah, blah, blah.

"Would you say that Judge Malloy might be holding a grudge against Mike Collier?" Preston Powell asked.

Back to George Blount—a close-up, displaying the fact that his left nostril was considerably larger than his right. "I wouldn't be able to comment on that, but she did warn me, just last night, that I'd better watch where I park in *her* town. She said she was, and I quote—" with his fingers he made little quotation marks in the air "—none too friendly when it comes to handing out parking sentences, unquote."

Preston Powell came back on camera, grinning as if he'd uncovered the hottest news story of the year. "You heard it first right here. Judge Lilly Malloy, in her own words, is none too friendly when it comes to handing out parking sentences. Now back to you, Brandy."

The camera went back on Brandy Bartlett, a pale, washed-out blonde with bright red lipstick, and she was grinning, too. "Stay tuned for further developments and breaking news on Malloy versus Collier."

"Oh, no," Lilly moaned, falling over backward onto her plush carpet. Next they'd be calling it Lillygate!

Deepening the Sunday morning do-do

MIKE WATCHED THE MEDIA circus in Lilly's yard from his jail cell, the television courtesy of Roger Jackson, who was on duty and had dropped it by Mike's cell on his way out to Lilly's house to restore some order. "She's in a real mess out there," he said, handing the black-and-white twelve-incher over to Mike.

"Lilly's a mess magnet," he replied, rigging up a wire to the bars as an antenna. "And somehow I always seem to be in the center of that mess."

"Well, my story got picked up by a wire service and I've been asked to do a follow-up, if that's okay with you."

Dropping back onto his cot, Mike shrugged. "The ball's already rolling, so I hope it's going to pay enough to make it worth your while. And make sure they give you the byline right underneath the header and not at the end. Something like Mike Collier Screws Up the Life of Lilly Malloy One More Time, by Roger Jackson."

"You in love with her?" Roger asked.

In love with Lilly? That thought had crossed Mike's mind the first time around, but only for a minute. Then he'd caught her red-handed at something she wasn't doing, which he would have discovered she wasn't doing if he'd done his job thoroughly. Which he hadn't. So any shot at love had gotten kicked out the window when Lilly got kicked out of law school. The second time around the love thought did cross his mind again, but only for a couple of minutes before she was packed off to jail. Out the window, part two. And now this time, no way, no how was that window opening for him, no matter what he felt for her. So there was no use dignifying the question with an answer, because any answer he had didn't matter. "I'm just trying to set things straight. Guess you could call it trying to pay up my tab."

Roger laughed. "Looks to me like that tab keeps getting bigger and bigger all the time. And after this morning, buddy—well, all I can say is I wouldn't want to be in your shoes the next time you come face-to-face with the good judge, because those shoes might end up being parked *right here* under *that cot* a whole lot longer than you counted on."

"Well, at least I'm safe from her in here." Mike chuckled. "I *am* safe from her in here, right?" He watched the news report, saw George Blount make an ass of himself—something that apparently came naturally—then Mike turned his attention to an eye-in-the-sky view of Lilly's house, wondering how she was doing inside, and if she was plotting her next move against him, or more aptly put, her revenge. "Juanita, could I have a phone, please?" he called.

"You're not gonna try calling her, are you?" she asked, handing her own personal cell phone in to him. "Because that would be suicide, Mike. Believe me, that lady will keep you locked up in here for harassing her. You know that, don't you? That you're gonna have to send someone after your bed-room slippers 'cause you ain't never going home if you call her?"

Mike grinned. "Well, if she does, at least I know I'll have great company and the best-tasting blueberry muffins any prisoner ever did sink his teeth into." He punched Lilly's number—the private one he prayed she would answer.

"All that flattery and a buck won't get you squat because I can't let you out till she tells me to. And I'm not holding my breath on that one, Mikey." Laughing, Juanita returned to her post at the desk and resumed her crossword puzzle.

"Come on, Lilly, pick up," Mike muttered through the first three rings. "Lilly…"

After the fourth ring he heard her voice mail: "This is Judge Lillianne Malloy…."

No way he was going to leave a message. She'd erase it once she heard his voice and he really needed to talk to her. So he dialed again and held his breath through the first two rings, then came a tentative, "Hello?"

"Lilly?" he said cautiously.

"Yes?"

"Don't hang up...it's Mike."

Dead air. Not a word from her, but he didn't hear her click off, either. Good sign. "Look, Lilly. I'm really sorry about all this. This isn't the way things were supposed to have turned out. I was just trying to prove a point, shake up some publicity for me—*not you*. And I wasn't lying when I said I don't have the money for the fine, because I don't."

"You're sorry, Mike? I'll just bet you are. So sorry, in fact, that you told someone I threatened to leave you in jail."

"Wasn't me," he declared. Bert Ford had picked a fine time to wake up. Probably one of Mike's esteemed rivals had slipped poor old Bert a twenty for the inside story. Something Mike might have done himself at one time. Hell, who was he kidding? The instinct was still imbedded. He'd have coughed up twenty-five. "Look," he continued, before she had a chance to respond. "I've been watching the news—"

"A television in jail, Mike? Guess I shouldn't be surprised about that, should I?"

Sucking in a breath, he forged on. "We'll talk about that later. Okay?"

"And the phone you're using? Can we talk about that later, too, Mike? And all the other things you get away with...have always gotten away with?"

"Would it help if I said I'm sorry?" he asked.

"You already did and it didn't."

Nothing was going to get through to her and he couldn't fault her for shutting him out. Reverse the situation and he'd be doing the same thing, only a whole lot bigger. Lots of shouting and accusations, threats and name calling. But that was him in a pinch. Lilly in a pinch was classy. Always had been, still was. "Look, Lilly. I have an idea, so please don't hang up until you hear me out."

Dead air again. But no hang up. "You know when I told you I sleep under my printing press—well, that's almost the truth. I do live in my building—a little apartment upstairs in the back. It's not much, pretty run-down, since I haven't had time to do anything with it, but maybe you'd like to use it until some of this blows over. Nobody will think to look for you in enemy camp and, obviously, I won't be there."

"You don't think a few dozen of the people in my front yard will follow me over there?" she snapped.

"I was watching an aerial of your house..."

"An aerial? They have a helicopter up taking pictures?"

"Yes, and from what I could tell nobody's out back, not in your backyard or your alley. I think you could just walk out."

"My car's out front."

"I'll have Jimmy meet you out back, if you want to go. So do you?"

"Okay."

No argument, no hesitation, and that caught him off guard. He expected something from her, and getting nothing other than an easy acquiescence told him how desperate she was. Mike cursed himself for that because Lilly never acquiesced easily to anything, which was a big part of what he liked in her. Even admired in her. He didn't want that to change, didn't want to be the one responsible for that change. "You're sure?" he asked.

"Like I have another choice? They're pounding on my door and banging on my windows and it's not going to stop anytime soon."

"I'm really sorry about this, Lilly."

"Not as sorry as you're going to be," she said, then hung up.

Ten minutes later, with an overnight bag in one hand and a leashed basset hound in the other, Lilly skulked out her back door, through the back gate of her postage stamp yard and right into Jimmy's car. "I'll get you over to Mike's apartment, Your Honor, as soon as I deliver this burrito to him," he said. "It's his lunchtime."

"Of course it is," Lilly said, sinking down into her seat. And she wasn't even surprised that the burrito came first.

5

Every Sunday evening needs a hovel to make the day complete

"SO NOW WHAT DO WE DO?" Rachel Perkins picked the green peppers off her fourth slice of pizza and tossed them back into the box along with all the other ones from her first three slices. Barely over five feet tall, with short brown boy-cut hair, a killer bod—if you liked a perfect one hundred pounds and a smile that could whip the world—she was always the chipper one in the Lilly-Rachel duo, the optimist, the one who snapped Lilly out of her glooms even when Lilly didn't want to be snapped, like now. "You're hiding out in his apartment like you're the criminal, you've got Mike's lawyer out walking your dog. He's kind of cute, don't you think?"

"Mike?"

"Jimmy."

"You think he's cute?"

"Maybe."

Even in the dark, Lilly caught the smile on Rachel's face. Innocent, hopeful. Man, had it been a long time since she'd smiled like that over anyone. Maybe since the first time she'd smiled over Mike. "He's cute," she said. "And single, I think. Want me to call him and have him bring us a Wong's number three?"

"I just said he's cute," Rachel snapped. "That's all."

"Yeah, just like the first time I saw Mike I thought he was cute. Take it from me, that's *never* all." Years of personal experience speaking here, and with Mike it still wasn't *all* no matter how much she denied it. And she denied it a lot. "So I could call him for you, maybe figure out a way to get him over here...Jimmy, not Mike."

"Mike, not Jimmy, you mean. Want another beer?"

"Sure, why not." Lilly listened to Rachel bump her way from the combo living, dining, bedroom into the combo kitchen, laundry, junk room. With five pieces of pizza down and soon three beers, Lilly was certainly taking out her frustrations in food tonight. She was entitled, since when it came to Mike there were a whole lot of frustrations.

"Jimmy said everybody's cleared off your property now," Rachel said, tripping over the boxes, stacks of books and clothes on her way back to Lilly, carrying two more bottles. "Maybe you could go home." Dropping down cross-legged on the floor, she handed over a beer, then grabbed up the slice of pizza she'd already depeppered. "Or maybe we could go to a hotel or something, if you think they'll come back to your house later and bother you."

"I'm half-buzzed, Rach. So are you, and we can't drive in this condition. And can't you just read the headlines if I got caught out in public sloshed? Judge Nabbed on Drunken Bender. No, I'm not going anywhere tonight and besides, the only thing I feel like doing is sitting in the dark and moping, so this is dandy...just dandy." Impossible apartment—no hot water, no light, every corner cluttered with unpacked boxes, all kinds of things going bump in the night. Not the Mike style she remembered. Used to be he was all swank and cush, every amenity at his fingertips. Now this, and she had no place else to go. She deserved to mope in the dark and she was glad Rach had come to her rescue, to eat pizza, drink beer and...well, keep those little voices in her head from turning into something more than voices.

"Well, you think Jimmy might need some help walking Sherlock? You can't go over there, but maybe I should just call and see. I mean, he can be difficult, you know. Maybe having somebody he knows there..."

"Who's difficult? Jimmy?" Lilly was feeling the buzz more and more. Getting mellow and sleepy, with the scent of Mike all around. She used to love going to sleep with that scent, waking up with it. His bed...the one she was staring at right now. Hot and sweaty...gasping, moaning. Fumbling in the dark, ripping off his buttons... His body...she could see it, almost feel it.... "I'm beginning to feel pretty tired," she said, not sure if she was feeling the effects of the booze or the effects of remembering Mike.

"Then lie down before you fall down," Rachel said. "Go to sleep."

Lilly didn't feel like lying down or sleeping. Her body was tired, her mind jammed with a whole flock of emotions she couldn't even begin to sort out, but she didn't want to lie down, shut her eyes, make it all go away. "I've got to deal with this in the morning, Rach," she said, stumbling over to the recliner—she'd seen it there earlier, when there was still light in the apartment. "And somehow I don't think he's going to make it easy on me."

"Can't you just release him?" Rachel asked.

"No, I can't just release him if he doesn't follow the conditions set down by the court." Plopping into the recliner and shoving it back to its farthest position, Lilly shut her eyes, but not to sleep. To think.

Unfortunately, an easy solution didn't spring to mind. There was nothing easy about Mike, and no easy way to deal with him.

"So can't the court change the conditions of his release?" Rachel continued. "Isn't there something Jimmy can do?"

"Maybe you should call him and ask," Lilly teased.

"See how you are? I make a perfectly good suggestion and you twist things around like a lawyer does. You're no fun when you're being a lawyer, so I'm going to bed. No more

Mike-in-jail talk, no more Jimmy." Rachel flopped down on the bed and kicked off her shoes. "Nice," she murmured, falling back into the pillows. "You ought to try it."

"No more Mike-in-jail talk," Lilly agreed. "Can't promise you anything about Jimmy, though." The nice drowsy effect of the beer was rolling down to her toes. She was finally relaxing, feeling a little more lethargic and a whole lot more willing to concede the evening to sleep. Yawning, she said, "I just wanted to do my job, Rach. That's all. Not get involved in something like this. But whenever Mike's meddling around in it, he really screws up my life. And it's never my fault! And I don't want to try his bed."

Lilly heard the telltale squeak. Same mattress. She knew the sound. She remembered the sound...their sound...their squeak...and so much more. "Would you lie still!" she finally snapped, after one squeak too many. All the relaxation and drowsiness drained right out of her. "And stop all that squeaking, for heaven's sake."

"It's big enough for four. Sure you don't want to share?"

"Been there, done that." And done that, and done that.

"In this bed?" Rachel squealed. "You're kidding! Do you think he changed the sheets?"

The Monday morning that should have been struck from the calendar

NEXT MORNING the courtroom was packed, and Rachel was sitting front and center, but only for moral support, she told Lilly. Yeah, right. Lilly knew her best friend was like the rest of them out there—gawking and eager and hoping for fireworks. "Tell Pete Walker to shut the doors," Lilly instructed her clerk. Tisha, she noticed, was dressed way over the top even for Tisha—barely-below-the-buns tight skirt; nipple-hugging Free Mike Collier T-shirt, sans bra, of course; new yellow streaks in her brown hair; gobs of makeup. "I don't want anybody else in the courtroom. And put on another shirt before you go out there!'' One without Mike's face emblazoned over a pair of 36C's.

"Big crowd," Mayor Lowell Tannenbaum said, strutting through Lilly's private door. "Too much publicity with the case, Miss Malloy. Way too much." He shook his head, sniffed, hiked his shoulders. "Guess it'll die down once you let him out this morning."

Shrugging into her robe, Lilly merely stared at him.

"You *are* going to let him out, aren't you?" His eyes started bulging.

She pulled up her hair and fastened it at the back of her neck with a black hair twisty, tucking a few stray strands behind her ears.

"Miss Malloy... *Judge* Malloy?" His voice went girlie.

And she put on her black glasses.

"It's political suicide," Lowell bellowed. "Political freakin' suicide, I tell you!" He reached up, ran his fingers through his comb-over and dislodged that one multitudinous hank of several hundred thin hairs, which, when set free, turned out to be ten inches long. It dangled just above his left ear all the way down to his shoulder. Between the hair and the tooth, Lilly didn't know where to look, so she spun around, grabbed a stack of case folders from her desk and headed to the door leading into her courtroom. "I'm not a politician," she said, opening it. "I'm a judge presiding over a court of law and I'll do what my job requires from me. Nothing more, nothing less." Then she stepped out as Tisha yelled over the noisy crowd, "Court's gonna start now, so everybody stand up for Judge Lilly Malloy!"

Come on down, Lilly thought. *The price is right!* Except nobody applauded her entrance. Of course applauding would have been tough since there were two hundred people jammed into that little courtroom that had never, during her jurisdiction, seen more than seventy or eighty. Leaving no room to get the elbows up and the hands together, thank heavens, even though Tisha was working the crowd—smiling, posing, wiggling, bouncing, looking as if she was on the verge of doing some cheerleading.

"Court is in session," Lilly announced, banging her gavel as she sat down at her desk. "No cameras, no recording devices of any kind and please turn off all cell phones. If your cell phone rings it will be confiscated by the bailiff." Her stare was fixed on the clock over the door at the back of the room, not the wide-eyed horde. "If you have a matter before the court today, you will be called when it's your turn. When you're called, please step forward promptly, hand any supporting paperwork to the clerk, Miss Freeman." Tisha stood up, tugged her skirt down and waved at the crowd. Every male spectator in the room—about one hundred fifty of them—waved back, and watched Tisha wiggle back into her chair.

Lilly continued, "Do not, let me repeat, *do not* step over the yellow line unless you are asked to do so. Should you step over the yellow line without permission you are subject to arrest, jail and-or a fine. There are no exceptions." She drew in a breath and finally scanned the crowd. Mayor Tannenbaum had squeezed into a spot in the rear, his hair plastered back in place, and Ezra, of all people, was seated near the door, looking properly serious and somewhat amused. Other than those two, and Rachel, no other familiar faces loomed. Since there were thirty-seven cases on her morning's docket, she supposed most of the people there were Mike fans, media and multifarious gawkers.

"I feel that I need to say something else before we start. This is a court of law and all matters here will be carried out as in any court of law. I will not tolerate outbreaks of any sort. Now, I realize that most of you are here because of recent events surrounding one of last week's defendants. I'm sure he appreciates your interest and support, but let me warn you. His case will be heard the same as all others before the court, and handled in a manner according to the law. You have no influence or favor in my court." She glanced at the row of women all wearing Free Mike Collier T-shirts—none wearing them quite as provocatively as Tisha had—and took in a steadying breath. It reminded her of a rock concert, and she expected them to faint dead away the instant Mike walked in. "So please control yourselves at all times and be respectful of all those who have cases that will be heard today. If you disrupt the court, you will be removed." *I should be so lucky*, she thought, pondering the ways she might be removed from her own court.

Shutting her eyes, really wanting to crawl under the desk instead of starting the session, Lilly decided there was no point putting it off any longer, so she slid her hand over to the pile of case folders and laid her fingers on the top one. It was Mike's—had that familiar burn to it... Well, at least it felt like it was burning. Should have been burning, as hot as he'd become these past few days. Slowly, she pulled it across the desk to her, then opened it. Ostensibly studying it for a moment, as though she hadn't memorized what was in it, Lilly finally glanced across the room to Pete Walker, her bailiff, and gave him the go-ahead nod.

He nodded back, then disappeared through the side door. Two minutes later he reappeared with Mike—Mike still in handcuffs, and still in his orange jail jumpsuit. "Geez," she whispered, as a wave of gasps rolled over the crowd. Jimmy was with Mike, looking awkward, nervous and not at all sure he even knew where he was. Tall, lanky and seeming more like a nervous defendant than an attorney, Jimmy finally spotted Lilly and beamed at her, even raised his hand to waist level and gave her a little miniwave with his fingers. "Geez," she whispered again. *This can't be happening.* "Counselor," she said, fighting the impulse to get up and run away. "Please approach the bench *with your client*."

"Me?" Jimmy asked, pointing to himself while looking

over his shoulder, just like a kid who hoped the teacher was calling on someone in back of him.

What was Jimmy looking at? Lilly wondered. A means of escape? And who could blame him. "You," she affirmed. Then she glanced at Mike, who was twisted around acknowledging the crowd with a smile. "Mr. Collier, please bring your attorney forward...now!"

"What's the meaning of this?" she hissed at both men as they faced her at her desk. "You shouldn't be in cuffs and you shouldn't be in that orange suit, Mike. That's not court protocol here and you've sat in on enough court cases to know it." Then she glared at Jimmy. "And you should know it, too, Counselor." Then back at Mike, glaring bullets. "So what are you doing?"

"Just having my day in court," he said casually. "That's all."

"Jimmy?" She looked up at him, hoping for a rational answer, but he turned around, staring at the crowd like a proverbial deer caught in headlights. Stage fright?

"His first trial," Mike said, shrugging. "Big day for him."

"This isn't a trial, Mike, and you know it. You plead and pay, then get out of my court."

"Well, I won't plead and I can't pay. And I won't apologize to the court...nothing personal, Lilly. I'm sorry about what I'm doing to you, but not sorry about what I have to do." He glanced down at her and a hint of softness crossed his face. That was the look that always earned him the benefit of the doubt, even when he didn't deserve it, like now. "But this is the way it's got to be. And I didn't mean for you to be in the middle of it."

"Mike..." She shook her head. "You do know what I have to do, don't you?"

He nodded, smiling.

Damn the smile, she thought. Why did he always have to

do that? "Last chance." With her eyes still on Mike's, she said, "Jimmy, can't you talk some sense into him?"

"Sure. About what?"

Earth to Jimmy. Lilly actually caught herself wondering if she should advise Mike to seek other counsel, since his counsel didn't seem to be here in the cognitive sense. Well, she thought about it for two seconds, then dismissed the idea. Mike would make too much of it, think she actually cared. Which she didn't. "Look, just step back Mike, and take Jimmy with you."

Mike still smiled at her. No pheromones jumping out or anything like that. Just a simple smile that squeezed her heart. Man of principle, she thought. A little off-center, but of principle, nonetheless. But damn it, why did *his* principles always come back to bite *her*.

"Mr. Collier," Lilly began once they were back at the defendant's podium. "You've been convicted of failure to pay nineteen parking tickets. Plus, you were charged with contempt of court. To relieve yourself of these charges, it is the decision of this court that you shall pay the fine as stipulated previously and in addition apologize to the court for your behavior last Friday." *Please, Mike, just do it. Get this over with and do it.*

"I'm sorry, Your Honor. I will not pay and I will not apologize for something that was not my fault."

The crowd gasped and someone in the back of the room shouted out, "Mike's the man!" Lilly banged the gavel, not even bothering to see where the offender was sitting because her eyes were glued to Mike's. As his were glued to hers.

"One last chance, Mr. Collier." *Please...*

He shook his head and the undercurrent of spectator rumblings hushed. "I can't do it, Your Honor. I will not pay and I will not apologize," he said quietly. Then he shot her his typical, careless Mike Collier grin. "So I'm prepared to face the consequences. Do what you have to do."

Well, what did she expect from him, anyway? Mike never

was exactly normal in what should have been normal reactions. That was one of the things she always liked about him...had liked, in the _way_ past tense. Maybe even one of the things that had attracted her so much, past tense again. Mike wasn't exactly the renegade man, but definitely someone who marched to that other drum. Well, that other drum came with consequences this time. Sorry, Mike. "Then for starters I'm tacking on another thousand dollars to cover the contempt of court charge as well as additional court fees."

"Which I won't pay, Your Honor."

Of course he wouldn't. She already expected that. Digging down deep for a bridled smile, she continued. "You've made your intentions quite clear to the court, Mr. Collier, so I'm sentencing you to one hundred sixty hours of community service to be determined by the—"

"Won't do it, You Honor," Mike interrupted. "No fine, no community service—not that I have a problem with community service, because I don't. But it's still a sentence for something I shouldn't be sentenced over. So nope, no community service."

A rumbling went up from the spectators and Lilly banged her gavel. That refusal from him actually did surprised her. She'd spent a fair amount of time reading the sentencing guidelines to find it. "What did you say, Mr. Collier?" she sputtered. It was a reasonable sentencing alternative, the one she thought for sure he would take. And now... Well, now there was nothing left. Time to go bottom line, and she wasn't feeling as good about it as she'd thought she would when she'd considered all the choices.

"I said I won't do it. No community service."

Lilly looked over at Jimmy, hoping he had an answer, a suggestion, a solution, a compromise...anything, but he was combing his hair. Still, she did what any good judge would do under the circumstances. "Counselor, would you like a moment to confer with your client?" Standing and adjusting his bright red necktie at the same time, Jimmy turned halfway to the crowd, halfway to Lilly, and asked, "About what, Your Honor?"

Lilly shook her head. If this was the defense Mike wanted... "To advise Mr. Collier that this option will keep him out of jail, but if he refuses it, the only thing remaining for me to do is sentence him to another jail term."

Jimmy looked at Mike. "What she said."

Mike looked at Lilly and winked. And it was a wink. Nothing imagined. Just a good, solid wink anyone looking would have seen. But Lilly was the only one who could see his face. And she definitely saw the wink.

"What I said," he stated. His voice was loud enough that everyone in the courtroom heard. And another round of gasps and under-the-breath comments resounded throughout.

This time Lilly let the noise continue for nearly a minute while she came to grips with the next move. Big trouble, she told herself as her gavel came banging down. Really big trouble. And briefly her eyes came to rest on Mayor Tannenbaum, who was turning red and squirming some kind of dance in the back row. Another disgruntled customer, it seemed. "Then the decision of the court, Mr. Collier, is to sentence you to thirty days in the city lockup."

The Free Mike T-shirt section let out a collective scream and, despite Lilly's earlier instructions, cameras popped up and started flashing. Pete Walker stepped away from his station next to Lilly's desk and shouted, "Come to order," while Tisha tried to squeeze herself into as many of the shots being snapped as she could.

Sitting back, folding her arms across her chest, Lilly saw Mike actually mouth an apology to her. Fat lot of good that did, because the circus was back in town and she was the ringleader. Picking up her gavel, she pounded it halfheartedly and waited until Pete had threatened the crowd enough times to bring their roar back down to a quiet rumble, then she finished her sentence. "Mr. Collier, I'm going to release you on your own recognizance for the time being, pending an appeal, which I'm sure will be forthcoming."

She glanced hopefully at Jimmy, whose eyes were glued to Rachel. And Rachel only had eyes for Jimmy. So that was it! Lilly felt a little envious. She remembered what that first blush of love or infatuation felt like. It was so exciting, so consuming, as if there was nothing else in the world, no one else in the world but the two of them—Rachel and Jimmy, her and Mike a long, long time ago. And here in the courtroom Rachel and Jimmy were doing that duet right now. It was just the two of them, and nobody else existed. Too bad Lilly might have to kick her best friend out of the courtroom for being such a distraction. Of course, if she left Rach there, Mike would get the kind of preoccupied representation he merited. Sort of a devious way to manipulate matters that Mike deserved, but Rach and Jimmy didn't. And truthfully, all Lilly wanted to do was get this over with quickly. "I'll be forwarding the matter to the prosecutor's office later today, so when—"

"No appeal, Your Honor," Mike said. "And no release on my own recognizance. I just want to serve my time and get it over with."

Lilly shut her eyes. Dear God, Mike had found a way to make it even worse, if that were at all possible. Which, it seemed, it was!

"May I approach the bench, Your Honor?" Jimmy asked, finally prying his eyeballs off Rach.

Good! He's going to object, offer a compromise or something to make this thing go away, Lilly thought...no, she prayed. So, cautiously, she let out a little sigh of relief. "Approach," she instructed, crossing her fingers under the desk.

And Jimmy approached. "I was wondering, Your Honor, since Mike's going back to jail, which means the media's going to be chasing you again and you'll probably be hiding out—and Mike said you can stay on at his place as long as you want, by the way—should I just keep Sherlock over at my house for a while? Maybe Rachel could bring over some of his toys."

"Sherlock?" Lilly was the one with the deer-in-headlights stare this time. And it lasted into the fifteen minute recess she called after she slammed the gavel on the desk and closed the Mike Collier case once and for all.

"Get him in here," she hissed to Tisha, who was loitering in the private hallway outside Lilly's office, batting her eyes and bucking her 36C's at Felix, who was the *Journal*'s photog for the day. Like that would do her any good! "Mike Collier. I want to see him *right now*."

Lilly was hunched down onto an old couch in her office, still in her black robe, when Pete Walker brought Mike in, still handcuffed. "Leave us alone," she instructed Pete.

"You gonna have him uncuff me first?" Mike asked, kicking a metal folding chair right up to Lilly's couch, then sitting down.

"No," she snapped. "You want to do this the hard way so I'll oblige."

Mike arched his eyebrows wickedly. "Didn't know you were into handcuffs, Lilly. Adds a whole 'nother dimension to you."

"Handcuffs and duct tape, if you don't shut up." He was too close. She could feel it…feel him…

"Wanna do it on the floor, Lilly? Right here, right now?"

No, not that again! "Mike…" Damn, she couldn't remember what she wanted to say. *Think, Lilly, think!* She chanced a glance at him and he was studying her…studying hard. Then the hot flash hit. She jumped from an even 98.6 up to a roaring 105 in a heartbeat. And the sweat baptizing her face caused her glasses to slide down to the end of her nose and right on off into her lap. *Get him out of here,* her last shred of sanity screamed. *Before you* do *do it on the floor, right here, right now.*

"I've got to get back to court," she stated with finality. And she meant it in more ways than one.

"It's still there," he said, grinning. "Isn't it? That *thing* we always had going between us. Admit it, Lilly. You're feeling it right now."

"There's no *thing* between us, Mike. Not now, never was."

"Look, Lilly. I really screwed up twice. I'll admit that and I don't expect us to go back. Although—" he chuckled, and his suggestive eyebrows arched again "—there were some mighty good moments, weren't there?"

"You know, I really hated you," she said, the fever suddenly lessening. "Still do, when I think about what you did to me...what you caused me, what you took away from me. Everything I'd worked for, everything I was achieving.... I can't get it back, Mike. None of it. And yes, that second time I did fall for your apology and there was even a moment I thought... Well, it doesn't matter what I thought because before I had time to sort us out I was in jail. Funny how that happened. Another night with Mike, another professional catastrophe in my life. So I won't go through that again. I don't know what you're trying to pull with this parking ticket grandstanding, but you're not going to get away with it. Not in my court. Not in my life."

"We need to talk, Lilly," he said, suddenly serious.

"I've said everything I intend to say. You want to go to jail for a month, that's your business. You know what it'll take to get you out, but it's your choice. End of conversation, Mike." She stood and headed for the door back into the courtroom. And as she opened it...

"Shake those sexy hips, you judgely vixen."

Great, just great! she thought, catching herself shaking them just a little.

6

Later Monday morning, same ol', same ol'

"I THINK YOU KNOW the drill by now," Roger Jackson said, leading Mike back to his cell.

Mike smiled. "What can I say? I like the digs here better than where I'm staying." But thirty days! He'd expected another three or four days, maybe a week, tops. But a whole damn month? Lilly was certainly in rare form with that sentence. Maybe she called it strictly by the book, but her book was packing a mighty big wallop these days and she was obviously getting a kick out of throwing it at him, over and over and over....

"Think maybe it's time you find yourself a good lawyer?" Roger asked, opening the cell door. "One who's a little more familiar with a law book than Wong's take-out menu?"

Laughing, Mike stepped inside the cell—*his cell*—looked around, found the tin of fresh-baked chocolate chip cookies—courtesy of Juanita Lane—sitting atop the television, and popped open the lid. "Jimmy's doing just what I need him to do, which is pretty much nothing." He took a bite, offering the tin to Roger. "And I really don't want him getting the notion to play lawyer right now." Not because Mike wanted to fester in jail for a month. He didn't! But above everything else, he had Lilly to consider, and any other lawyer would have been going after her with a vengeance, since this whole mess was splattered everywhere in the news. That kind of publicity could get him an A-list lawyer who'd have him out of there in minutes, but that certainly wouldn't help Lilly. And this was all about helping Lilly, so keeping her out of it meant keeping Jimmy in it. "I think Jimmy's doing fine on the Wong takeout, since I don't intend on eating jail food for thirty days," Mike quipped.

"Thirty-one," Roger corrected. "August has thirty-one days. So what gives with Lilly anyway, Mike? I know I only report on the jail beat, but I'm sensing something else here, something you don't want to talk about. And since you *claim* you're not in love with her, which I don't believe, by the way, what's the deal?"

"Other than the fact that every time I get near her I screw up her life?" Dropping down on his cot, Mike shrugged. "I'm not sure what gives yet, but when I find out I'll give you the story, okay? In the meantime, would you ask Juanita to rustle up a glass of cold milk for me? Can't have chocolate chip cookies without cold milk."

Roger did just that and Juanita, now thoroughly under Mike's spell, rushed to his cell with milk and a cell phone. "Anything else, Mikey?" she asked cheerfully.

"Marry me?" he asked, grinning through the bars. "As soon as they let me out of here, we'll run away together. Tahiti, Jamaica, Detroit?"

"Could we make it end of next month, Mike? My grandson's thirteenth birthday is coming up in a few weeks and I promised to take him to an NFL game. After that I'm all yours." She winked. "If you can handle it."

Mike grinned. "Juanita, love. By that time I'll have been behind bars so long I'll have forgotten what it's like to be with a real woman such as yourself." He winked back. "So you may have to teach me a few moves, if you know what I mean."

"See how you are, Mikey? Performance anxiety already. After a whole month in here God only knows how you'll be in bed. And I can't be wasting my time with—" she lowered her head and gave him a deadpan look over the top of her glasses

"—an incompetent. Sorry, but that's the way it's got to be. A woman my age needs a man who can perform every time, every place. Not someone she's gotta teach."

"You know you're breaking my heart," Mike said, clasping his chest.

"Better yours than mine." Juanita blew him a kiss, then went back to her post. "Ten minutes on the phone, then I need it back," she called. "Rules, you know." As if any of them applied to Mike.

Ten minutes to do what? he wondered. He wasn't hungry, so no need calling Jimmy. Fritz was flittering his leadership skills over the meager newspaper crew—probably flittering the *Journal* right into the ground—so no one there to call, either. But Mike had ten minutes, plus thirty-one days. *You've really done it this time!*

He was thirty-three years old and it was time to quit messing up. He needed to drop anchor in the place in life where he wanted to be. And what he had now was almost it. Close to it, anyway. That's what he'd thought for the last few months, as his paper struggled for survival, and always seemed to keep afloat—just barely. The life he wanted...most of the life he wanted. The life he wanted except without Lilly. Hell, he'd never expected to see her again and, until he had, he had been making do just fine. No, it wasn't the way he would have chosen things, because *things* would have included her in some way. But he had been getting along without her.

Then suddenly, Lilly appeared, and everything changed.

"Lilly," he said to her voice mail. "Will you have dinner with me tonight? Say, around seven. I think we should try to settle some problems between us and I do need to talk to you about..." No, the less said the better. "Just call this number back and leave word with Juanita if I don't answer."

His next call was to Lowell Tannenbaum's voice mail. "This is Mike Collier and I'm still conducting business, even though I'm in jail. You said you wanted an interview and I can fit you in this afternoon at one. I'll have my photographer here to snap some shots." Mike smiled. One Tannenbaum signed. Drag him in and see what turned up. Even if the mayor didn't want to meet with him face-to-face, he'd never, ever turn down a photo shoot. "My deadline's three o'clock, by the way, if I want to make tomorrow's edition." One Tannenbaum sealed. "Front page story." And one Tannenbaum about to be delivered.

The mayor showed up early, as it turned out. Hair combed over into an almost-swirl on the top of his almost-bald head, then plastered in place, and all dressed up in a crisp brown suit, crooked brown bow tie, theatrical makeup with rosy-red lips, Tannenbaum was ready for who knew what when he arrived at Mike's cell. Juanita was escorting him, making faces at him behind his back as she let him in. "Met up with your photographer, Felix, outside." Lowell sniffed. "We did our photo shoot on the steps of the building. Thought if they turned out I might use them for my campaign pictures, if that's okay with you."

Felix snapping Tannenbaum—now, that's a campaign moment sure to convince the voters, Mike thought. "Have a seat," he said, pointing to the gray metal chair across from his cot. "Tell me what's on your mind." He grabbed his pen, poising himself to write, or doodle. Some days being a journalist really sucked—a sentiment that had nothing to do with being in jail.

The mayor arched his skeptical penciled-in eyebrows. "What's this about?"

"Just trying to get a story." Mike needed an antacid to swallow down with those words.

"About what?" Tannenbaum adjusted the crease in his trousers, pulling up the cloth enough so there was a gap between his brown socks and the hem, revealing an inch of pasty-white flesh.

"Anything you want to talk about. Your fiscal responsibility platform..." Maybe that would get the ball rolling. Get him to spill something. Problem was, jail was limiting. If the mayor walked out, Mike couldn't go after him, couldn't hound him. So he was treading on eggshells, trying to lull Tannenbaum into a feeling of superiority, which shouldn't be too hard, considering it was, after all, Lowell Tannenbaum. "I think the readers should know more...."

"So, you're finally coming around. Figured you would." The mayor settled back in his chair, sniffed, hiked his shoulders and prepared to expound. "Yep, figured you would once you had a chance to think about it. Especially after you found out you've got your parking place back, with a Reserved for Mike Collier sign to be erected there first thing next week. It was all a big mistake..." Sniff, hike.

Yeah, right, Mike thought, doodling a black cloud over the likeness of Tannenbaum he'd sketched. The lightning bolt coming out of the cloud was aimed right at his pinhead. "A big mistake that got a lot of publicity. Made people take note of the parking ticket situation here in Whittier, didn't it? I mean, Mayor, I've done some looking, and someone's really keeping on top of all the illegal parking."

Tannenbaum sniffed and hiked again. "That's just the way we do things around here. I know you've been away from here a long time, Mike, but we try to keep our town affairs neat and tidy." He smiled, then reached to smooth his left eyebrow, interrupting his pretense momentarily to stare at the eyebrow pencil smudge he'd just put on his thumb. Popping a small compact out of his pocket, Mayor Lowell Tannenbaum took a look at his face, checking his eyebrow for smears. Convinced he was smudge-free, he added, "Anyway, I wanted to run through the highlights of my platform for the next election, if you don't mind."

"Fiscal responsibility," Mike said, not bothering to write down a word. He didn't have to, since everybody in Whittier already knew, word for word, the rhetoric that was about to suck the oxygen out of his jail cell.

"Fiscal responsibility." Sniff, hike. "And the financial books are open for anybody who cares to come down to my office and check them out. Monday through Friday, nine to five. I've got nothing to hide and the good people of Whittier know that. First time any mayor has ever done that." He frowned at Mike. "Are you writing that down—the part about how no mayor has ever done that before? It's important, Mike."

Mike nodded, blinking to keep his glazed-over eyes from freezing that way. "Got it," he lied.

"Fiscal responsibility, Mike...." And the mayor yammered on about his political agenda for the next twenty-five minutes, nonstop. A string of well-rehearsed utterances of which Mike recorded only enough to plump out the puff piece he'd be writing. Mostly he just doodled and forced himself to stay awake, or at least not snore when he dozed. Then finally, when the Tannenbag of hot air seemed to have deflated just a bit, Mike jumped to his feet, extended his hand to Lowell and thanked him. "Just one more thing, Mayor," he said, hurrying the man into the corridor. "About these open books that anyone can come to see..."

The mayor nodded. Sniff, hike.

"Just where would all the money come from that keeps them balanced, keeps them fiscally responsible?" He gave the mayor a sunny grin as he swooped in for the first pickings. "I think the readers would like to know where the big sources of Whittier money are, don't you?"

Caught a little off guard, the mayor ran this hand through his plastered comb-over and loosened it. It fell over his forehead, then down in his face, but he recouped quickly and brushed it back into place with a stroke that appeared well-practiced. "The usual places, of course. Taxes, city fees like dog tags and building permits." That said in his nervous, girlie voice.

"Parking tickets?" Mike asked. His voice was casual, but the stare he fixed on Tannenbaum was anything but. It was a dart, zeroing in on the target. "Like mine?"

"General disregard for the law *like yours*, don't you mean?" Tannenbaum snorted. "Except you don't seem to be paying your fines like everybody else does, do you? Instead, you're costing the taxpayers approximately one hundred fifty dollars a day by refusing to pay." And he didn't sniff, hike. "But if you'd like to take a look at the books, feel free. In fact, I'll be happy to have someone run them over to you, since you can't go to them." He smiled. "And won't be able to for quite some time, it seems." Sniff, hike.

Juanita escorted Mayor Lowell Tannenbaum out of Mike's cell block while Mike dropped back down on his cot and munched a chocolate chip cookie, thinking about what Lilly might like for dinner tonight.

Monday evening back at the hovel, or not!

"IT'S A DATE," Rachel said, throwing Mike's few hanging clothes into a pile on the floor, then hanging up her and Lilly's clothes in their place. Lilly, in the meantime, was busy prying a board off the window over the kitchen sink, trying to let in some light. "A guy asks a girl out to dinner, Lil, and that's usually called a date...or in prison I suppose it's called a conjugal visit."

"What's the point of sentencing him if the rules don't apply to him?" Lilly snapped, pulling back on the board to give it one last chance to surrender before she went at it with whatever tool or weapon she could find in the apartment. "And it's not conjugal."

"Yeah, well, the evening's still young, girlfriend. You've got lots of time to make it happen."

The board finally gave and Lilly went back-stepping all the way across the room, holding on to it. "Stop it, Rach. It's not funny," she panted. "And I'm not going, so quit nagging me."

"I think you should. I mean, I won't be here this evening. Got a date, so you'll be here all by yourself...in *this* place, still trying to fix it up, like it can be fixed overnight. Which it can't, and you know that, but you're using it to avoid what really needs fixing. And you know what that is, even though you won't admit that, either, and that's all you're gonna do all night—avoid it. So do you want to come with us?"

"A date? That's fast work, isn't it? Who with? And I'm *not* avoiding anything!"

"Jimmy. He's kinda cute in a bumbling sort of way. And smart, even though he doesn't show it too well. We're just going out for pizza and a movie. No big deal, so you're welcome to tag along. And you are too avoiding it, Lilly Malloy. Instead of thinking about Mike, you're renovating his apartment."

The last thing Lilly wanted was a pizza and movie—in public—especially as an interloping horn-in on somebody else's first date. Therefore, an hour later, as she sat alone in Mike's decrepit warehouse apartment, debating between her frozen dinner choices—the one with assorted breaded chicken parts and the one with all-white breaded chicken parts—she wondered what Mike would have offered her from his jail cell. A Wong's number three, maybe? Or a burrito?

It was already past seven, way too late to accept his invitation, not that she'd been inclined to do that. But if she had, she was too late, even though she did want to talk to him...only to find out why he was doing what he was doing, and to see if he'd changed his mind about paying up and getting out. As those lame excuses rolled around in her head for several more minutes they must have become convincing enough, even to her, because at seven forty-five, all decked out in her best holey jeans, one of Mike's plaid flannel shirts that hung halfway to her knees, plus a baseball cap under which she tucked all her hair, Lilly set off for the jail. As she walked, she prayed no one would recognize her. She looked more like she belonged camping under a railroad trestle than presiding over a court of law.

Howard McCray, on guard duty for the evening, recognized her right off, though. He didn't even bat an eye when she pecked on the glass to be let inside the locked-up-tight city hall. Instead, he gave her a friendly wave and scrambled right over to the door. "Nice evening for a walk, Your Honor," he commented, as Lilly scribbled her name on the sign-in roster. "Little warm for that flannel, though, isn't it?" he continued. "Course, it does get a might chilly later on, if you intend on staying into the night."

Lilly shook her head. "I won't be here long," she said, rushing past him before anybody spotted her. "I just need to...to go over some court records. Maybe check in on somebody over in the jail, if I have time." Like all night, she thought.

"Happy conjugating, and I don't mean with verbs," he called after her.

"What?" she sputtered, spinning around.

"I said, make sure you sign out when you leave."

Cal Gekas was on duty when Lilly wandered into the cell block without even putting on the pretense of first stopping by her office. He was playing cards with Mike through the bars, eating chocolate chip cookies. "Looks like she made it," Cal commented, scooting his chair back, then pushing the small computer desk on wheels away from the door. "You'll be wanting this table, right?" he asked.

Mike pulled the table inside, and by the time Lilly arrived at his cell, it was laid out with a nice spread of fettuccini Alfredo, tossed salad, bread sticks—all served on green-and-white china sitting atop a red-and-white checkered tablecloth. "Sorry I couldn't manage the wine," Mike said. "But jailhouse rules. No alcohol." Holding out the gray metal chair for her, he waited several seconds while she hesitated outside in the corridor. "It's still warm," he said. "I figured you'd be late so I had it delivered just a few minutes ago."

"Cozy," she commented, finally stepping inside.

Cal Gekas closed the door behind her. "Sorry, I can't leave it open, Your Honor, but we've got rules. The cells have to be locked." Then he skittered away.

"Rules," Lilly commented, her back to the bars. "Interesting how they work, isn't it?" She hadn't intended to be let in. In fact, she'd intended on staying in the hall, a good ten paces from the iron bars, well into Mike-safe territory. "Use the ones you like, discard the ones you don't."

"Care for a bread stick?" Mike picked one up and waved it at her. "Lots of garlic butter, nice and warm."

"I didn't come here to eat." The words were emphatic, even if her conviction wasn't. Truth was, she didn't know why she was there and the fact that she was scared her, and not just a little. It always started like this with Mike, something innocent and simple. A meal, a cup of coffee, a glass of wine. Then the next thing...well, that was never so innocent and simple.

"Suit yourself." Mike took a bite of the bread stick and Lilly almost winced over how slowly he chewed it. Lingering, deliberate...his mouth moving so seductively... She remembered his mouth on her, all over her.... The kisses, the way his tongue slid up and down...over the hollow of her throat, across her shoulders, through the valley between her breasts, then down, down, down.... "Oh, God." Lilly's eyes suddenly flew wide open. Had she just moaned out loud? She braved a look at Mike. He was dishing out two bowls of fettuccini, much more caught up in the Alfredo sauce than in her. And she sighed in vast relief, gritting her teeth against any more moans, out loud or otherwise. "I'm not staying," she insisted, still pressed to the door and really meaning it.

"Sure you are." He placed her bowl of pasta on the table, then sat on the edge of his cot and gestured her over to the chair across from him. "Otherwise, why are you here?"

"I'm here because..." Geez, she didn't know why she was there. And he knew she didn't know. It was written all over his grinning face. "I'm here because I wanted to thank you for letting me hang out in your place while the media's still after me." Not good, not bad and apparently not convincing, because his only response was taking a bite of fettuccini. And the noodle...omigod, the noodle passing through his lips so...so— "Oh..."

"Oh, what?" he asked, wrapping another noodle around his fork, then holding it up to her.

Oh, great...oh, no...she'd moaned out loud. "Oh...it looks good and I haven't eaten anything since breakfast." Not the best comeback, but it was the only one she had, since watching him twirl that noodle was distracting every single one of her otherwise sensible senses.

"Then eat." He stood, walked over to the jail door.

"You're my prisoner," she protested as he rubbed the noodle lightly across her lips. "This is highly irregular," she mumbled, almost giving in, wanting to give in, fighting to give in. But she wouldn't, couldn't. Not the noodle—*his noodle.* "And this is against the rules, I'm sure."

"Even a judge has to eat sometime," he said, his voice so quiet and low it sent shivers up her back. He knew just how to use that voice on her—she had a history with that voice. His give-in-to-me-Lilly voice. It always worked and she always did.

But not this time. And that resolve didn't come just because they were locked in a jail cell with a guard camped down the hall. The *Lilly Beware!* alarm was going off in her head. It was the one that shoved her way past the moment into the aftermath...the aftermath of every moment they'd ever had together. An ugly aftermath where she ended up on the blunt end of receiving something she didn't deserve, something all wrapped up in Mike's own unmindful brand of gift wrap. That thought, that realization took hold, at least momentarily, and she grabbed the fork out of his hand and ate the noodle—*his noodle*. "Pretty good," she said, finally pulling herself away from the door and moving over to the table. "And I am hungry, Mike. Starved, in fact. Could I have more salad?" And for the next ten minutes Lilly ate without saying a word, while Mike sat back, arms folded across his chest, watching her.

"Got any cannoli?" she finally asked, after wiping her mouth. "Or tiramisu?"

He held out the tin of cookies, smiling as Lilly looked them over and took out the three largest. "Jimmy's out with Rach, in case you didn't know. Pizza and a movie. Got milk, by the way?"

"Have you ever looked into the parking ticket situation here in Whittier?" he asked, finally digging into his own fettuccini. "How many are issued per week or per month? And what kind of revenue they're bringing in?"

"Back to that?" she snapped as he chewed and swallowed. "You had your chance for a lighter sentence, Mike. I did everything I could, but you decided on jail, and it's over with now, so deal with it."

"How many parking ticket cases, on average, come through your court...say, each week? And what percentage is that compared to all the parking tickets issued?"

Chewing up his next bite, he went for a third, and for some strange reason, Lilly wasn't affected. Not at all. In fact, he was just another person sitting across the table chewing his food. Nothing sexy about it. No Mike effect. Strange... "I've never counted," she replied, narrowing her eyes. "You working on some kind of appeal, after all?"

Shaking his head, he reached across the table for another bread stick. "Just a story idea in mind. Trying to do some fact gathering."

"About parking tickets?" Now she was beginning to wonder. Mike went after headliners, not the mundane back page items, and parking tickets were back page at best. "Come on, Mike. I know what kind of stories you get yourself involved in and you're not interested in parking tickets outside the fact that you got nailed for a bunch of them. And the mayor, by the way, has given you back your parking spot, so you don't even have a gripe anymore."

"Not a gripe," he said. "Just a grudge."

Smiling, Lilly stood. "Well, that's life, Mr. Collier. And you've got thirty days and twelve hours to think about that grudge."

"How many parking tickets did you process today, Lilly? And how many more never even made it into court?"

"You don't give up, do you?" Walking to the cell door, she turned around to face him and found him standing directly behind her, almost pressed into her. Biting her lips to keep back the moan or the sigh or the little lusty giveaway she knew, from past experience, was trying to escape—one that would inevitably betray her by sneaking out when she least expected, or wanted it to—she grabbed on to the cell doors behind her and locked her eyes on the floor. "My offer of...um, community service or paying the, um, fine still stands if you want...." Glancing up just a little, not sure why she did it other than to see if he was glancing down—which she really didn't want him to do because that would be the start of something she didn't want to start—Lilly was ambushed by his intense stare, the one she remembered oh so well. Seeing it, she tried to dodge it, tried to look back down at the floor before it snared her, but in that moment their roles reversed and she couldn't get away. He was decreeing the judgment over her and she was the prisoner. And she had no breath to fight the sentence he was doling out, no will to resist it.

Mike's kiss was as spirited as it was good—as good as it ever had been. The familiar feel of his tongue, the remembered taste of him—he evoked everything in her so fast—the fire that sprang up before they drew their first breath during the kiss, the hunger that pounded for more before their lips even parted. And now, like always, his firm mouth demanded an answer from her...an answer she offered with a voracity that belied her reckless need, one that had erupted with their very first kiss years ago and rushed back now, so many years later.

"Mike," she murmured, trying to fight through the torrid fog to push him away. She had to...had to break free. But as if he knew she was struggling to wage that battle, he countered by lowering his lips to her neck, then around to the hollow of her throat. Unfair advantage. Mike knew that made her go weak in the knees, and he chuckled low and suggestively while she fumbled for an even harder grip on the bars behind her, her fiery clench on the cold metal turning it hot as she struggled to keep herself from melting into his arms.

"You always did like that," he said, unbuttoning the top button of her shirt, then moving his mouth to her exposed shoulder. "And you loved this, didn't you."

Reaching low, Mike wrapped his hands around Lilly's waist, into the hollow of her back. Then he kneaded her there for a moment, slowly and methodically, until she moaned, not caring that he heard the pleasure he was giving her. "Remember what came next?" he whispered in her ear. Lowering his hand to her derriere, he cupped her in a firm hold, then pulled her away from the iron bars and into his hips, where she felt the iron of his erection against her pelvis. Instinctively, her arms went up to wrap around his neck, as they'd done so many times before.

An ingrained reaction to Mike, one not to be controlled. She knew that and she knew he knew.

"Remember, Lilly?" he whispered again, his voice so rough with sex it dragged every ounce of her own need to the surface.

And she did remember...every vivid detail. What came next and what came after that, all the way to the afterglow, then into the next liaison, because with Mike, once was never enough and, as often as not, she was the one begging for more. More...that's what she wanted now. She wanted *more* so badly she ached all the way through for it...for Mike. And when a groan of growing arousal escaped Mike's own lips as he pressed himself even harder to her—so hard they shared the same heartbeat—she knew she was close to begging for more, begging his hands to stroke a path under the flannel shirt, along her ribs, to her breasts.

Lilly also knew if they didn't stop right then, they wouldn't, not even in jail. That part of their history was undeniable. But oh, how she didn't want to stop, even though he was the one who finally did.

"No more," she choked out, bringing her hands up to Mike's chest and pushing him away...but not before she brushed the back of her hand across his cheek. "We can't do this, Mike. Not here, not anywhere."

Smiling, he obliged willingly, for which Lilly was grateful, since every bit of will she could muster against Mike was spent in pushing him away, and there was no more left in store lest he begin again with the intense stare that always started it all.

"So can you check the records for me? See how many parking tickets get processed a week?" Mike asked, traipsing back over to his cot, as cool as he'd been when he was eating the bread stick moments ago.

"You never change, do you, Mike?" Straightening the flannel shirt and buttoning it up to her throat, despite the fact that

it was a ninety-degree August night outside, Lilly took in a
steadying breath. "It's always about your compulsion to advance your career. And somehow, I'm always the one getting
run over by that compulsion." She turned to the bars and
yelled, "I'm ready to leave." Then she spun back around to
Mike. "Not this time."

When Cal Gekas let her out, and Lilly walked away, she
half expected to hear one of those little voices calling out a
sexy suggestion or innuendo. But the only thing she heard
was the occasional squeak of her rubber-soled running shoes
on the concrete floor. And for some odd reason, she felt disappointed.

7

Living at the hovel and other Monday night woes

"WHAT DO YOU MEAN, he sort of kissed you?" Rachel poured a glass of orange juice and handed it to Lilly. It was after midnight, the printing press downstairs was sputtering and wheezing to get out the morning edition—the one where Lilly's decision to jail Mike for a month was once again the headliner—and she and Rachel were sitting at his table, eating a snack of Twinkies by candlelight. "He either kissed you or he didn't. Mouth to mouth, lips to lips, tonsils to tonsils. Remember?" She puckered up and play-smooched at Lilly. "It hasn't been that long, has it?"

"Okay, okay. So he kissed me." *Boy, did he kiss me.*

"And you did what?"

Lilly winced. She didn't want to admit her part in this. As a judge she would have called it inadmissible. But it wasn't, because she'd done the deed in question. And her lips were still a little swollen to prove the point. Tag 'em as evidence—they gave her away. "I let him, and before you jump all over me with more questions, it was just once."

"That's all? You let him do it one time?" Rachel laughed. "You never were a good liar, Lil."

"So it was a little more than *let*. No big deal." No way was she admitting to encouraging him or even responding to him. And absolutely not a word about the *enjoying it* part.

"I'm betting on a whole lot more... Wait! No way! You didn't do *that*, not in the jail cell?" Rachel squealed. "Lilly,

even for you that's way off the radar." Then a wicked little
smile crossed her lips. "So did you get caught?"

"No," Lilly sputtered. "I didn't do *that*." *Woulda, coulda.* "I
kissed him back a little, but that's as far as it went." *Wanted to
really bad.*

"Good thing, or they'd be stopping the presses downstairs
right now, changing the headline to Judge Caught Cavorting
in Jail." Rachel shook her head. "Serious stuff, sweetie, and I
don't know what to tell you except remember who he is, and
be careful."

"It was a kiss, for heaven's sake, and we stopped. That was
it. No more. Then he started asking me about parking tickets.
And that's weird, even for Mike."

Rachel grinned at her friend. "Sure it wasn't some sort of
strange jail pillow talk?"

Lilly shook her head and took a drink of juice. "Who knows
what he was doing?" she finally said. "But he was doing it
alone because I left."

Rachel pulled her legs up to keep her feet from dangling,
and sat cross-legged in the wooden kitchen chair. "So tell me,
was it as good as it always used to be?" she asked, unwrapping her second Twinkie.

"We were in jail, Rach! Nothing happened."

"But you wanted it to. Some good, hot outlaw sex behind
bars. Hey, I could think of worse places." She tossed Lilly a
mischievous wink. "I've seen some of those prison movies."

"He's not an outlaw," Lilly argued, plowing into *her* second Twinkie. "And it's jail, not prison."

"Jail, prison. You've got *the thing* going again and it's just a
matter of time." She pulled the last Twinkie from the box.
"Splits?"

Lilly shook her head. "It's all yours. And no, I don't have
the thing going again. He just caught me off guard. That's all."
Off guard, out of control, hot to trot. Call it whatever, Lilly
was deeply aware that the chemistry between them hadn'

simmered down. Once, even twice with Mike—years ago—could be explained, sort of. But being swooped into that curse three times? Well, maybe it wasn't exactly some unconscious professional death wish, but close, and she was beginning to wonder if she truly was one of those women who could be attracted *only* to the wrong kind of man—the kind of man who was bad for a woman in every way that counted, which attracted her all the more. Because Mike was bad for her in every way that counted.

She'd scoffed at that idea two times before, when Mike was busy hacking away at her career piece by piece—intentional or not—and she'd chalked it up to youthful naivete, lust and a whole lot of other superficial, crazy mixed-up emotions and hormonal reactions. But now? What was this time about? *Hello, Lilly! You don't have an answer, silly or otherwise, and it's beginning to scare you because your Mike-Collier hormones are whacked-out again.* "He just caught me off guard," she echoed, trying to reassure herself—and failing.

"He caught you off guard?" Rachel laughed. "Let's see. He asked you for a rendezvous in his jail cell. Then even though you said you wouldn't go, you did, and spent all evening there with him, eating his food, drinking his wine—"

"No wine," Lilly interjected, as if that made a difference, since all it took was water to get her in the Mike mood.

"Okay, no wine. But you ate his food and somehow got yourself into a position where he kissed you, you kissed him back and you still want to claim that he caught you off guard. I would submit that, since you have prior knowledge of how your little ol' libido acts in close proximity to one Mike Collier, there is no unintentional catching off guard. *If* you were caught off guard, it was only because you wanted to be, and I rest my case." She smiled. "So what's the verdict, Judge? Did I win?"

"I ought to throw you in jail with him."

"Yeah, then you'd get to come visit *him* on the pretext of visiting me. I'm sensing a pattern here, Lil."

Shaking her head, Lilly released a big, discouraged sigh. Rachel was right, of course. There *was* definitely a pattern there. "So what should I do, Rach? Other than keep him locked up."

"Marry him."

When Lilly looked for the usual grin on Rachel's face, the grin that came after one of her typical outrageous statements, it wasn't there. Her expression was dead serious, her eyes full of a meaning Lilly refused to decipher.

"You *are* kidding, aren't you?" Lilly sputtered, not sure how else to respond. And to that, Rachel merely shrugged, then crammed the rest of the Twinkie in her mouth.

LOVE MIKE? Me in love with him? Not a chance. Rachel is so wrong about this one I ought to go over to the bed, shake her awake and tell her so. Let her lose some of the sleep I've been losing ever since she just casually dropped "marry him" on me and went to bed.

It was four in the morning and Lilly was so far from sleep she was considering rounding up her caseload of defendants and getting a good, early start on the day. Might as well, since Rachel's words wouldn't let her sleep. That, and the fact that her best friend might have been serious.

No, she *was* serious. Lilly just didn't want to see it. Some best friend! *Here I am in the middle of a crisis and what does Rachel do? "Marry him, Lilly"...marry him...marry him!*

Even the wind-up clock was conspiring. Tic, tock...tic, tock...marry Mike...marry Mike....

And what did Rachel and the clock know about it, anyway? You had to love someone to marry him, right? She didn't love Mike. Never had...had she?

No, I don't love Mike. Don't love Mike...

Tic, tock...marry Mike...marry Mike...love Mike.

Tuesday morning is as good a time as any for all you-know-what breaking loose

THE HALL OUTSIDE Lilly's office was literally flooded with reporters the next morning as the courthouse opened for business as usual. Except there was nothing usual about the mob descending on Lilly's court. They were so thick she could barely squeeze her way through them, and poor Pete Walker, her court bailiff, wasn't having much luck clearing them away, since he stood a whole head shorter than most everyone in the pack, and no one really even saw him. But he was frantically waving his night stick in the air, jumping up and down and shouting for everybody to clear the corridor.

Tisha Freeman seemed to be the only one enjoying all the hubbub, posing and smiling when the cameras pointed, and answering questions she shouldn't have been.

"Does Judge Malloy have a sexual bias?" a reporter yelled out.

"I don't know which way Judge Malloy goes concerning sexual things, but if she does have a bias it's certainly nobody's business but hers," Tisha responded, batting her contact-colored violets at the questioner.

"Does Judge Malloy have a history of sentencing men more unfairly than women?" someone else yelled.

"No, she doesn't sentence men any more unfairly than she does women. Everybody's treated the same in Judge Malloy's court." Then Tisha slowly moistened her pale pink lipstick with her tongue.

Great, Lilly thought, trying unsuccessfully to push her way to the front of the crowd to take back whatever Tisha was giving out. No sleep all night, she was late for work this morning, then Tisha was babbling away to the press. Could this day get any better?

"What do you know about Judge Malloy being arrested and thrown in jail?" came the next question.

Tisha continued, "If she got sent to jail once, I'm sure she deserved it just like anybody else would. Judge Malloy wouldn't stand for impartiality. She's not impartial in her courtroom and I'm sure she wouldn't be in jail, either. That's just the way she is."

"Wait," Lilly yelled from somewhere in the middle of the pack. "Let me explain...." No one even looked at her, and it was quite clear that no one was interested in what Lilly had to say, not while Tisha was putting on a much better show.

The next questioner demanded, "And do you know how Judge Malloy received this appointment to the bench?"

That one almost stumped Tisha, and Lilly was about to breathe a little sigh of relief over the pause in witless answers when a lightbulb lit up over Tisha's head. "I think because the robe from the last judge already fit her, so they didn't have to get a new one...new robe, not new judge." She giggled. "Although they did get a new judge. And her robe is kind of big, so I guess she could wear bulky clothes under it to fill it up. But if you want to know what's under her robes, you'll have to ask her. I never talk about anybody's underwear, or whether they wear it. And if Judge Malloy doesn't wear underwear under her robe, that's her own business. Nobody else's, unless she wants them to know." Tisha turned her face to a television camera, caught sight of Lilly, who'd almost succeeded in shoving herself to the front of the mob, and waved at her. "They've been asking me all kinds of things about you, but you don't have to worry, Judge Malloy. I'm not telling them anything that could make you look any worse than you already do."

A tight smile crossed Lilly's lips. "I'll just bet you are," she muttered under her breath, girding herself for the equivalent of the perp walk down to her office.

Cameras flashed, questions were shouted. "We hear Mike Collier paid his fine this morning and got out of jail," one reporter yelled at her. "Can you tell us how you feel about that?

Would you rather have him locked up than out on the street?"

Lilly glanced at Tisha, who was raptly engaged in occupying the attention of one young male photographer who seemed to be taking an awful lot of close-ups of her, and not necessarily of her face. "Mr. Collier's release was within my original stipulations, and well within the law," Lilly said, almost gritting her teeth. She didn't know Mike was out; nobody had told her. "I'm glad he finally came to his senses and paid his fine. And as far as having him back out on the street—that'll save the Whittier taxpayers some money, which is good for the city."

"But in light of his early release, do you still believe your sentence was fair, considering his offense was *only* parking tickets?" another reporter called out. "And would you throw him in jail again, say, if he parked in a no-parking zone even one more time? Or does he have to get a certain number of tickets before you'll lock him back up? And what would that number be, if you'd please be specific, Judge Malloy."

The hairs on the back of Lilly's neck bristled. That was Mike's voice. He was buried somewhere in the passel of reporters and no one had even noticed him there. "Let me answer the second part of the question first." She ran her hand through her hair, realizing that she hadn't yet pulled it back for her courtroom look. Naturally, the cameras were snapping away, catching Lilly, not Judge Malloy—a distinction she preferred to make. "Yes, I'd do it again if that's what the law called for, and the number of tickets is irrelevant. If Mr. Collier shows up in my courtroom again, and throwing him in jail is my only sentencing alternative, then he'll go back to jail. It's as simple as that. No one here in Whittier is above the law, including Mr. Collier, and if you print that as a quote, please highlight it in case he's reading." Lilly finally found Mike standing in the back, leaning against the wall, smiling at her. "And it was a fair sentence last week, by the way, just as it will be the next time Mr. Collier finds himself in my traffic court. Of course, the best solution for him would have been to obey the law in the first place, then we wouldn't be forced into the position of wasting so much time and effort and tax-payer's money over this. But he didn't, so the consequences are his choice, not mine."

"But don't you have a vendetta against him? Shouldn't you have recused yourself from his case, given your past history? He did get you kicked out of law school, didn't he?" And so the questions went as Lilly jostled her way on into her office and finally slammed the door on everything and everyone. *All this over parking tickets,* she thought, as the picture of her dear little judge career sinking through the floor popped to mind.

Slipping into her robe, and yes, she was wearing under-wear, her hair back, glasses on, all in an attempt at her usual judge effect, Lilly grabbed up her stack of case files and headed off to work. This morning there were no crowds. No one at all except the usual people pleading their cases, thank heavens, because she was fighting back the yawns and forc-ing herself to keep her eyes open. The Mike Collier furor was over, and for that she was glad. Even so, when the side door opened and Pete Walker walked in, a bit mussed from his hallway encounter, Lilly did hold her breath for a fraction, half expecting to see Mike even though the logical part of her knew he wouldn't be there. Probably wouldn't be caught even close to the courthouse, since he was once again a free man. And as she banged her gavel down on the opening of law and order as usual, startling herself into full alert, the normal colorless routine seemed a bit more colorless than usual for some peculiar reason.

Parking tickets always started her day, and the plead-and-pay defendants usually went by quickly. Except lately, when the sheer numbers of them seemed to be ganging up on her. This morning there were a whole succession who could have simply paid their fines at the cashier and gone home. But there were many who didn't, which meant that in most cases, coming to court and paying the additional costs actually doubled their initial penalties. Not smart at all, but some of them insisted they just didn't know, while others insisted on having their day in court.

Strange, she thought. Really strange.

Eventually, by the afternoon session, when the parking tickets were behind her and those with speeding tickets were lining up to be heard, the whole parking ticket issue was long gone from Lilly's mind. That is, until she took a fifteen minute break midafternoon and found Mike lounging in her office on her couch, shoes off, feet up, reading what appeared to be files. Stacks of them.

"What are you doing in here?" she hissed, taking off her glasses.

"Signed out some court records, but I can't take them out of the building, and I remembered you had a couch. Since you're in court, I figured I'd just come on down here, stretch out and do some reading." He grinned. "You don't mind, do you?"

"Get out," she growled, heading to a minifridge for a can of soda—her midday sugar boost. "And what was that all about out in the hall earlier—'Do you still believe your sentence was fair since his offense was only parking tickets?'"

"Just trying to get a story, that's all." He grinned. "And it was a damned good answer, even if I don't agree with it. And I will quote you. Not sure I'll read it, though."

"Who paid the fine for you, Mike?" Lilly asked, taking a swig of her orange soda. "I know you don't have that kind of money, so who anted up?"

He shrugged. "Don't know. Juanita just said I was all paid and good to go, so I did."

"And being the top-notch investigative reporter that you are, you didn't bother to check? You weren't even curious?"

"Actually, I did check, and I still am. But there's no record. Just an anonymous contribution from a fan, I suppose."

"There's always a record," Lilly hissed. "And you know that."

"Then be my guest and find it so I can thank him...or her." Grinning, he reached over to the table at the end of Lilly's couch and grabbed his reading glasses. "So now, if you'll excuse me, I've got to get these files back by the end of the day and I've still got a lot of reading to do."

Lilly took another drink of her soda, then set the can on her desk. "Why do you always do this to me, Mike? Why do you always simply force yourself on me?"

"If you're not going to finish that soda..." he replied.

"Fine, drink it. I don't care... I don't care what you do as long as you keep it away from me. Okay?" Robes whooshing behind her, Lilly marched over to the door into the courtroom, stopping before she opened it. "We're not friends, Mike. Not lovers. Nothing."

"That wasn't nothing in the cell last night," he said. "In fact, I'd call it something."

She spun around. "That was a mistake."

He grinned. "Some mistakes are good, aren't they? And we've had our share of whoppers. Admit it, Lilly."

He's trying to mollify you and you know it, her logical self was screaming, and for once she heard it. He *was* trying to mollify her and he was so damn good at it. She had war wounds that still bore scars. But she wasn't about to let him do it to her again. "What I'll admit, Mike—" she said his name with as much venom as she could invoke "—is that you're good in bed. Good? No, you're great. A marvelous work and a wonder. And what girl doesn't want a night like you're capable of giving every now and again, a night with someone who has your, shall we call them, advanced skills. And while I regret pretty much everything else about us, I don't regret the sex. But that's all you are to me, Mike—good sex, great sex, the best sex I've ever had. But I'm not in the market anymore. At least not in your market." She wrinkled her nose and gave him a coy little smile. "So knock yourself out on my couch with those files as long as you like, help yourself to anything in my fridge and keep remembering that while it was good for me, it was every bit as good for you. *But you're the one who blew it.*"

Slipping into her courtroom, Lilly collapsed against the door to let her shaky knees and skipping heart quiet down before she banged her gavel on yet another humdrum session. Just before she did so, she recalled the look on Mike's face moments ago—dumbfounded, one she'd never seen there before. And it was so good on him.

But what was even better was being the one who put it there.

"WELL, LILLY," Mike muttered, trying to refocus on the umpteen pages of facts, figures and boring statistics piled in his lap and on the floor. "You've added a new dimension to this *thing.*" And he liked it. Liked it a lot. Used to be she was sexy. He chuckled at the understatement. Sexy as hell was more like it. But she always tilted a little toward going with the traditional flow. Not a big distraction in their bygone relationships, such as they were. But she had new proportions now— good ones, exciting ones, ones that were going against the flow, going against her flow—and that made her even sexier than her former sexy-as-hell self. And *that* was definitely a problem for him because the third time wasn't going to be a charm for anyone if it came with the final blow to Lilly's career. Which it could, if he wasn't careful.

But man, oh, man. She sure was a formidable sparring partner these days and under different circumstances, he'd have been first in line volunteering as her punching bag—just for the thrill of the confrontation. If anything, that was better than the sex. But he had to keep his head, had to get those kinds of thoughts out of it, because the more they took hold, the more he was distracted. And he couldn't afford even the most negligible of Lilly Malloy distractions. So the only punching he did was her phone number. "You're right," he said to her voice mail. "It was every bit as good for me." He was about to click off when a few more words flew out. *"Better*, since I was the one fortunate enough to be with you and all you got out of the deal was me." Well, not exactly what he'd meant to say. A little too revealing, probably. But she'd find some way to twist them into fighting words. And that held a lot of promise.

Smiling, Mike turned his vacillating attention to the parking ticket records for the past several months. *So what gives?* he wondered. "What's going on in your court, Lilly Malloy?" he mused aloud. "And how am I going to get you out of it, whatever it is?"

The records showed a profitable business, for sure, but only becoming huge, actually tripling, since Lilly's reign in a black robe began. Lilly's reign in a black robe... Then—oh, no—Tisha's prophetic words came back to distract him. *And if you want to know what's under her robe...* He knew. Boy did he know, and that thought was where his concentration ended.

Tuesday evening deep down lonesome

"...GOOD FOR ME." Lilly tried to erase the message but hit the wrong command and ran through Play one more time. "You're right. It was every bit as good for me."

Tisha huddled over Lilly's desk, sharpening pencils Lilly didn't use, looked at her, grinning. "Anybody I know? He sounds cute," she said. "Hot date tonight, Judge?"

Lilly shook her head. "Wrong number."

"I wouldn't mind getting a wrong number like that once in a while." Ducking behind the door, Tisha emerged a minute later wearing a getup only Tisha could wear—short, tight, her belly ring showing, the French flourish tattoo at the small of her back revealed. Lilly knew men went for the package, but at her thirty, looking at Tisha's twenty, she suddenly felt old because the only thing running through her mind was *How does she sit down in something like that?* Glancing at her own sensible black slacks, she decided *Not comfortably*, and comfort was good. Way back when, before Mike, during Mike, she'd had a dose of Tisha's life, maybe not to the same extent, but she'd had some moments. And now comfort was what she wanted. Boy, would Tisha be in for a rude awakening in another few years.

"Next time, if he leaves a number, give it to me, okay?" Tisha said, pulling two more belly rings out of her purse.

Now, that would serve Mike right, Lilly thought. Or would it? The image of Mike hooking up with Tisha on a blind date made her wonder what he was looking for these days. Flash or comfort? Maybe some of both? "Have fun," she said, even though from the looks of Tisha, that was the indisputable object of her evening.

"Yeah, I plan to," Tisha replied, scurrying out the door. "Soon as I can find me a date."

Find a date... Lilly and Tisha were in the same boat. Hard to believe. But Lilly hadn't had a date—a real date—since her last date with Mike. What was that? A year ago? And last night in the jail cell didn't count even though it came close to ending the way their last date had ended. That thought made Lilly shudder as she hung up her robe.

"So why haven't you dated?"

She spun around, but no one was there. Just the stupid voice again, asking a stupid question...stupid since the answer was obvious. She didn't date because she didn't want to. Nothing to do with Mike. Just not enough time to get her career up and going and have anything left over. Sherlock was about as much as she could, or wanted to, handle. Some lazy attention in the evening, clean water, a bowl of food, an occasional walk around the block. All the man her life needed.

"Care for some dinner? I stopped over at the deli for a couple of sandwiches. You like turkey breast, right? With mayo and tomato?"

The voice again, and Lilly didn't fall for it. Her back was to the door and she didn't turn to look because he wasn't there, wasn't getting ready to proposition her down to the floor again.

"Lilly? I asked if you'd—"

She shook her head. "You're not here, Mike. No sandwiches, no mayo and tomato."

He laughed. "If I'm not here, then where am I?"

"Somewhere I'm not."

"Rachel moved your things back to your house," he said. "You could have stayed at my place a while longer."

"And you'd have been happy to sleep under the printing press, right?" she asked, shrugging into a cotton jacket. "Who paid your fine, Mike? I was just beginning to like the idea of having you locked up and out of my hair for the next month."

"Like I said before..."

"Well, the case is over. Somebody paid your debt to society, so we don't need to keep meeting like this, do we?" When Lilly finally turned around to face Mike, he wasn't there. Unlike the other times, though, she knew he had been.

And now that he wasn't, she felt a little...empty.

8

Salami, banana peppers and Wednesday afternoon

"WHAT FILES DID Mike Collier recently check out?" Lilly asked the clerk of records.

The clerk, a tired, sixty-something who looked as though she'd rather be doing anything other than this job, punched a few computer keys, then tapped her fingers impatiently on the desktop while the sluggardly computer churned out the log. "Looks like it was all parking tickets," she said, getting ready to hit the button that would send that record back into the void from which it came.

"Wait," Lilly said, stepping around the desk. "I want to get a look at that."

The woman spun the screen away. "Aren't you the judge who locked up Mikey?" she asked, her cranky eyes mellowing as his saintly name rolled off her lips. Then the crankiness snapped back into place. "Locked him up for parking tickets, didn't you?" she hissed.

Great, another fan. Mike strikes again. How did he do that...*always* do that? Without exception, without fail, without effort, he smiled and they fell at his feet. Yeah, right. So she fell, too, but that was different. *Watch it, Lilly. You're rationalizing. You were as bad as the rest of them when it came to Mike and you know it.* Worse, because she not only fell at his feet, but also into his bed.

"Didn't you?" the clerk demanded.

Snapping out of Collierland, Lilly nodded, deciding that silence on the matter of Mike Collier was definitely golden, since nothing she could say would tarnish his perfect gold halo. "And I just need a peek at the list of files he was going over." But the cranky eyes didn't mellow, not one iota. "Just for a minute, that's all."

No response. Not even a blink.

"A few seconds."

"Gotta have permission," the clerk finally snapped. "That's the rule and I don't break the rule, not even for a judge." Then she—nah, she wouldn't have—but it did sort of *look* like she curled her lip and snarled like a pit bull.

"Who gave Mike Collier permission?" Lilly ventured, wondering if Mike's growling watchdog had all her shots.

"Me."

"You?" Lilly dug down deep for a sweet smile. "So how would I go about getting your permission—" she twisted to take a look at the woman's name tag "—Edith?"

Edith reared back in her chair, letting out a rumbling, exasperated sigh. She was primed to snatch her minute of power, Lilly decided. Probably did it every chance she could. "You ask me," Edith answered, her voice as hard as cement. "*Politely.*"

Resisting the urge to rumble out her own exasperated sigh, Lilly put on her best polite behavior, even though it obviously wasn't as good as Mike's, since Edith's cranky eyes were, if anything, even crankier now. No, not merely cranky. Vengeful. Bloodthirsty. "May I look at the records please, Edith?" she asked, her voice so gooey sweet she felt sticky. "The same ones Mike looked at."

"He didn't belong in jail, you know," Edith growled, hitting the screen's On button, then spinning the monitor around for Lilly to view.

Lilly checked over the log, the one Mike had pulled files from, and except for the fact that every last file on it was for a parking ticket, she couldn't find much else of interest there.

Just more of his obsession to prove he was right? she wondered. His crusade to save his parking place? "He didn't ask to see anything else—say, speeding tickets?" she asked, scanning down the entire run. Hundreds and hundreds of parking tickets, that's all. "Or any other traffic offenses?" Nothing there would make good headline news, let alone back page. No drunk driving arrests, no property damage. Frankly, Lilly was baffled. Parking tickets were the least significant of all traffic offenses on the law books, yet they were the majority of traffic offenses committed in Whittier.

"No!" Edith snorted. "And he did go out and buy me doughnuts and coffee for my trouble." She eyed Lilly's submarine sandwich, still in its bag. "That Mike Collier knows how to treat people nice."

Lilly took in a breath, clutching her sandwich to her chest, and forged ahead. "These are just from my court, right? And only since I've been on the bench?"

Edith snickered. "That's right, Your Honor. Your court, every last one of 'em. And I'm guessing Mikey's got something interesting in mind, digging into them like he did."

"You wish," Lilly retorted, jumping back lest the pit bull attacked. As it turned out, Lilly didn't requisition any files. No need to right now, since she'd turned up what she was looking for—something where all roads led to her court. Instead, she thanked Edith for her time, and yes, she even surrendered her submarine sandwich, then did a speedy retreat while the woman was still inspecting the condiments.

Lunchless now, with only fifteen minutes left until court reconvened, Lilly decided to give up on the idea of food, go for some sun and clear her mind of everything—parking tickets, Edith, Mike. It was a respite she'd earned, despite the occasional clumps of noontimers bustling along, glaring at her. She knew the glare, of course. It was the one all the Mike fans gave her these days.

All hail the conquering Collier. She did have to hand it to

Mike, though. He'd found his life here, his friends, his support. And that was nice. Something she'd like to do, too. Lately, though, that dream was slipping even lower than a remote possibility, and she wondered if she should start updating her résumé, again. Real soon!

Another clump of Mike fans wandered by, so Lilly shifted her gaze to avoid theirs, catching a glimpse of Mayor Tannenbaum across the way. He seemed to be filming something. Probably a campaign commercial, Lilly decided, immediately wondering if he'd applied some concealing foundation to the tooth.

Moving to a spot closer to the Tannenbaum exhibition, Lilly decided watching him was as good a way as any to occupy her last few minutes of recess before going back to work. So trying not to be too obvious, she gave him a casual glance, one that turned into a full frontal stare when he started flapping and waving his arms—either doing the chicken dance or trying to fly—followed by some finger pointing. Wagging his index finger at the camera, he leaned into the shot, giving that skinny digit a good, sound shaking. Then he backed away and smiled. Oh, no—the tooth, front and center. And it stayed especially conspicuous as he jammed his hands in his pants pockets, reared back and laughed.

Then, his hair. Was it her imagination or...? No, there was more of it today, but it didn't look as much like a toupee as it did an attempted thickening of the real crop. And it was darker than usual, a nice rich brown to match his suit. Omigod! Not hair out of a spray can? Too bizarre, she thought, trying to quit watching. But she couldn't, not for another five minutes as he went through the rest of his motions—one-arm pushups, pantomiming his way out of the box, singing like Pavarotti and step-dancing at the same time. Well, not really all that, but he did pull a big white Pavarotti-like handkerchief out of his pocket and wipe his eyes. The emotional climax, Lilly guessed, laughing so hard she needed a corner of that handkerchief, herself, to wipe away her tears. "You need to kiss a baby, Lowell," she said, not loud enough that he could hear. "Can't end it without the baby."

"Why torture a poor baby?" Mike said, dropping down on the wall next to Lilly.

"First the mayor, now you. All I wanted was some fresh air and fifteen minutes alone." She hadn't seen Mike coming or she would have gone back to her office. The town really wasn't big enough for the both of them, she thought, watching him set two cans of soda between them.

"Funny how we keep bumping into each other like this," he said, pulling an Italian submarine sandwich out of a brown paper bag. It was sliced in two and he handed half to Lilly. "Your soda's the orange. That's what you like, isn't it?"

"And you assumed I would have lunch with you, *why?*" She opened the sandwich, looked at the condiments, then closed it again.

"Edith called, said you were looking at the records I pulled, and that your submarine was better than my doughnuts." Popping the top on his soda, he took a swig. "I figured since you were checking records, you were getting curious. So I thought I might take a chance that we could spend a few civil minutes together and talk about it. And I'm feeling really civil today. How 'bout you?"

"Civil, yes. Civil toward you, no way." But the sandwich— it was her favorite, the exact same thing she'd sacrificed to Edith. And she was hungry. "Okay, I've got ten minutes until I have to be back in court. You get five of them. That's all, Mike. *Five,* so you'd better make them count." Then she took a bite of the sandwich.

"Okay, then. It started with the parking tickets, and before you say anything else, yes, I did really get mad when they took away my parking place. My spot was the only one on the street zoned out, and I know you're not going to admit it, but that's wrong. So I decided to dig for some dirt. Yeah, revenge. Anything I could use as leverage that would get me my parking place back."

"And you found something?" She was staying noncommittal, but Mike did have a point about it being wrong—a little point, anyway.

He nodded. "At first it didn't seem like anything—lots of parking tickets all over town. But the more I dug the more parking tickets I turned up. Three times more than any other town this size in the state of Indiana. Or anywhere else in the Midwest, for that matter. And some of these people, Lilly, they're repeat offenders—over and over, as if they *like* paying the tickets."

"Nineteen times?"

"Okay, so it happens. But my tickets are different."

"Yeah, protest tickets."

He smiled. "Something like that. But you've got to admit it's strange."

"Well, maybe we've just got an epidemic of lazy parkers like you. Busy people who find it easier to pay the fine than hunt down a legal parking spot. And you don't exactly have a lot of dirt, Mike. Nothing that would stand up in court, anyway." Taking a drink of soda, Lilly went back to her sandwich—salami, Genoa ham, pepperoni, banana peppers, black olives, provolone, lots of tomato and onion, hold the lettuce— Mike had remembered all that right down to the oil and vinegar dressing. Amazing how he grasped the details but not the big picture. "So what's the bottom line here? I've only got another minute."

"You're cutting me short? I thought I got five minutes, not four."

"That was before I had onions on my breath. Got to gargle before I go back to court. Never know who might be stepping over my yellow line and getting in my face." She gave him a wicked little smile. "Then getting himself thrown in jail."

"I always liked you with onions on your breath." He gave her that wicked little smile right back.

"Now that's real romantic."

"We were, Lilly. For a time, anyway. The first time. The second time was...well, for old times' sake, I guess. But we had fun together, even if you don't want to remember it, and lots of romance."

"And you have a strange way of ending a romance," she said, standing, wiping her mouth on a paper napkin, crumpling it, then tossing it at him.

"Bottom line, Lilly, is that the parking ticket disbursement in Whittier is a front for something else, although I haven't been able to put my finger on what that is yet. And a lot of it's getting filtered through your court, meaning, like it or not, you're in the middle of it." Then he added, "And I don't want you to be anywhere near it. But I am investigating, and I'll get to the bottom of it, then..."

"Then blow the lid off it with my name linked to it, whatever it is, and pretty much end my legal career altogether. Haven't we done this before, Mike?" Calm on the outside, anything but on the inside, she wanted to plunk herself back down on that wall and stay there. Spend the rest of the day in the sun, forget there was a court inside waiting for her to preside over it, forget that there was another lurking misdeed, misdemeanor or malfeasance with her name on it.

A hard lump formed in her throat, one that could so easily explode into tears. But she wouldn't cry. Not for Mike, not about Mike, not in spite of Mike. So she fought to swallow it back. Fought hard to lock away her emotions, all emotions. But when she looked into his eyes she found so much compassion there. So much that for a moment Lilly let herself believe it was genuine, that he really *was* concerned about her. That was a dangerous moment, though, filled with so much of their past, so many of the times she'd truly believed in him, so much of the hurt when she'd learned she couldn't. "I'll take care of it," she said, fighting the emotion. "I always have."

"You can't, Lilly. Not this time. Not in your position."

He stood, maybe to put his arms around her, maybe to walk away—Lilly didn't know. But she instinctively stepped back from him, out of arm's reach. "I've survived before," she said, all her barriers flying up to block him out. "And I'll survive this time. Just watch me." Finally, the emotional edge was gone. Lilly was back in control.

"I'll keep you out of it, Lilly," he promised, reaching through her iron opposition to take her hand. "You have no idea what I went through when I started digging around and found out you were in traffic court, and it's your court that seems to be the center of whatever's going on. What are the odds?"

"About one hundred percent when the two of us get together," she snapped, yanking back her hand. Moment of weakness, letting him get that close. But it felt so good, so comforting, so...right.

"I wanted to tell you, even tried, but..." He shrugged. "Timing's everything and I guess ours is always pretty lousy...except in bed."

Same old Mike. Same old predictable Mike. She braced herself to walk away from him. No point staying, since she knew what came next. But as she turned to leave, he reached out and took hold of her arm. It was a gentle hold, one she could have pulled out of, but she didn't. And it raised goose bumps up and down her arm, goose bumps he could see, could feel, if he wanted. "You always have to reduce it to that level, don't you? One step forward, then throw Lilly on the bed."

"I like to think of it as elevating it to that level. And you'll have to agree it was a pretty high level sometimes." Then his hand gently stroked her goose bumps, causing even more.

"So tell me what *you* think I should do, Mike? Tell me how *you* think I should cover my backside so this *whatever it is* doesn't take me down, and so you don't *accidentally* take me down, like you've been known to do when you get rolling on a story. Which you will, once you figure it out." She looked at his hand on her arm. Still goose bumps. Oh, how she loved that touch. How she'd missed it.

And that sloppy sentiment scared the bejeezus out of her!

"Well, trust me for starters." He glanced over at the mayor, who was shaking hands with the crowd of six or seven innocent bystanders who hadn't been fortunate enough to escape his Tannenbaum tentacles. Normally, the noonday courtyard was bursting with activity, but when the mayor came out to play everybody there escaped to other, safer ports—across the street, behind the Dumpster, under the bushes—except those poor, ill-fated few. "And don't trust *him*, no matter what." Mike nodded toward Tannenbaum.

"Who? The mayor? He's strange, but that doesn't make him dishonest...does it?" She glared across the way at him. "Do you think?"

"I don't know yet, but my gut tells me he's involved." Mike finally released his hold on Lilly and tossed the empty soda cans into the trash. Following her up the steps to the city hall's front door, he continued, "All I'm saying is to be careful. Okay? I'll keep digging and I won't do anything until we can figure out a way to shield you."

Lilly spun around. "I don't trust you, Mike. Not because you're dishonest, because you're not. I don't trust you because a big story's going to jump right out at you and that's all you're going to think about when it does, no matter what you've promised me. Then, after the fact, you'll say 'Oops, Lilly, I'm so sorry, I didn't mean to do it.' And I can't overcome that again, Mike. More than that, I shouldn't have to."

"I deserve that."

"You bet you do, and a whole lot more. But the problem is, even though I don't trust you, I have to. So I will. But it's conditional, Mike, and I'm wise to you now." A poison-packed smile skimmed her lips. "And if you take me down this time... Well, let's just say what's going to happen to *you* puts a new spin on the old saying 'misery loves company,' and leave it at that."

Still Wednesday afternoon and no place to hide

MIKE CONTINUED STANDING there for another few minutes, watching Lilly enter the building. God, he loved her when she was feisty. Of course, he loved her every other way, but feisty was the best. It was sexier than anything ever called sexy in the history of the world, for starters, but it also made her glow in ways he'd never before seen. Confidence for sure, as well as a striking intensity claimed part of that glow, but most of it was simply Lilly being Lilly on her own terms. That made her happy.

And that made him happy.

Lilly was right, of course. She had no cause to trust him. He sure wouldn't, if he were in her shoes. But she was beginning to let him back in—just a little—and this was the first time in years he'd felt a tweak of hope. No, he wasn't deluding himself into thinking that anything big would come of it. Right now he wasn't looking for big with Lilly. He was looking for whatever he could get, and it didn't matter what. A scrap was good, if that's all she tossed out. Then maybe, just maybe, he could take that scrap and build it into something that would prove to her there was so much more between them than great sex and jousting. Both were part of the same thing, actually, but that was a huge leap in logic she wasn't ready to take yet.

No, Lilly wouldn't believe what he'd finally come to understand. And to be honest, there were times he hardly believed it himself. Not after so many years of thinking that anything but love was really love. So who was he kidding here? Not himself anymore. And Lilly? Well, she might come around in due time, he hoped. Dear God, did he hope.

"How's it feel to be a free man?" Mayor Tannenbaum called, spying Mike near the building. He was flitting over, which was the last thing Mike wanted. But he'd been distracted and this was his payback. Probably Lilly-sent.

"Food's not quite as good on the outside," Mike answered, wishing there was some way to simply disappear into thin air before the man reached him. But too late, with the prospect of a captive audience, one in the media at that, the mayor promptly launched into the Tannenbaum trot to get himself over there.

"Well, I heard you had a few conveniences our other prisoners don't normally get. Guess it pays knowing how to work the system, doesn't it?"

Mike forced a thin smile. "So I've been told."

"Saw the spread you wrote about me. A little cropped, wasn't it? Hardly anything in there about my platform, Mike. I expected better from you, especially after I gave you back your parking place."

"It was a human interest piece, Lowell. People really go for them. Makes them feel like they have a personal relationship with the person they're reading about. In other words, get to know the man first, then the platform." Mike wanted to reach around and pat himself on the back for that pack of prevarication, but instead he said, "Great picture, by the way. Really did you justice."

The mayor beamed over that whopper, opening his scrawny little lips into a toothy grin that allowed the sun to shimmer off the obvious. Mike thought about putting on sunglasses so the tooth glare wouldn't blind him, but his cell phone rang and he turned sideways, indicating a private conversation might be coming up. The mayor actually took the hint, closed his lips over the tooth and strolled away.

Lilly's number came up on the caller ID. "Been thinking about me?" he asked, instead of answering with hello.

"Not you. But what you told me."

Mike looked inside the front window to see if he could find Lilly in there somewhere, gloating over his being trapped with Tannenbother, but the sun beating down on that side of the building was as blinding as the Tannentooth, so he simply waved, figuring she'd see it if she was there. Prickles on the back of his neck told him she was.

"We need a strategy," Lilly continued. "Something more than researching the files. Something proactive."

"And you're suggesting what?"

"Nothing, Mike. I'm not suggesting anything because I'm not the one who gets involved in these kinds of things. That's what you do, so you're the one who gets to come up with the plan. And don't go getting any ideas that because I've agreed to work with you I'll agree to anything else, because I won't. There's nothing between us except a partnership of convenience. I get my butt cleared, you get a story. That's it."

"And a gorgeous butt it is...sorry, it just slipped out." No, it didn't, but what the hell. It was a damned gorgeous butt. Soft, round, a sumptuous pale white that never saw the light of day... And a man could dream, even if he couldn't touch.

"You get your story and that's all you get, Mike. Understand me?"

"Yeah," he muttered, his mind still back on sumptuous pale white.

"Mike?"

"Huh?"

"That's the way it's going to be. Nothing else."

"Oh, sure." But his mind was still on far more pleasant places when he heard the gavel bang in the background and realized their conversation was over. Lilly was back in her basement now, business as usual.

And Lilly's gorgeous butt or not, he was in serious need of a gorgeous strategy real quick.

A berry busy Wednesday night

"I DON'T KNOW IF I need an attorney or not," Lilly said to Ezra. They were eating hamburgers and sitting out on her sundeck. It was a cool evening, uncommon in Indiana during August, and Rachel was out with Jimmy again, a regular occurrence lately. Odd couple, Lilly thought, but kind of cute, and they did get along so well. Not like her and Mike. She'd actually considered inviting Mike to dinner, too. Thought about it for, like, two seconds before she came to her senses. She needed calm, reasonable reassurance, and that was Ezra. Mike was all about sizzling and being on the edge and a whole lot of un-certainty. He was the reason she needed calm, reasonable re-assurance. "It's like I told you. He thinks something's going on in my traffic court—something illegal—and he says he'll fix it and keep me out of it when he figures out what it is. But I don't trust him, Ezra. Even when he means well, I'm the one who ends up going directly to jail without passing home and collecting my two hundred dollars. Between us, I'm scared to death of playing Mike's version of Monopoly because no matter how it starts, he ends up with all the hotels while I go bankrupt. And there's not much left in my starting-over bank anymore. If I go bankrupt again, I may not make it back."

"Well dear, the only thing I can advise is that you be careful in your judicial decisions. Make sure they're squeaky clean, which I'm sure they are, and you'll be fine. You've got good judgment, even though you haven't always used it in the past. But use it this time, and trust yourself. Oh, and just in case this gets out of control, I'll start a file so there'll be a pa-per trail on record *before* anything happens. Other than that, all I can say is go with your gut instinct."

Just like Mike does, she thought. "You know, my second

choice in college was animal husbandry. Maybe I should be training monkeys at the zoo instead of presiding over a court." Then she laughed. "Not much difference sometimes, is there?" Lilly grabbed Ezra's empty glass and went inside to pour him more lemonade, only to find Mike sitting at her kitchen table. "How'd you get in?" she hissed.

"Door's open. I knocked, you didn't answer."

"So you broke in."

"So I let myself in. You really should keep your door locked, Lilly." He chuckled. "You never know who might wander in off the street."

"I have company, Mike. Invited company, and it's not you."

"And I haven't been interrupting you, have I? You don't happen to have another burger you could throw on the grill for me? Spent all my money on lunch."

One nice evening with Ezra down the tubes. And she didn't want to fight, not with Ezra here. So she pointed at the fridge. "In there. But you cook it, not me." Then she went back outside and handed Ezra his drink. "We've got company," she said.

"You mean Mike Collier? I saw him wandering around in your kitchen an hour ago."

"And you didn't tell me?" Dropping back into her deck chair, Lilly kicked her feet up and didn't look at Mike as he traipsed outside carrying his treasure trove of raw meat, onions and cheese to the grill.

"Figured you either knew he was here and didn't want me to know, or you didn't know and wouldn't want to. Either way, not much point saying anything about it, ruining your evening."

"Men," Lilly sighed. "Can't live with them, can't keep them in jail forever."

"Evening, Professor," Mike said, saluting Ezra from across the deck.

"Mike," Ezra responded cordially.

"Anybody care for another burger?" he asked, turning up the propane flame.

"We're getting ready for dessert." Lilly watched him grab the spatula and toss his burger on the grill. Such ease. Everything Mike did was easy, and she envied him his style. Always had. Maybe that was another of the things that attracted her to him. It sure was what attracted everybody else to him—not in a sexual way, but in the way that people simply liked being around him, doing things for him, being part of his aura. It was genuine, a gift—one that blended so seamlessly with everything in his world, and rocked the world of everyone around him. But it was also a gift he knew how to work when he needed to. "I have some berry cobbler inside."

"And it's great," he said, tossing an onion slice on the grill.

"You ate the cobbler?"

"A little. Kind of surprised me, I've got to admit. I never pegged you for a good cook. Did you know that Lilly could cook, Professor? Because after all these years, I sure didn't."

Without cracking a smile or a frown, Ezra looked directly at Mike, saying, "My relationship with Lilly has encompassed *many* aspects of her talents, young man. One among the many being cooking. But in the interest of accuracy, and because you have a history of making the wrong assumptions and accusations—which you have done again, I might add— I made the cobbler. And if you intend on getting Lilly out of this mess as you claim, I'd suggest you acquaint yourself with *all* the facts before you go out on a limb, which it seems is where you quite often find yourself when it comes to Lilly. Discover who *did* make the cobbler before you lay the credit, or the blame, on anyone, young man."

Lilly wanted to high-five Ezra for his remarks, but he folded his arms over his chest and stared at Mike the whole way through the grilling of the hamburger. It was the stare of an overly protective father, one whose daughter was too

good for any boy—or man. Mike must have recognized the
stare, probably one he'd seen on every father of every girl or
woman he'd ever dated, because when the burger was done,
he made a hasty getaway back into the house to eat it.

"Sorry," Lilly said to Ezra. "He just keeps turning up
where you don't want him, like a mosquito you never can
quite swat. It's always buzzing around your ear, but somehow manages to evade the blow. And that's Mike, always
buzzing around your ear, never getting smacked. Of course,
you knew he was in Whittier, so you probably expected him
to start buzzing around, didn't you?"

Ezra laughed. "Pleading the fifth, my dear. And could I
have one more lemonade for the road?" He held out his glass
for a refill, noticed it was half-full, then dumped the contents
over the deck rail into the grass.

"Pleading the fifth my butt," she laughed. "You're as
scheming as he is." Grabbing the glass from him, she headed
to the kitchen.

"Take your time, dear. No need to hurry back. *Especially if
you get a better offer from someone inside.*"

"Ezra!" she sputtered, spinning back around to him, not at
all sure if she'd heard his voice or that other voice. And the innocent arch of his wooly eyebrows didn't give her an answer.
"With or without ice?"

*"Whichever gives you enough time on the kitchen counter with
him."* Lilly blinked her eyes, shook her head. "Doesn't matter,
dear," Ezra replied. "Whichever's easier for you."

Opening the fridge and pulling out the pitcher of lemonade, Lilly spat at Mike, "Why are you here?"

"Thought we might get into a strategy session. Didn't
know you had company, but I've got all night. No money to
take a gal out on a proper date these days, so unless I'm working, my time's free and, as it turns out, I'm free all night."

"And what's that supposed to mean?" *Stupid, leading ques-*

ion, she reprimanded herself. *Give him an opening like that and he'll take it.* Lilly fixed her eyes on Mike's lips for the answer because she knew if she didn't, the answer might not be what he said. Of course, his answer had as much likelihood of being something he *did* say that she didn't want to hear.

"Not working. Paper's already put to bed."

"What?" Surely he hadn't just been direct with her. Not Mike.

"I said I'm through for the day."

Simple as that, she thought. And that made her nervous. "So the part about all night…"

"You trying to lead me into something?" he asked. "I'm just here to work."

Lilly listened for something else, his innuendo, her little voice—a challenge, a naughty little suggestion. Something…anything. But nothing. Just a head full of quiet. So she answered, "After Ezra leaves," then carried the glass of lemonade outside to him.

"*And the only strategy I want to discuss tonight is upstairs in my bedroom, sweet cheeks.*" Only Lilly didn't hear that one. Mike did, and he blushed.

9

Wednesday night and it's back to the berries

"YOU THINK I SHOULD DO what?" Lilly almost choked on her last bite of berry cobbler. Ezra had deeded his share over to Mike and abandoned her to Mike's cobbler-grubbing clutches. But she'd be damned if she'd let Mike have his fair share of the cobbler, or anything else. Not in her house, not in her life. So she ate almost half of the darn thing, and this last dish wasn't because she wanted it so much as she didn't want Mike getting it. And he would have, just to spite her. This was the battle of the berries and she was going to win it since she'd dished out the portions herself and hers were twice the size of his. All's fair in war and berry cobbler.

"You've got to be kidding. I mean, you really think I could do something like that to Tannenbaum?" Now she was bloated and on a sugar high that would have her dancing on top of the table if she wasn't careful. Of course, better dancing on the kitchen table than what the voice suggested she do on the kitchen counter. At least, she'd thought it was her voice suggesting that, not Ezra. "Explain that to me one more time, okay?" she continued, wiping the berry stains from the corners of her mouth, both happy and miserable at claiming her victory in the berries war.

"It's simple. Tannenbaum's the key. It starts and ends with him, but I don't know what comes in the middle other than lots of parking tickets. So that's what we need to find out." Pointing, Mike said, "You missed a spot, left side...."

She dabbed.

"A little more to the left...lower."

She dabbed some more.

"Didn't get it. Want me to..." Sitting next to her at the kitchen table, Mike reached for the napkin but Lilly reared back, not actually slapping his hand away, but the slap was certainly implied. "Hey, I was just trying to help," he said, grinning.

"Yeah, right, like you've helped me before." She knew *he* knew exactly what he was doing. One touch, even the innocent wiping of berry cobbler, and Mike would expect their strategy session to adjourn to the hot tub, the boudoir, the washing machine or some other such place where stripping naked was the protocol. Because that was *their* protocol. Close encounters led to closer encounters led to... Nope, wouldn't go there, wouldn't even think about going there. "Just keep it professional, okay? Here and now. Lowell Tannenbaum."

"Here and now meaning there's no more history between us?" Mike asked. "My slate's clean?"

"You wish."

"So let me get this straight. I have to keep our relationship strictly professional, here and now, but you get to hang on to the history, including the parts that weren't strictly professional—you know, the good parts? And you get to bring out the bad parts anytime, anyplace and beat me up with them whenever you want. Doesn't seem real fair, since you get to keep all the good stuff and I get, well, a partner with cobbler on her face." He laughed and grabbed Lilly's cobbler bowl, then carried it over to the sink. "But if that's the way you like it..."

"Not like it, Mike. That's the way I demand it. And you know why. You're doing it right now, as a matter of fact." Disarming her again...and again...and again.

"So it's Lilly's law or nothing?" he asked, turning around to her. "That's it?"

Trying to wipe away that berry smudge, wherever it was
she stated seriously, "Lilly's law, and you're right. That's it."
It was hard to appear serious, though, when there was an er
rant stain lurking somewhere near her mouth.

"Higher and a little more to the right."

She dabbed.

"Got it. See how nice it is when we work together?"

"If we'd truly been working together, Mike, you would
have warned me about the possibility of a berry stain before
was stained. But you waited until it was too late. Like al
ways."

"Spoken like a true attorney," Mike laughed.

"Spoken like a true Mike Collier survivor," she retorted
"And just in case you're interested, a *future* Mike Collier sur
vivor."

"That wounds me," he joked, clasping his chest.

"Good." She shot him a tantalizingly mocking smile. "I
meant it to."

They stayed in the kitchen to mull over the Tannenbaum
strategy, not because it was comfortable in there, but because
it wasn't. Straight-backed wooden chairs were much more of
a restriction to unprofessional tendencies than the cushy,
overstuffed couch in the living room, and Lilly felt much
safer sitting straight-backed on a big ol' wooden restriction
next to Mike than sinking down into a big ol' cushy tempta-
tion with him. Picky distinction, she knew, but one that might
actually allow her to get through the rest of the evening with
her clothes on, her resolve intact and a strategy to save her job
in hand. Win, win, win. "So getting back to the plan, you
think I should be the one who finds out what Tannenbaum's
up to? And just how would I go about doing that?"

Mike laughed. "Well, do you find him sexy?"

"About as sexy as foot fungus. Why?" Then she looked at
the wicked sparkle in Mike's eyes and the berry cobbler in her

belly churned. "No...Mike, hun-uh. I don't know what you're thinking, but I don't like it."

"I was thinking that you could probably seduce the information out of him. Well, maybe not in the real sense of seduction, but maybe flirt in the sense that he thinks you'll go through with something. When he's convinced, you'll be in a position to gain his trust, which is exactly what we need—his trust. Just make him putty in your hot little hands, Lilly. And believe me, I know how that feels."

"You mean the other way around, don't you? That *I* know how it feels," Lilly snapped, glancing down at her hands. And they *were* hot. Sweating, in fact. "This plan...you've sunk even lower than I thought you could possibly sink, which was somewhere *under* the slimy things under the rock."

"Enough about my apartment." Mike laughed, adding, "But I liked what you did with the place. Haven't found my shorts yet, but who needs 'em? And you left an undie in my drawer, by the way. Black, lacy, not much there. Remember it?" He reached into his jeans pocket, then came back empty-handed. "Sorry. Thought I had it with me."

Lilly shook her head. Mike was disarming her again. "Do you ever stay on the same subject for more than thirty seconds?"

"I don't really think there's any more than about thirty seconds worth of discussion about your black lacies, but if you want to try..."

"I've never owned black lace in my life, Mike, and you know that...er, used to know that." And the quick flash of who might have owned those panties jabbed her. Somehow, in all these years, she'd never pictured Mike with another woman. Sure, there had to have been—probably lots of them. Just not in her images, and now, having someone else—and her alleged panties—force her way in made Lilly queasy. Getting queasy over *that* made her even queasier. The implications were pretty clear, even to someone who refused to think about them, which was what she was doing—not thinking about them. But even in her court, those implications were admissible as proof...proof of something she didn't want pleaded anywhere near her.

"Well, if you'd like some I'd be happy to buy you a pair. I mean, I can't afford expensive gifts, but..."

"Let's just stick to Tannenbaum, okay?" Lilly growled, her voice as tight as a rubber band stretched to its limit and about to snap.

The instant he heard her reaction, Mike raised his eyebrows and shot her a look that told her he'd caught that little slipup—caught her overreaction to his teasing. And that wasn't good. "So it's your plan that I get to seduce him while you do what?" she hurried to add before he had a chance to dive into the ocean-size opening she'd just handed him.

"Watch?" A big ol' Mike Collier grin came with that suggestion.

"You wish." She grinned right back at him. "In your wildest fantasies, maybe. But I do have a better plan and it involves *you* doing the seducing while I get to videotape you in case I ever need to use it against you. And maybe he'll like you in black lace panties." Scooting back her chair, Lilly stood and headed to the stairs.

"Blackmail? Bad girl, Lilly." Mike arched his eyebrows without cracking a smile. "And just when I thought you were beginning to trust me."

"Yeah, like you really inspire trust. Good night, Mike. I'm going to bed. Sweet Tannenbaum dreams. And lock the door on your way out, will you? Can I *trust* you to do that?"

"Second room at the top of the stairs, Mike. And hurry up. I'm hot!" He opened his mouth to respond, then shut it. That invitation was way too good to be true.

Thursday morning wee hours and the basset needs a bath

MIKE KNEW HE SHOULDN'T, knew exactly what would happen if he did. But that illusory invitation kept bugging him while he did the dishes, scraped the grill clean and watered the pots of petunias and begonias on Lilly's deck. He even thought about giving old Sherlock a bath, but at two in the morning, Sherlock was knocking out some pretty hefty zzzzs in his doggy bed and probably wouldn't take kindly to a good scrubbing. So now, two hours after Lilly started knocking out her own zzzzs, two hours after he should have been locking the door behind him, Mike was looking at the stairs as if they were a castle that was his to conquer. Problem was, the reward at the top wore double-plated chain mail and came with a mighty sharp javelin, one she wanted to use on him in the worst kind of way.

Damn it, she was difficult. And damn it even more, she was worth it. So no stairs. Not tonight, but another night? He hoped so—truly hoped so—because this would be his very last chance with Lilly, and he didn't want to blow it. His life without her would be... No, he wouldn't think about that, either. And he wasn't thinking about it when he sacked out on her couch for the rest of night.

Still Thursday morning, basset still needs a bath

"I WAS THINKING," he said, when Lilly wandered down to her kitchen the next morning, "that we could always make sure you're in a situation with the mayor where the two of you wouldn't be alone." Mike rose up from the sofa as she passed by, grabbed his T-shirt off the coffee table and tugged it on over his head. "What's for breakfast?"

"Whatever's in *your* fridge back at *your* place," she said, breezing on by him.

"I slept on the couch," he said, realizing his jeans were too far away to grab without getting off the couch, and he wasn't wearing underwear because he just hadn't had time to do a load of laundry lately. Luckily he'd found the pink coverlet in the hall closet last night when he turned in or Lilly would really be embarrassed right now seeing him in, well, his morning condition. He smiled. But then, maybe she wouldn't be.

"Apparently," she called from the kitchen.

"Didn't think you'd mind."

"Didn't think to ask, either, did you?"

He heard some door-slamming, decided it was a good time to wrap himself up, head to the bathroom and grab a quick shower. No, she wouldn't make him breakfast. But even Lilly wouldn't begrudge a man a quick shower, and it would be nice to have some warm water, since his gas service was turned off for a couple of missed payments and all he'd had for the past month was cold. So with the pink coverlet wrapped around him, Mike hurried up the stairs and into the bathroom, turned on the shower and hopped in as soon as the spray was warm.

It was a nice feeling, the fact that he was in a real shower and not a moldy three-sided plastic stall. And it was nice that it was Lilly's shower—her body wash, her shampoo, her puff. An orange disposable razor peeked out of the shower caddy, and he envisioned her shaving her legs with it—long legs, beautiful legs...legs leading all the way up to...

"No point daydreaming about that," he muttered, grabbing the bottle of strawberry-and-kiwi body wash and squirting out a big glob on his chest. "Ain't gonna happen." Then in mid-lathering he heard the bathroom door creak open. And that surprised him. He'd hoped she might, but never expected that she would. So maybe, just maybe...

Her footsteps on the creaky wooden floor were getting closer; he could hear them over the water. She was trying to surprise him, a thought that *really* excited him. And through the translucent shower curtain he could make out her form, not the detail, but the blurred image of her, which was all he needed, really. The anticipation. The expectation. The wild imagination. She was getting closer...and closer...until—

Mike threw back the shower curtain to welcome Lilly in and... "What the hell!" he shrieked at Jimmy, who was standing there bare-butt naked.

"What the hell!" Jimmy shrieked right back at him.

Downstairs, Lilly handed a cup of coffee to Rachel, and smiled. "Jimmy was expecting you in the shower, wasn't he?" she asked.

Rachel nodded. "But somebody was already in there so I came down to fix us some breakfast. And Mike was expecting you, I'm guessing?"

"I guess so. So which do you want, cereal or eggs?"

LILLY WAS OUTSIDE the bathroom door when Mike finally emerged, looking properly subdued and still a bit red-faced. Holding out a cup of coffee for him, as well as his pants, she remarked, "Never would have thought Jimmy was your type." Casual remark, eyebrows arched in disinterest, straight face, no laughing. "Although I've got to tell you, Rachel's pretty crushed that you got to take a shower with him before she did."

Mike was wrapped in a towel this time, not the pink coverlet, although from the peek she'd got of him in the coverlet, and what she recalled was underneath it, she thought he did look pretty good in pink, all things considered. And good in a green bath towel, too. With droplets still glistening on his chest, his hair all slicked back and wet, Lilly knew, without a shadow of a doubt, she should have stayed downstairs in the kitchen eating cold bran flakes. But Jimmy had run through there after his close call in the bathroom, thrown Mike's jeans at her, the ones Jimmy had grabbed to cover himself when he made his getaway from Mike, bidding Rachel a hasty, if not humiliated, goodbye on his way out. And somebody had to bring Mike his pants, didn't they? But it should have been Rachel, because Lilly was already beginning to feel the wobbly kickback that came from being so close to an almost-naked Mike Collier. And for Lilly, *almost* naked was as bad as totally. Just like in horseshoes, it counted. *That* she knew from experience.

"So when you get your pants on...what the heck, wear a towel, come on downstairs and have some cold..." She glanced down the full length of him—didn't want to, didn't mean to, couldn't stop it. Chest to toes, toes to chest...remembering... "And have some cold shower, er, cold cereal, and we'll..." *Do it on the kitchen table, use the butter....*

Dear God, shut my mouth before I say it out loud. "Talk," she muttered without opening her mouth even a smidgen. *"And maybe you'll reacquaint me with your tattoo, big boy."*

Without a word, Mike turned and went back into the bathroom to dress, but before he closed the door, he dropped his towel and all she could see were the lips, that artist's rendition on his spectacular butt. And she wondered...nah, couldn't be. No way. Hun-uh. Maybe? No, she hadn't said it aloud.

Or had she?

"You're kidding, aren't you?" Rachel squeaked over her bowl of cereal. "He wants you to sleep with the mayor, that little squirrelly guy?"

No, Lilly hadn't mentioned the dropping of the towel, especially since... Well, she might have accidentally asked for it. Some things were private, even from Rachel. Mike's butt being one of them.

"Seduce, not sleep." Lilly's bran flakes were getting soggy, but she wasn't hungry. The reason, while she sure didn't want to admit it, was that Mike was right. Not about her seducing the mayor, but about her getting close to him. Made perfect sense, and she'd tried most of the night to come up with something other than seduction to fit the bill. Tried, couldn't, and that, along with the fact that it was Mike's idea, was ruining a perfectly good morning. So was her reaction to Mike in a towel. And without.

"So what's the difference?" Rachel asked casually. "Do you have any fresh fruit for the cereal?"

Pointing to the fridge, Lilly grunted, "Peaches in the bottom drawer. And the difference is seduction is enticing or attracting. Going to bed is what comes after that. And one doesn't necessarily lead to another."

"Yeah, right," Rachel snorted. "You really need to get out more often."

"Well, it doesn't have to..." And she was pretty sure she could beat Tannenbaum two out of three in a good arm wrestle if it came down to that.

"So you lead the mayor on...have you seen that tooth of his? You're not going to kiss him, are you?" Rachel cringed. "And that hair." Then she shuddered. "I think you'd better come up with a plan B, girlfriend, because plan A's enough to make you quit eating for a month. Can I have your cereal, since you're not eating it?"

Lilly absently pushed her bowl across the table, her mind foundering on kissing the mayor. His lips, hers... That's where the brakes went on, where she went into shock, and that's where she stayed until Mike sauntered in, fully clothed, and grabbed up the box of bran flakes. "Morning, ladies," he said, his casual Mikeness turned on to the full charm setting. Bending, he gave Rachel a kiss on the cheek. "Nice to see you again."

"Nice to see you, too," she replied, then laughed. "But that's not what Jimmy was babbling when he ran out of here a few minutes ago. You and Lilly want to be alone?"

Mike glanced over at Lilly, who still hadn't spoken. "Nope. Any fruit to go with the cereal?"

Rachel pointed to the fridge. "Peaches in the bottom drawer."

Mike fixed his bowl of morning bran and dropped down into a kitchen chair between Rachel and Lilly. "So what's wrong with her?" he asked Rachel, referring to Lilly.

"She went into a coma when I asked her if she'd have to kiss the mayor."

Mike took a bite, then glanced at Lilly. "Probably not." And that snapped her out of it.

"Probably not? That's all I get? A probably not! More like no way I'm going near that man's tooth no matter what, and there's no probably about it," Lilly snapped. "Or sleeping with him, or running my fingers through his comb-over or anything else. If I do this, and that's a big *if* because I haven't decided, I'll flirt a little but that's where it stops. Flirting, Mike. Not kissing."

"That's pretty well limiting the seduction then, isn't it?" Mike asked, reaching across the table to the orange juice carafe. "No kiss, no fingers, no bed…what's left?"

"Anything but actual physical contact." Lilly grabbed the glass of juice he'd poured for himself and drank it down. She wasn't much of a hard-liquor drinker, but a little vodka bracer in it might have been good just about then.

"So do we get to go shopping for sexy clothes?" Rachel asked eagerly. "'Cause what Lilly has isn't exactly sexy." She laughed. "Unless you don't wear underwear under your robe, which, I think, is probably the image half this town has of you now."

"Well, thanks for reminding me of that one, like I hadn't forgotten it." Lilly grabbed the second glass of juice Mike poured for himself, took a drink, then let him have what was left, which wasn't much.

"Actually, I hadn't," Mike added casually. "Thought about it a lot last night, kept me awake for minutes."

"Minutes? All I warrant is minutes?"

"You want more from me? I mean, I'd be glad to give it my all but that court clerk of yours called me on the cell phone in the middle of the night. She wanted another T-shirt and I'm betting she didn't intend on wearing a bra under it."

"So you took it to her?" Lilly asked, fighting not to sound too interested.

"No, I pruned your hedges. Take a look."

"And you really want me to believe you chose yews over hers? Yeah, right." But she did want to believe that, so she peeked out the window and sure enough, a whole hedge of orderly yews. Oddly, she was relieved. Didn't want to be, didn't like to be, but she was.

"I've always chosen yours over anybody else's, Lilly. Which is why I'm here letting you eat my breakfast and not out delivering a T-shirt and being somebody's breakfast."

Lilly spun around from the window to reply, but she couldn't dredge one up out of her little stash of Mike Collier comebacks. She was caught off guard, dazed, startled. Years ago those were the words she'd wanted to hear, but now? A response to them just wasn't there, and he was waiting for it. Oh, how he was waiting. His eyes were glowing, his smile challenging. He was chomping at the figurative bit and here she was, empty, devoid of rebuttal, her mouth open with nothing to say except...except... "Um..."

"Excuse me." Rachel jumped in, clearing her throat. "We were talking about shopping, remember? Sexy clothes? Seducing the mayor? So when are we going?"

"Whenever Mike convinces the merchants to sell to me, 'cause I'm not up to another round at Big Bob's," Lilly said, spooning a peach slice out of Mike's bowl. "Something to do with their favorite son being thrown in jail by...well, me! Forget the fact that he was guilty. That doesn't matter around here. And when I throw him in jail suddenly my size isn't anywhere to be found in Whittier, not in dresses, shoes or ice-cream cones." She took another of his peach slices, then another, until she'd eaten them all.

"Guilty maybe, but with extenuating circumstance." He looked over at her. "Have you got any more peaches?"

"Nope, fresh out. I hear they're having quite a special on them down at Gilroy's Market, though. Didn't you write an article on it or shouldn't you go do that right now?"

Lilly rose and headed to the stairs. Time to get dressed for work. Ten minutes later, she dashed down the stairs, dressed in black slacks and a white blouse. Plain, simple, no fuss no muss under the robes. Mike was gone, probably to the newspaper. So was Rachel, probably to Jimmy's office. So Lilly patted Sherlock, made sure his bowl of water was full, his dry food topped up and the board was out of his doggy door so he had access to the yard when he wanted it, then she went to the fridge to grab the last peach—the one she'd hidden from Mike. But it was gone!

"Damn you, Mike Collier!"

Thursday morning, oh to be back home giving the basset a bath

"THE MAYOR'S WAITING to see you," Tisha whispered before Lilly was all the way inside her office. "He's been here for...like all morning, and he's creepy. He keeps moving his hair all over his head, like that's going to do any good."

Lilly looked at her watch. Eight o'clock. Court didn't start until nine. Of all days to be early! "Want a chance to get to know him better?" Lilly muttered, trying to figure a way out of the meeting.

"Better? Hello...I don't even want to know him worse, which is way better than I want to know him to begin with."

Lilly's head swam with that answer and she didn't bother going back to unravel that which didn't bear unraveling. Instead, she sat down behind her desk, pondering her next move. *Can't go over it, can't go under it, can't go through it, guess I'll have to go right to it and get it over with,* she decided, wondering whether or not to hide under her robes. They were a daunting reminder of who she was, but her mission, should she choose to accept it, was stilettos. So the robes stayed off, and the figurative stilettos went on. "Send him in," she finally said, praying for a twister to whisk her off to Oz.

"Miss Malloy..." the mayor said, marching in and straight over to Lilly's desk. He was wearing his usual brown tweed suit, white shirt, brown bow tie, brown lace-up shoes. Probably brown socks, too, but Lilly wasn't going anywhere near his pant legs to check it out.

"We need to talk," he continued.

Lilly gulped. Time to take one for the team. At least, wander out onto the field and size up the opposition. "Call me Lilly," she said, smiling and... No, she didn't do that, did she? She didn't bat her eyelashes at him? Please God, no. Taking quick stock of all her facial features, she did find her eyelashes still batting around in the breeze, but in her defense, only a little. "Don't you think it's about time that we..." She gulped again. "Lowell... I can call you Lowell, can't I?" And the eyelashes did it again, but only for an instant. She was going to deserve a medal of honor and a better pension plan for pulling this one off.

The Tannenbaum bow tie bobbed up and down on the Tannenbaum Adam's apple. "You certainly can, Lilly." Then he smiled at her, parting his lips so unexpectedly Lilly barely escaped the bright rays bouncing off his tooth. Her eyes automatically dropped to his chin, just a few millimeters into much safer territory. "And you're right. It is about time."

"So what can I do for you...Lowell?" Eyes still anchored to his chin, she prayed he didn't move anything else into her line of vision.

"I wanted to talk about Mike Collier. I understand he's been nosing around, looking at parking tickets. Have you heard anything about that? I mean, since it's your court, I thought maybe something might have gotten back to you or maybe he'd mentioned what he was doing."

Bingo! She hadn't doubted Mike about the Tannenbaum connection, but this proved that Mike's digging was striking a major mayoral nerve. "Sorry, Lowell, and if I knew what was going on you can be sure I'd come to you." And that was no lie. She'd be there with a bailiff who had great big handcuffs with Tannenbaum's name on them. "But I don't. Oh, and do sit down. Standing's so formal between friends, don't you think?" Also, on his duff they could go eye to eye without her risking any accidental eye-to-tooth gawking, an impulse that was getting desperately hard to drive back. The more she resisted, the more her eyes fought her.

Lowell nearly leaped into the chair across from Lilly's desk, then he crossed one leg over the other, straightened the crease in his trousers and tugged at the sleeves on his jacket. Lilly looked down and saw two inches of white skin where his pants and socks didn't meet. Then her eyes traveled to the broomstick-skinny ankles inserted into great big feet. It just never got any better for the man. "I'd be curious to know where you heard about what Mike's been up to, if you don't mind telling me?"

"A clerk down in records," he gushed. "Don't remember her name, but she mentioned it to someone who mentioned it to someone who told my secretary who, of course, brought it to my attention. Said Collier was checking over records, parking tickets issued in the past."

Lilly fought back a smile with a forced and necessary sober frown. Good old Edith knew the fastest route to the mayor's ears, it seemed. Which meant Mike had already set this *strategy* into play. He could have told her about it, though. Would have been the reasonable thing to do. But reasonable wasn't necessarily synonymous with Mike Collier. Silly her, it was *never* synonymous with him. "I think he's probably still angry because he got caught and couldn't get out of it. I'll bet he's looking for something that'll prove he was right and everybody else was wrong." Lilly wrinkled her nose at him. "But don't you worry, Lowell. It's all taken care of." Then she wrinkled her nose again and he must have liked it because he smiled. "And legal."

"I'm glad to hear that, Lilly." Tannenbaum bounced his head up and down in agreement like a cheap bobble-head doll. "But I have to wonder if he's looking for something that could cause you more trouble than he's already done. After all, you two do have that history. I mean, I heard what they were saying on TV so I know none of it was your fault. But it does seem like too much of a coincidence that he's digging into your court records, and not the records of any of the other courts. Wouldn't you say so?"

So this is where he drags me into it? Where he throws it into my court? Yeah, right. Over his bony little buttocks! Lilly nodded her agreement at his blather, fighting hard not to do the bobble-head while at the same time coaxing her properly somber look into something more resembling distressed. "You really think so, Lowell? That he might be out to—" distressed turned to downright pained, and she deserved an award for her performance "—get me again?"

"As your friend, I thought it my duty to warn you."

Friend? More like a matter of convenience weaseling itself in at the opportune moment, and Tannenbaum, little weasel that he was, was jumping on for the ride. "So, are you a married man?" she caught herself asking. Hadn't meant to, but it just slipped right out.

His face blanched. Actually drained to white before he shook his head.

"Well, I'm having a few friends over tomorrow evening— eightish." Eightish? First time something like that had ever wiggled through her vocal cords. But apparently it was working, because Lowell's eyes were beginning to bug. "If you'd care to stop by."

This time he nodded as he blanched even more. It was a

jerky nod, born more from shock than response, one that displaced his comb-over by a good inch.

"Maybe we'll have a few moments to put our heads together and talk about what *we're* going to do about Mike." Emphasis on the *we,* and she actually did wink—just a trifling one. But it caught his attention, because he choked. "Casual," she continued. "Cookout. Just an evening among friends." Now all she had to do was round up the friends.

"Um..." was all he managed to get out before Lilly stood.

"Look, Lowell, I've got to run off to court now. But I'll see you tomorrow night, won't I?" And the dratted eyelashes went at it again, right about the same time her nose wrinkled at him.

"Um..."

"Good, can't wait. Remember, eightish." Lilly grabbed her robe on her way into the courtroom even though no one would be allowed in for another forty-five minutes. She needed time alone, time to rally and regroup, time to plan her own private Mike Collier strategy. And Tisha was correct about the mayor. The honorable Tannenbaum was...creepy.

"I'm having a party tomorrow night," she said as Tisha wandered by Lilly's desk with a stack of folders for today's cases. "Eightish...er, eight. Want to come?"

Tisha popped her gum. "Cool. Want me to dress up or something?"

"Mike Collier's going to be there." Lilly smiled, and her nose wrinkled, but this time as part of her devious grin. "Wear anything you'd like." *Look out, Mike, Tisha's on your tail....* And it served him right!

10

Friday night whines and wine and other such annoyances

"WELL, I DIDN'T THINK fast enough on my feet, so sue me," she snapped at Rachel. Balanced precariously on the top of a stepladder, Lilly finished hanging the last paper Japanese lantern above her deck, then climbed back down and looked up at it. Not bad, really. Pretty, festive. Kind of made it seem as if she was getting ready to have a real party instead of putting on an elaborate camouflage to pseudo-seduce the mayor. "But I didn't want to be alone with him, and I thought this was as good a way as any to make my first move." She shuddered. Her move, translating into inviting Tannenbaum to the trumped-up cookout, the thought of which was twisting a knot in her gut. "And here I am getting ready for my first *move* in who know knows how long, and look who I'm moving on." She shuddered again. "I need a real life, Rach. Promise you'll beam me into a real life if I even look like I'm starting to find *the tooth* attractive. Okay?"

Rachel laughed. "But you've been complaining about how long it's been since you had a date. So maybe this will get you into the mood for a real one, or at least give you a little hint about how it's supposed to be done just in case you and, say, Mike...or anybody," she added quickly, "want to actually do something that takes a move."

"Me and Mike? Whose side are you on, anyway?" Lilly snapped, whooshing into the house to hunt down the plastic tablecloth. Mike was in the kitchen, sitting at the table drinking a bottle of beer, looking relaxed and cozy and fitting in like it was his spot at the table. Wearing jeans and a plain white T-shirt, he looked good, but then, Mike always looked good. That was part of the problem, Lilly reminded herself, trying to ignore him. A big part.

"I let myself in," he said casually. "You don't mind, do you?"

Lilly didn't answer. No need. Mike did what he wanted to do and telling him to knock next time was a big waste of breath. So she simply shook her head and kept on going. Then on her way back with a plastic Hawaiian-style table-cloth, she stopped in the kitchen long enough to grab the bottle from Mike's hand, take a swig of it, hand it back, then head on outside. "His plan, my beer and all he does is just sit there," she muttered to Rachel. "Sit there and watch me do the work."

"Well, did you ask him to help you?" Rachel grabbed one end of the tablecloth from Lilly, helping her flap it up and down to straighten it out. "You and Mike have lots of problems, Lil, and I know he caused them and you were the one who took the hits. But I think that if you two would just talk things through maybe it wouldn't be so bad anymore. Maybe you could call a truce or something, at least until you get the mayor seduced and find out what's going on."

"Not seduced."

"Okay, persuaded. But my point is, you and Mike need to communicate better, since you're working together. And no, I'm not expecting you to go back to the way you used to be, or anything even close to it. I thought that since the two of you are living in the same town, though... I mean..." She huffed an exasperated breath. "Lilly, he's trying to get you out of this mess, isn't he? Trying to help you. That should count for something, but you're being stubborn...and bitchy."

"Bitchy?"

Rachel nodded.

"Traitor," Lilly snapped, sliding the tablecloth into place. "I thought you were supposed to be my best friend."

"I am, and best friends also get to be critics, especially when the person they're criticizing is…"

"Bitchy," Lilly supplied.

"All I'm saying is that if Mike doesn't know what he's supposed to do, he's not going to do anything, because if he asks you, you'll just snap his head off or hand him his you-know-whats on a platter."

"On a platter?"

Rachel nodded. "A silver one. And it's not like you haven't done that before."

"Guess it's just a natural reaction to loathing and despising someone," Lilly retorted, laughing.

"Hun-uh, girlfriend, and you know it. Which is why you won't talk to him now except on the defensive, or to argue. 'Cause you're afraid of your real natural reaction, and it's definitely not loathing and despising."

"You always manage to get back to that. I make one little mistake and you just keep—"

"My third graders do better math than that," Rachel interrupted, holding up two fingers.

"Okay, so I make a couple of little mistakes, and that means—"

"You know what it means," Rachel interrupted again.

"Will you let me finish talking?" She loved Rach, but the problem with the two of them being so close for so many years was that she couldn't get away with anything. Couldn't lie, couldn't hedge, couldn't even dodge the issue. Especially about Mike.

"So will you just go talk to him and see what happens? In fact, I'm going to run out for ice and go pick up Jimmy right now, so you two can be alone." She scrunched her nose. "All alone. Just you and Mike and that little voice…"

"Get out of here." Lilly wadded up a paper napkin and threw it at Rachel. "Before I throw you in jail."

It took Lilly five more minutes to finally wander into the kitchen, and when she did, Mike was still sitting at the table, but his laptop was open and he was working on something, typing fast and furiously, his strong fingers attacking the keys with a passion she remembered. He always had an intensity like that when he worked, as though he was writing a Pulitzer contender. And that intensity was still there. She could see it, feel it. The air was charged with it and Mike was so wrapped up in what he was doing he didn't even know she was there watching him. Glasses on, sliding a ways down his nose, a frown popping over the top of them, this was the serious side of him she'd rarely seen. Certainly, their first relationship go-round hadn't been about the serious side of anything—at least not for him. And even now, including those few nights in jail, it hadn't worked its way out. Too bad, because she liked it. It was good on him. It added a depth he apparently tried to keep hidden—the kind of depth that spelled commitment and forever. One that scared her to death. And yeah, getting back to the basics—it was sexy, too. The deep, brooding kind of sexy she'd never gotten from him before.

But she liked the other side of him, too, the happy and casual Mike, always smiling, always with a glint in his eye. The charmer. The one who always melted her. Still melted her. The one who could have been her commitment and forever a long time ago.

For a moment, Lilly pondered both sides of the man, then stopped herself before the topic became too penetrating. No point. She'd already read ahead to the last page—twice—and the ending never changed. So taking in a deep breath, she braced herself against pretty much everything typically Mike Collier and asked him, "Wanna cook my brats?"

He looked at her over the top of his glasses. "And I thought that was all over between us years ago."

"Bratwurst," she snapped.

He winked. "Call it whatever you like."

"Why do I even bother?" she huffed.

"Because you know what to expect," he replied. "And you want what you expect, otherwise wouldn't keep coming back for more."

He had a point, but she wouldn't admit it—not to him, not even to herself. She always did go back, even when she promised herself she wouldn't. That frustrated her as much as Mike did. More! "Skip it! I'll just ask Ezra."

"I'll guarantee you won't like his brats half as much as you'd like mine. You'll have to admit that in the past we've had some mighty good brats together. Spicy mustard, maybe a little sauerkraut for some extra kick. Ezra's a mayo kind of man, Lilly, and I'm telling you his brats will bore the hell out of you, and you'll come looking for mine, because you're spicy mustard all the way, with a little sauerkraut thrown in just to make things tangy. So yes, I'll cook your brats."

Heaven forbid she should mention the burgers and steaks. "Thanks," she mumbled instead.

Nodding, Mike went back to his work, his attention *so* not on Lilly now, especially after such an in-depth exchange over bratwurst, that it actually made her a little uncomfortable. And, of course, being uncomfortable about being uncomfortable made her even more uncomfortable. She wasn't used to Mike ignoring her. Most of the time she wanted him to and he wouldn't, but now that he was and she didn't... "So what are you working on?" she asked, sitting down, thinking about sliding her chair closer to his so she could take a peek. So she could wiggle her way back to the periphery of his universe was more like it, but there was no way she'd admit to that one. Geez, that vexatious little thought made her even more uncomfortable.

"It's an article about the new interstate and how it's going to affect the farmers who will be forced to sell their land because of it, and what kind of impact that agricultural loss will have on the area as a whole." Then he smiled and the glasses came off. "Nothing about parking tickets. Other things do go on in Whittier, believe it or not."

"Do you like writing about interstates and farmers and the broken scanner at Gilroy's Market? I mean, that's not the person you used to be, and I'm having trouble imagining you doing this. It's just not what I expected."

"We all change, for better or worse," he replied, dead serious. "I always wanted to be a good journalist, not a sensational one. But somewhere along the line I got that confused. And this piece about the impact of the interstate—that's good journalism. Not sensational or exciting, but good...solid. It gets to the heart of what will happen to the people here—like one man who will lose fifty acres all told—and presents the facts such as the fiscal impact that will come of an interchange—gas station, minimart, motel, restaurant. Commute times will change, emergency services will change. And most important, in the end I'll be only the messenger on the story, not the person making, twisting or interpreting the news, which is what a journalist's supposed to do. So do I like writing about the broken scanner at Gilroy's Market? Guess that all depends on if somebody actually pays $790 for that can of cling peaches. That's news."

She smiled. "Or three thousand dollars for nineteen parking tickets."

"And I suppose you still want that apology from me." He chuckled. "Trying to invoke Lilly's law again?"

"Nope. Not tonight. I just want someone to do the grilling. Lilly's request. And somebody anted up three grand to get you out of that apology. Did you ever find out...?"

Mike shook his head, turned his attention back to his computer screen to save the document, then shut down. "So how does your *date* like his steak?" Mike's mouth curled into a wicked grin as Lilly dashed upstairs to change into her best cookout casual. Not-so-short white short-shorts, blue tank top, legs shaved, armpits shaved, hair tied up in a pony-tail...she was ready to go, at least she thought she was until she stepped into the hall outside her bedroom and Mike handed her a tube of glossy red.

"I know you never wear the stuff, so I went out and bought some on my way over here."

"Why?" she asked, pulling off the lipstick cap and looking at the color. Not just glossy red like the label stated, but really, really red. Bordello and bodacious. And she wondered if she needed some seamed, black, fishnet stockings to go with it.

"'Cause a fellow likes a gal with red lips." He grinned. "Luscious, moist red lips."

"The kind of gal you blow up or the kind you pay by the hour?"

When Lilly greeted Mayor Tannenbaum at the front door promptly at eightish, the first thing she noticed was that he noticed her lips. So Mike was right about that one! Right didn't mean his idea was a good one, though. Because it wasn't. Risking a glance at Tannenbaum, she cringed. He looked like a starving man who was on the very brink of de-vouring something. Her lips!

"Hi," he said, the spittle of lechery beginning to collect in the corners of his mouth. He licked his own lips.

So maybe this was going to be easy, after all, Lilly thought. "Lowell." She pronounced his name in a pucker, which wasn't easily done for a man in a yellow plaid shirt, green knee-knocker bermudas, white legs, brown socks and san-dals. "I'm *so* happy to see you...*so* happy," she repeated, kind of liking the sound of it as it billowed through her lips. But she was in a quandary whether to pucker them next or lick them or just bat her eyes at him. Or maybe go beyond the call of duty and try all three. Indecisive moments like this made her appreciate the power of her gavel. One big bang on the

wooden block and her intention was clear. No fuss, no muss
"Please come in."

He mumbled something, Lilly wasn't sure what, anc
handed her a box of wine as he stepped inside. "The bes
wine to be had in a box" was what she thought he said, bu
instead of asking him to repeat himself she thrust the wine a
Rachel, who was passing through looking for Jimmy, ther
latched on to the mayor's arm, keeping her eyes properly
fixed to the knobby white knees bobbing three inches below
his shorts and three inches above his socks. "Mike Collier':
here," she said quietly, leading him to the party outside
"He's like that, you know. Just does what he wants to do. Bu
I wanted to warn you so you wouldn't be surprised. A man ir
your position...well, you deserve that."

Tannenbaum tittered something that sounded like a con
dolence or an apology or some such—*I'm sorry, I'm pasty, I'm
not a crook*—as she foisted him on Mike at the grill, then scur
ried to the nearest Tannenbaum-free zone, which turned ou
to be behind Ezra.

"That's the one?" he asked, fully engaged in a ribeye on a
bun. "I'd venture to say if he's got a scam going on, the
money isn't being appropriated to wardrobe." Ezra, dressec
in white twill slacks and a blue-and-white Hawaiian prin
shirt looked over at Tannenbaum, who was standing almos
shoulder to shoulder with Mike, watching him cook. "I thinl
poor Mike needs some rescuing."

Lilly smiled. "I think poor Mike can take care of himself.'
And payback was becoming sweeter and sweeter by the min
ute, she thought, as Tisha finally effervesced on to the scene.

"Will you look at that," Rachel whispered. She was hang
ing on to Jimmy, nudging him in the ribs, when his heac
turned, just like every other man's there did, including Ezra's

"Hi, everybody," Tisha called from the doorway. "Sorry
I'm late but I couldn't decide what to wear. Is this okay?" She
spun around, showing off her bikini top, one so skimpy that a

sneeze or a breeze or a hard stare would snap it right off her. And her shorts redefined the term short-shorts. They rode low at the waist, way down below her perfectly flat belly— *damn her for that belly,* Lilly thought—revealing not one, but three with jingling bells on them, belly rings. And not only did the shorts ride low, they were cut high in the leg, revealing enough of her derriere to let everyone know it was as toned as her belly. *Damn her for that butt,* Lilly thought.

"Hi, Mike," Tisha said, wiggling her way right over to him, past Juanita Lane, Cal Gekas and Roger Jackson, all from the jail. Roger's wife, decked out in prim capris and a flowered cotton blouse, slapped her husband on the arm when Tisha breezed by him, brushing her largely unclad breasts against his arm, and his eyes bugged out of his head.

Mike, who hadn't turned around from the grill to see Tisha coming yet, finally did, gasping, "Jesus Christ!" He dropped the burger he was flipping and it landed with a splat on the deck. Looking at Lilly, his eyes pleaded for help, explanation, rescue, anything. But Lilly merely shrugged at him and smiled. A smile of conquest she knew he comprehended.

"Going to be a good party, after all," Lilly whispered to Rachel, who was yanking on Jimmy, trying frantically, and without much success, to drag him out of Tisha's line of sight.

On the opposite side of the deck, Tisha managed to squeeze in between Mike and the mayor, who was already shoulder to shoulder with Mike. When she was finally where she wanted to be, she nudged her hip into Tannenbaum, pushing him away. So the mightless Tannenbaum, with two cups of wine in hand, plus a burger, chased Lilly back down as Ezra scooted into the shadows, leaving her to face the mayor all by herself.

"Please, let me help you," she said, watching him set the plate down without dropping the burger, but not so the cups o'wine. The cheap grape stuff sloshed onto the plastic tablecloth, dribbling down to his white, knobby Tannenknee.

"Oh, dear," he murmured, looking down at the splash
over at Lilly, then down at his leg again.

You wish, she thought, pretending not to notice *the look.* Bu
the second thought that came knocking on her brain re
minded her what this party was really about, and it wasn'
partying. So she gritted her teeth and reached for a pape
napkin. *For the good of the team,* she said to herself, grabbing
up her cup and downing the rest of the wine in it before she
martyred herself for the cause. *Hell, for the good of my career*
Then she zeroed that napkin in on his knee, went in for a
slow, steady landing—God forbid her hand should veer of
course—and commenced the dabbing. It was a quick dab, re
ally, crucially placed only over the actual knob of the knee
not a millimeter above or below it. And it was a perfect tech
nique—one that caused the stupefied mayor to suck in a
sharp breath and hold it until he nearly passed out from as
phyxiation. "All done," she said, witnessing the fact that he
was beginning to turn blue. "Lowell...take a breath now."

And he did, of course. The old one quavered out, floun
dered a bit until he was finally able to suck in some fresh ox
ygen. Then another breath and another... Breathing in the
throes of passion was what it sounded like, and she didn'
know if he was about to hyperventilate or—No! Not going
there. Not even going close to it.

"Missed a spot," he said, much to her relief, then pointed to
the tiny splash just above his knee. It was hidden by the hem
of his bermudas, but he pulled them up enough to reveal i
and sure enough, there was a drop of wine in need of Lilly's
personal attention. The horny little worm! He shut his eyes—
he actually shut his eyes and waited with a warped little smile
to let her know that in his book this was considered scoring—
probably something close to a home run.

The only thing that got Lilly through the second dabbing
was a quick glance across the deck at Mike and Tisha. Her
36Cs were crushed into his arm, sort of trapping it in place as

they gyrated up and down, making it pretty damn difficult for him to flip that burger. He was trying to maneuver away from her, but there was nowhere to go except over the rail. And from the looks of Tisha, she'd go right on over after him.

That little satisfying twinge of revenge got Lilly through the mayor's next dabbing, hoping there wasn't yet another hidden spot of wine still awaiting her in yet other uncharted Tannenbaum territories. "Let me get you some potato salad," she offered, jumping up from the bench before Lowell could squeeze out a yes or no. He was, apparently, still basking in the afterglow of the dabbing, still a bit breathless and, thankfully, speechless.

When she returned with his food, Lowell's bermudas were hiked up not quite as high as Tisha's shorts, but high enough that his skinny white thighs were glinting at her almost as much as his tooth did. *God, give me strength. The man wants another dabbing.* "I have to go take care of something inside the house, but I'll be right back. Promise."

Fleeing into the house, Lilly met Mike shoulder to shoulder in the doorway. He was trying to get away from Tisha as hard as she was Tannenbaum. It was a tight fit in the frame together, but they both got through it at the same time. Lilly headed straight to the stairs. Mike followed on her heels, and when they reached the top, they looked at each other and laughed. "So was it good for you?" Lilly asked.

"As good as it was for you."

"I was going to hide in my bedroom for a few minutes."

"I was going to hide in the john."

"Lock the door this time," she said, opening her bedroom door. She hesitated for a moment, then against her better judgment, turned back to Mike. "Come on," she said. "But keep *this* door unlocked."

So he followed her into the bedroom and dropped onto her bed as she plopped down on an embroidered chaise on the other side of the room. Safe distance, she thought. And the door was not just unlocked; Mike had left it open. No voices popping into her head, either.

Plenty safe for a few minutes, anyway.

"SAW YOUR HAND UP HIS pants," Mike said. He'd wanted to laugh when he saw Tannenbaum's reaction to Lilly. Poor man, he could only dream. "Nice touch, judging from the look on his face." Mike remembered the touch, and it *was* nice. Better than nice.

"That's what he thought." Pulling her feet up, she kicked off her shoes. "So did Tisha, from what I could tell. I think she's got a thing for you, Mike. And she dressed just for you—you know that, don't you?" Lilly wrinkled her nose. "Her Friday night specials."

"Maybe she'll loan you some Friday night specials like that for your next date with the mayor," he said, kicking off his own shoes and pulling his feet up on her bed. It wasn't made. The pink sheets were crumpled and he could smell Lilly's scent on them—the faint trace of sweet soap she still used. He'd always loved that on her, and was glad she hadn't changed it because so much else about her had changed. Oh, she was still Lilly. But Lilly with an edge. And a sharp one at that. "She was a nice touch, though. Let me rephrase that. She would have liked a nice touch."

"You know what they say about variety. Just thought you might like a little."

"You just thought you'd make my evening miserable. A little get even with Mike, and I'll admit, you're getting pretty good at it."

"So did I?"

"What? Make my evening miserable? Yep, about as miserable as yours."

"Then my work here is done." Lilly laughed. "And you two looked so cute together."

"You know who I look cute with, Lilly. And it's never been

Tisha's type, which is why you set us up. But I did kind of like the belly rings, so I'll forgive you. Ever thought about..." He shook his head. "Nah, your belly is perfect the way it is. An inny, if I remember correctly?" Had they ever simply talked like this before? he wondered. Pleasant conversation only for the sake of pleasant conversation? It was nice, and maybe if they'd tried it years ago...

"Forgive me?" she laughed. "Isn't that twisting things all the way around—twice, if I remember?"

"Memories are such subjective things, aren't they?"

"You call them subjective, I call them gospel, and even if I do decide on getting a belly ring, you'll never have a memory of it. So don't go getting any ideas." She raised her eyebrows wickedly. "About anything."

Ideas? He was full of them, but they were so far off, if ever. "Well, it looked to me like Tannenbaum had some ideas about making a little memory of his own. I don't suppose you happened to learn anything while your hand was down his pants, did you?"

"Technically, my hand was up his pants, not down. And the only thing I learned is that he's in desperate need of some time in a tanning bed and a little exfoliation on his skin."

And Tisha's hand had been on the verge of getting down his pants every time he'd let up his guard. Tisha—Lilly's revenge. She knew that type scared the bejeezus out of him. Always had, and he had to hand it to Lilly—she was getting a nice, sharp edge to her, one he liked a little too much. Everything she'd always been, plus that edge—what a package! Too bad he'd blown it for them so long ago.

Still, this was good right now, sitting here and talking, getting along almost like they were friends. He wanted her back as a friend, not that they'd ever been real friends, because they hadn't, not in the way they should have been. He'd spent their first weeks trying to do what all horny young men want to do with someone as gorgeous as Lilly, and once he'd done it he'd slammed shut the door on pretty much everything else. And it was only after that he'd realized that while the sex was great, and he missed it—damn, how he missed it—he'd missed Lilly even more. That was an ache that kept on nagging him even now, after all these years, when he thought about what kind of friend she could have been. A friend and so much more. "Maybe you and Lowell and Tisha and I could double-date some night. Pizza and beer... Is she old enough to drink, by the way?"

"Drink and do a whole lot more." Lilly shot him a wicked little grin, one that zinged right to his heart. "If you want."

He wanted, absolutely *wanted*, all the way down to his bones, but not with Tisha. And he was going to have to get over the cold, cruel truth facing him that it wouldn't be with Lilly, either. Not now, anyway, and maybe not ever. And that didn't exactly make his heart go zing, but it did make it ache a whole lot more. "What I want is some of the wine in the box. What kind of protocol is there about drinking it straight from the container? Do I have to put it in a brown paper bag like I do my bottle of wine when I'm hanging out on the street corner on Friday nights, drinking, bumming spare change and cigarettes?"

"How destitute are you?" Lilly asked, forcing a frown.

"You're not going to offer me a loan, are you?" He was beginning to know that look, actually anticipating it at odd, unguarded gaps in their customary skirmishing. "Because I'll swallow my pride and take the cash if you absolutely insist." And he held back his grin, imitating the forced frown she was giving him.

She let loose a sharp laugh. "Fat chance. I was just wondering about the vagrancy laws here in Whittier, and if they'd apply to you. And I believe there is an ordinance about drinking wine from a box on a street corner on a Friday night."

"Punishable by throwing me back in jail, I'm guessing."

"Something like that."

"Admit it, Lilly," he goaded.

"Admit what?"

Her face took on an innocent expression. He recognized that, too. And he felt the arousal. No, not the sexual kind, although that wasn't too far off, but the kind where every last nerve ending in his body was beginning to tingle, and every synapse in his brain starting to wake up. "Admit that throwing me in jail felt good. That you loved the power and the control you had over me because there was nothing I could do to stop you. And that if you had the chance to do it to me again, you would."

"You forgot something." Her face was dead serious.

"That you'd throw away the key?"

"Well, that too, but you left out the most important part. That if I had the chance to do it again I'd do it...with glee."

"Glee?" he asked.

"Glee."

"Glee," he repeated.

She nodded. "For me it was better than sex."

"Better than *our* sex?" He watched her face, didn't miss a twitch, and that question stopped her. She was grappling for the next comeback. It wasn't on the tip of her tongue, not even close. He had her, and that might not happen again. So this was a good place to end the conversation and leave the room. Jumping up, Mike grabbed his shoes off the floor and headed to the door. But just as he entered the hall, he heard her draw in a little breath, so he braced himself for the zing. And she did let him have it.

"No, Mike. Nothing was ever better than *our* sex. Which is why you should be eating your heart out right this very moment, since all you're getting from me is wine in a box."

Even though he didn't turn around, he knew the smile on her face. Felt it in his heart, and sticking like a dagger in his back.

11

Friday night still, will it never end?

"SO YOU'LL HAVE DINNER with me tomorrow?" Lowell Tannenbaum asked, his Adam's apple bobbing up and down in eager anticipation. "There's a nice little diner right across the street from the cement factory."

Nice little diner, her foot. Lilly could just imagine it, and every picture ended with Lowell practically sitting in her lap.

"I could pick you up—"

"I'll meet you there," she insisted. Bad enough she was having dinner with him in a crowded little diner booth, but no way was she getting in a car with that man, too.

"Really?" Tannenbaum looked positively apoplectic. "You're really going to meet me there? Like, a date. Just the two of us?"

"Really," she said, holding on to her front door. "The two of us." She'd concede that much, but not the date part. That would drag him all the way back in the door, and she'd only just now succeeded in getting half of him out. With the door firmly in her grasp if he tried so much as a kiss, a handshake, heaven forbid a grope, she'd bash him. *Oh, I'm so sorry, Lowell. I didn't mean to slam it on your tooth...* "Seven o'clock good for you?" She really should pucker her lips, bat her eyes a little— give him a little icing on his wishful cake. She was all puckered and batted out, though, and she just wanted him to go home, to hike his size thirteens all the way to the street without so much as looking back. Yeah, right. Lowell Tannenbaum struck her as a looking-back kind of guy, the first clue being that his goodbye was already into its fifth minute, probably meaning he wanted more than a little frisky wine-dabbing to cap off his night. Just her luck—the illustrious little mayor wanted to go home with some bodacious, bordello red on his collar and—her skin crawled thinking about it—other Tannenplaces.

She had her door in a firm grip, however, so she was safe. "Good night, Lowell," she said for the tenth time, inching it at him, and at the same time glancing at Mike, who was standing in the next room, out of Tannenbaum's sight, arms folded casually across his chest, smirking at her.

"Maybe we could take in a movie afterward?" Tannenbaum asked, still fighting to hold his place.

In the dark, sitting next to him? Not a chance! "I'll think about it," she said, still pushing at the door. Unfortunately, a Tannenbaum clodhopper was in the way, so the door budged only about an inch. At that rate, the Malloy-Tannenbaum good-night was going to turn into a good-morning.

Why me? she thought, letting go her grip on the door just for an instant. In that moment Tannenbaum took the lapse as a sign from God that his evening was about to end in some serendipitous, bodacious bordello luck, so he stepped back inside the house.

"Maybe I could just wait until everybody goes home..." he began, creeping even closer to Lilly. "Then we'll be all alone so that we can—" he sniffed, hiked his shoulders, grinned "—well, do whatever comes naturally, if you know what I mean. Got any of that wine left, by the way?" Sniff, hike.

No, not the wine in a box! "I have a headache," she said, the first excuse popping into her mind. It was time to get him out of her house, get herself out of the scheme, get herself back to her job, get rid of Mike. Time to let what happened happen, then deal with the aftermath, if and when. Really, really stupid, letting Mike get her caught up in this mess, especially since she hadn't even seen any evidence of a mess. It was just his word, and on that rather nebulous word she was getting ready to seduce the mayor. And for what? Some kind of vague scheme that may or may not be happening. *You've lost it*, she told herself. *And now it's time to get it back.* "I'm sorry, Mayor, but this...this situation between us just wouldn't work out."

Not to be dissuaded, Tannenbaum took another step toward her, stretched out his hands and cracked his knuckles. "Sure it will. I have power, you have power. Can you imagine what all that will add up to, where it could put us? But only if we're together. And I have something that will fix you right up. A nice little massage, among friends, and in Whittier it pays to have friends, Lilly."

Well, that set of insinuations raised her eyebrows. "I like having friends," she replied, glancing over at Mike, who was giving her a thumbs-up. "But I don't really have any in Whittier yet...Lowellsy. At least none in high places." So the mayor seemed a little guilty about something. In and of itself that didn't mean anything—that was the lawyer in her talking. But she could take another step over into Tannenbaum turf, see what else he was dangling—and that was Lilly talking.

"You do if you want one," the mayor replied. He had the look in his eye of a cartoon evildoer twisting the end of his handlebar mustache as he tied a helpless female to the railroad tracks. And the train was definitely bearing down on her, or at least, he thought it was. "Like I said, I'm a friend if you want one, Lilly. Life in Whittier is so much better with a little help from a friend. So many things a friend can do—a friend in the right places." Sniff, hike.

Bingo! She was back in the scheme. Hook, line and Tannensinker. And that was both Lilly and lawyer talking, because the mayor was definitely hinting at something hinky here. "We'll talk about it tomorrow night. See what kind of friends we're going to become. Okay?" She found a promising smile for him, one that offered, but didn't give.

"Lilly," Mike called, stepping around the corner the same time Tannenbaum was swooping in for a kiss. Lilly assumed he was, since his lips were puckered and pointed straight at her. "I've been looking everywhere for you. Your mother's on the phone, she says it's urgent, something about an oatmeal recipe." He narrowed his eyes at the mayor. "Can't wait. She says your dad wants oatmeal right now."

"Sorry," Lilly said to Lowell, as he reined his lips back in. "But we'll pick this up tomorrow night. Let's make it six forty-five, and that way we don't have to wait so long to see each other." She wrinkled her nose at him, a wrinkling he took to be a good sign for he wrinkled back, then she left him standing in the open door as she dashed into the kitchen behind Mike.

"Oatmeal, Mike? My dad wants oatmeal? What kind of pitiful excuse was that?"

"Best I could come up with," he said, offering her a bratwurst. "Spicy mustard or mayo?"

"He's a pesky little thing," Rachel giggled.

"Who?" Lilly snapped, shoving Mike's brat back at him. "The mayor or Mike?" She glared at Mike.

Rachel sidled up to Lilly, whispering in her ear, "I said *little*, girlfriend."

"Ex-girlfriend," Lilly replied.

She laughed. "Well, your ex-girlfriend's going over to Jimmy's tonight, so you'll have your house all to yourself...just in case." And as Jimmy walked by, she grabbed his arm and waved at Lilly on her way out the door.

Shortly after Rachel left, the rest of her party guests bid their farewells. The jail crew followed Ezra out, and Tisha, who was in a bit of a snit because she couldn't find Mike, decided to cut her losses and go looking for a late date. Lilly didn't see Mike leave and she really expected to find him lurking somewhere in her house—in a closet, under the stairs, in her bed...but he wasn't there. And yes, she was a little disappointed that he hadn't had the courtesy to say goodbye. But that was Mike. In and out as he pleased. Her house, her life, her heart.

So here she was on a Friday night, the party over at...she glanced at the clock. A quarter of nine? Talk about eating and running. But here she was with lots of evening still to go and she was all alone. At least Rachel would end her evening happy, Lilly thought, trudging upstairs to bed. And start tomorrow that way, too. "Geez," she said aloud, too bummed to even undress before she plopped into bed to spend yet another night staring at the ceiling. A lot of that going on lately. Maybe a nice mural up there...

"Hey, Lilly."

No, not that again. Not tonight.

"Hey, Lilly, wanna consort in the court, boogie on your bench, grabble with your gavel?"

"Grabble?" she said. Great, here she was, nine-fifteen and she was talking to her voice. Bad enough it talked to her, but now she was talking back to it. And no, she didn't want to consort, boogie or grabble, whatever the heck that was. She didn't want to sleep, either.

"Hey, Lilly, wanna borrow the bailiff's handcuffs?"

"Hey, Lilly, wanna come judge this?"

Nine-thirty, and the voice was having a regular conversation now. *"Hey, Lilly, let's get ready to rumble..."*

"Enough!" she shouted, jumping out of bed. "I give up." She didn't know where she was going, but anyplace was better than being home alone with the voice. Maybe by the time she got back it would have laryngitis.

Friday night much later and things are looking up, finally!

ANYPLACE TURNED OUT TO BE the *Journal*. The voice drove her to it. It was a plot, a conspiracy. And she'd played right into its licentious little hands. She was weak, so weak, in fact, that by ten o'clock she was perched on a stool watching Mike work. The voice had won this round, but next time...

Mike was busy putting the final edits into the computer and sending them to press. He knew she was there. Glanced up at her, nodded when she came in, then went back to his work. It was almost an hour later, when the paper was finally put to bed, that he leaned back in his chair and spoke. "We're always just barely under the wire," he said. "Can't afford the proper help. Not yet, anyway."

He looked tired, Lilly thought. Not chipper, no glint in his eyes.

"Then the paper doesn't support itself?"

"Barely. I meet payments and payroll." He shrugged. "I get by."

"Ever thought about going back to Indy? Getting on the paper there again?"

He grinned. "You'd like that, wouldn't you? Getting rid of me? Packing me off to Indy so you could have the whole town all to yourself."

She grinned back. "I wouldn't hate it."

"Well, sorry to disappoint you, but I'm not going back. I'll keep things on a shoestring here for a year or so, sleep under my printing press if I have to, and the situation will turn around for me eventually. It's called investing in my future, something I've never done before. Of course, way back then my future was tomorrow, and the day after that didn't count. Times sure have changed, because the day after tomorrow is all I worry about. Care for a drink? You and Rachel raided my beer pretty good, but I think I have a couple left upstairs."

Lilly followed Mike upstairs to his apartment and staked her claim in his recliner. It was nice and cozy there, watching him make a cursory tidy-up of his kitchen. A dump was a dump, and Mike's place still was a dump, but with him in it, it didn't seem so bad. "I need a maid," he said, handing Lilly a beer.

"A wife," she said, instantly regretting the opening she'd just given him, and wondering where he'd take it now that he had it.

He didn't take it anywhere, surprisingly. At least not anywhere Lilly expected. "No woman in her right mind would settle down here," he said, sitting cross-legged on the floor across from her. "No man in his right mind would, either."

"It suits you…or at least, it could with a…"

"A woman's touch?" He laughed, almost bitterly. "I haven't dated anyone since the last time we… No woman's touch in my life since then. Haven't had the time, the inclination or the right woman."

This was getting too serious. Too personal. She didn't want to go there, didn't want to think about it. Mostly, she didn't want to know why he hadn't had the inclination, because if she did, the answer might be too close to her own reasons for doing pretty much the same thing. No time, no inclination, no man. And deep in her heart, so deep even the god of all things chocolate and irresistible couldn't bribe it out of her, was the niggling little truth, the one she didn't want to admit. Nobody compared to Mike. In the money or out of it, nobody even came close. At first she'd assumed that everything they had going for them was merely the sex. Good in bed and the rest didn't count. But so many other things did count, just not in ways she understood, or even wanted to understand. "So what's your plan?" she asked, trying to keep the conversation light.

"For starters, make things right with you."

"Not about me—about the paper. What's your plan about the paper?"

"For starters, make things right with you. Once that's taken care of, concentrate on the paper."

Not the words she wanted to hear. Too serious, and serious

scared her. It made her vulnerable and pliable and wishful. "So, are you going to be there tomorrow night?" she asked, glad there was another topic to skip over to. "The diner...my date."

"Don't like horning in," he said, grinning.

Back to safe ground. Finally! "Well, I suppose I could say something clever here like tell me one time when you didn't horn in. But we both know the answer to that one, don't we. So instead I'll just say...you leave me alone with that man and no penalty I'll impose on you will be severe enough. And I *will* hunt you down and punish you."

"Sounds promising." Finishing off the last of his beer, Mike stood and carried the bottle into the kitchen. He hunted for a trash can, couldn't find one, so he gave up and set the bottle on the counter. "Care if I make a few suggestions about that punishment? Remember that one night after we got drunk at that little Italian place downtown?"

Did she ever. They'd barely made it to the parking lot, and who would have ever guessed that all little black Mercedes looked alike in the dark? Boy, were the owners surprised! "Look, I'll go through with this, but so help me Mama Rosa's you'd better keep the Tannenwolf off me or next time the marinara sauce will be hot."

"Next time? Does that mean there's something for me to look forward to?"

Well, she'd opened that door. Far be it for him not to enter. "Tomorrow night, Mike," she snapped. "And that's it. If I can't get anything out of him tomorrow night, I'm out of it."

"So use me," he said, stepping away from Lilly. "You both have it in for me, so make that work for you." Crossing over to his bed, Mike dropped down into it and lay there flat on his back, sprawled out in the middle, staring up at the exposed pipes, duct work and beams in the ceiling. "But in the meantime, I don't think we can have any marinara delivered at this hour. Would some sweet and sour sauce from Wong's be okay?" He patted the bed.

"Hold your breath and count to...like, a billion."

"Hey, you can't blame a man for trying. Especially one who's already known the incomparable Lilly Malloy in the incomparable ways I have. I mean, what you do can make a grown man weep, Lilly. Do you ever think about—"

"No!" she snapped.

He raised his head and looked at her. "Well, I do." Then he dropped his head back onto the bed. "A lot."

The flush was beginning to rise up her neck. That was the way it always started between them. She shut her eyes, fanning herself, remembering... First the flush, then the full blaze. Hot...so hot, then clothes came off. He ripped at hers with the fury of a child unwrapping a gift from Santa—shedding her, in mere seconds, of everything but the droplets that shimmered between her breasts. His excitement was in going straight to the gift. But hers was in the anticipation of it—unbuttoning every button with bridled indulgence, inching down the zipper a millimeter at a time and watching him on the verge of exploding during her oh-so-slow pursuit. By the time she was ready to slide the jeans down, graze her fingers over his erection, but only as a promise of more to come, he was moaning. Soft moans, more like little gasps. And he bit his lower lip, trying to control himself as she played, and she loved to play. But he was always so eager to return the favor. And she remembered those favors...wow, how she remembered them! Now, that was a memory to keep a girl warm on a long, cold night.

Unconsciously, Lilly tugged at her jersey shirt, pulling it away from her body, and did some frantic fanning as the memories kept on dissolving her into the cardinal element of need and want and longing right there before *his* very eyes. Those had been good times, though, she recalled. Good times when their bodies came together, slick and glistening with

weat. Good times on the floor, in the bed, in the shower. It
never mattered when the burn to satiate started. It was always pure liquid fire, flowing down from her heart and up
from her toes. The strong muscles of his chest crushing into
her...him thrusting into her, her thrusting back at him.

Then suddenly, even as she stood on the other side of the
room from him, stood right next to the window fan that was
trying desperately to stir a little air in his musty apartment,
Lilly got so hot her clothes were soaked with perspiration.
The perspiration of arousal and desire, she knew. And Mike
knew, too, which was why she ran straight home to a cold
shower. Not a word to Mike on her way out. He didn't say a
word, either. But she heard him laugh.

Had he headed for a cold shower, too? she wondered, as
she let the chilly water cool her down. Or was she the only
one going way out on that shaky limb?

It was after one when she turned off the shower, turned on
the television and headed to bed. Maybe with all the noise going on around her, the voice would give her a couple hours of
peace and quiet. She hoped so, anyway, because her near-
orgasmic gig in Mike's apartment had totally wiped her out.

Drifting off, she figured she'd hear the voice or dream
about Mike, but the last thing she heard came from the television. "And I promise you continued fiscal responsibility if
you elect me to be your mayor one more time. Just look at the
money I've already brought into the city.... Have a plan...
more money...more money."

"Promises, promises," she mumbled just before the sand-
man hit.

if it's Saturday morning that must mean leather and stilettos

IF YOU'RE NOT GOING TO seduce him in actuality, then do it in
wardrobe," Rachel said, holding up a black skirt. It was

leather and way too short for sitting comfortably, uncomfort ably or otherwise.

Lilly jerked it from her hand and thrust it back on th clothes rack. "I have a reputation to protect, remember?" Th salesclerk, an austere forty-something, glanced over at Lilly didn't smile, didn't frown, didn't put a crack in her flat-sobe facade.

Lilly and Rachel glanced back, mimicking her expressio until she finally took the hint and busied herself straightenin; collars and cuffs on the other side of the shop.

"I'll bet you that little black skirt that nobody at the dine across the street from the cement factory's gonna care a hoc about your reputation, Lil," Rachel said, her voice a tad mor muted. She grabbed one in her size—a three, compared t Lilly's nine—and held it up to herself. "Want to buy it now or just put it on layaway?"

Lilly snatched that one from Rachel and thrust it back o the rack, too. "I almost did it last night," she said, droppin down into the chair next to the dressing room. "I mean, nc almost, but I could have. Not that I would have, but I coul have. And I was thinking about it, Rach. How we used to b how we could be."

"And you finally realized that you love him? Like I haven been telling you that all along?"

She glanced up at Rachel, who was holding up the blac leather again. "Just where did that come from?" she spu tered.

Rachel looked at the skirt's tag. "Canada."

"Not the skirt!"

"We have some lovely spandex," the clerk said, carrying pair of long spandex pants across to Lilly. "Body-hugging, s he'll get the idea, but not so revealing that he doesn't have use his imagination just a teensie." With Tannenbaum, Lil wanted a whole lot more than a teensie.

"Perfect," Rachel exclaimed. "In black."

"You're that judge," the clerk finally said to Lilly.

And Lilly slunk down in the chair. "I'm her evil twin sister."

The top Rachel selected for Lilly was a tight, sleeveless shell—white, with a plunging scoop neck. In fact it plunged so low, Lilly almost choked when she looked down. But this was sticking to the basics, Rachel claimed. Except for the underwear—a thong that would leave a definite barely-there imprint under spandex, and a bra that would push things way out and over. Lilly did choke when she looked down and saw that!

The total package came with Lilly's headstrong protest until they got to the stilettos. Lilly's big fear. Trying to wiggle, jiggle and balance herself all at the same time. "No way," she said, as the shoe clerk brought them out. Four-inch heels, simple, sexy and to die for, Lilly did concede to herself. And suddenly, she was showing off the whole package for Mike, watching his face for approval. Well, at least in her mind she was.

"Lil?"

"Huh?"

"I said, are they comfortable?"

She looked down at the shoes. Too bad Mike wouldn't get to see them. "They're fine," she said. Not that it mattered. Lowell Tannenbaum wouldn't care if she showed up in bare feet or shoe boxes, just so long as she showed up. Glancing at her watch, she realized that miserable undertaking was going to befall her in just under eight hours. *Don't the condemned always get a last meal?* "Let's go eat," she said.

"I, um, promised Jimmy," Rachel said. "But I'll call him. In fact, why don't the three of us..."

Lilly smiled. At least Rachel was getting on with her life. "You go on. Have a great time. I'll grab something and head on home." And count down the dreaded hours.

"But I'm supposed to be here helping you through this,"

Rachel said, taking the bag with the box of shoes in it. "Not out with him all the time."

"And you think helping me pick out spandex and stilettos isn't helping?" She chuckled. "Tell Jimmy that Sherlock misses him."

Outside the shop, Rachel tossed the shoes into Lilly's car, then stepped back. "I really like him, Lil. Jimmy...he's not like anybody I've ever met, and we just... I don't know."

"Fit?" Lilly supplied. She'd watched them, even envied how in such a short time that fit did happen. They'd simply come together and that was it.

"I think so. It's like I'm really happy when we're together, and I think about him all the time when we're not and I can't wait to get back to him. And it doesn't matter what we do as long as we're doing it together."

"Any little voices?" Lilly asked, chuckling.

Rachel shook her head, smiling the dreamy smile of a woman in love, and that's when Lilly knew for sure that Rachel was. It wasn't a crush or lust or a passing fancy. Rachel was in for keeps, lucky Rach. She glowed with it. It bubbled in her voice, sparkled in her eyes. Her gestures jumped and sizzled with the electricity of it. "I have the real voice," Rachel said almost reverently. "And I know he's not the deep, brooding sexy kind like Mike, but he's my kind, Lil. The kind I want every day for the rest of my life, and if I'm lucky, I'll have it."

"Rachel!" Lilly squealed, grabbing her friend for a hug. "It's a good thing you came to rescue me from Mike. I'm so happy for you."

"Me, too. I mean, I thought we were just...but we weren't. We talked about it last night...all night...." Rachel pulled back, wiping her eyes with the back of her hand. "And that's what you need to do with Mike, sweetie." she said, sniffling. "Sit up all night, talk to each other, listen. Figure out what you have that's good, and throw away everything else."

"Mike and I were always just..." Lilly said, shrugging. "And we still are just—"

"Then you underestimate yourself," Rachel interrupted. "And Mike."

"So if I buy you that black leather skirt as a what—pre-engagement gift?—will you promise to shut up about Mike and me for a few minutes?" A couple hundred bucks was a small price to pay to get off that subject. As happy as Lilly was for Rachel, and she really was thrilled for her, she was also a little blue for herself. She wanted that dreamy smile of a woman in love. She wanted to glow from being in love, wanted it to bubble in her voice and sparkle in her eyes. And she really wanted some jumping and sizzling.

Unfortunately, the only sizzling in her life was coming from the grill when she got home. Mike was there, cooking up some leftovers from the night before. "Would there be any point in asking you to observe the conventional custom of knocking before you come in?" Lilly asked, dropping her shopping bags on the kitchen table.

"I did, but you weren't home. All you have left is hamburger."

"So you just broke in. That comes with a longer jail sentence than parking tickets."

"Rachel gave me a key."

"She paid your jail fine, too, didn't she?" Lilly refused the burger and went for some salad in the fridge. "Always knew I couldn't trust her."

"Don't know who paid it. No paper trail."

"Yeah, right. You're just protecting somebody you don't want me to find out about." Grabbing a plastic container with various greens and tomatoes, she tossed it over onto the table, then hunted down a bottle of Italian dressing. "You don't want me tracking your influences in this town because you're afraid that someday, somehow, I'll use them against you.

Right? You're afraid I might crack the secret of the Mike Collier spell—the one you cast over so many unwitting victims?"

"Got a little grumpy going on?" he asked, slathering mayo and mustard on his burger. "I used to be good at fixing up your grumpies."

"Me, grumpy? What would I have to be grumpy about?" One bite of her salad and she was done with it so she shoved it across the table at Mike.

"Maybe something to do with Rachel and Jimmy. That is, if you were the kind of woman who wanted to settle down like your best friend's about to do. So are you, Lilly? Are you *that* kind of a woman? Happily ever after, white picket fences and kids?"

"I *am* settled down," she snapped. "And my life was going very nicely until you refused to pay your parking fine. Now look at it." She picked up the bag of clothes and pulled out her spandex pants. "I'll be wearing these tonight on a covert mission to seduce information from a mayor who may, or may not, be corrupt." Grabbing the stilettos. "Just look at these—I can't even walk in them. They don't work and it's all your fault, Mike. Every single time we get together I end up with something that doesn't work, and I just don't want to do that anymore."

He picked up the shoes, arching his eyebrows. "Sometimes the detours are better than the original directions we plan."

"Maybe for you," she grumbled, yanking the shoes away from him. "But my detours get detoured and just when I think I'm making the best of it somebody throws another orange barrel into the road and there I go again, new direction, new life."

"Did you ever want what Rachel has—what she's about to get?" He took a bite of his burger, then held it out to Lilly.

Shaking her head and pushing away his hand, she said, "You mean the happily ever after? Once, a long time ago."

"With me?"

Of course with you. Back when she was young and delusional. "Believe it or not, you weren't always on my mind, Mike." But he was.

"So if I wasn't always on your mind, that would suggest that I was at least sometimes on your mind? Right?" He grinned. "In what way, Lilly? Something good? Because we *were* good, you know."

"In bed yes, out of bed we were a calamity, Mike, and we never had the chance to find out if we could be something good out of bed."

"And that was a mistake. My mistake," he said quietly. All pretense and mischievousness dropped from his face. He was reflective, and reflective became dangerous and sensual. She remembered that look from before—it came just before the kiss. His eyes went soft, his smile gentle. Then she melted. He knew it, she knew it. It always worked. And always at that exact moment they were definitely something good, but afterward, in the other moments... Those were the moments she had to hold on to, no matter what else was going on inside her, and as he studied her now, and as she studied him, there was so much going on inside. Need, want...love. No, not love. She didn't love him, couldn't love him. Not again. But his eyes...so soft on her. Eyes so easy to love, eyes she was scared to love again.

Suddenly she was melting. Dear lord, how she didn't want to...and how she did.

Mike leaned across the table, raising his hand to brush her cheek, and Lilly surrendered to him, shivering at his tender touch. "Why were we always so good at this and nothing else?" she asked, snaking her hand around his neck. The moment was going to happen, had to happen. No fighting, no pulling back.

Moving onto Mike's lap, Lilly surrendered quickly into the lure of his lips. So soft and gentle, it was the kiss of a man who wanted to be remembered, the kiss of a man she wanted to remember. Constrained passion and courtly consideration, this kiss was meant to be nothing more. And it so easily could have been more. But this time it was a prelude, intended as a beginning—their last beginning, however it turned out. Lilly understood that, and felt her heart pounding hard.

As the kiss slipped away from them, Lilly didn't slide off his lap right away, didn't back away from him and say never again. Instead, she curled into Mike's arms and stayed there quietly as he stroked her hair. "Maybe the reason we're so good at this and nothing else," he said, his voice raspy, "is that we've never tried anything else."

If it's Saturday evening, that must mean spandex and stilettos

"I THINK ALL YOU HAVE TO do is show up and he'll be seduced." Rachel looked at her new black leather mini in the full-length mirror, then turned back around to Lilly, who was strapping on her stilettos. "He's a man, isn't he?"

"I kissed him," Lilly said, standing, trying to find her balance.

"Yuck. I thought you weren't going to go that far. I mean, Lilly, my heavens, that tooth. How did you ever—"

"Mike. I kissed Mike." Tottering over to the closet, she rummaged for a scarf, jacket, anything to cover up the low-necked, way-too-tight top she'd bought. It was a size five and she'd have sworn she'd picked out a nine. "And this time it was...different. Like it was our first time, or maybe our last. I don't know. But it wasn't like anything we've done before."

"And how would you feel if that was your last kiss?" Rachel twisted the skirt into place and smoothed it over her bottom. "Think this will work on Jimmy?" she asked.

"What I think is that Jimmy loves you and it doesn't matter what you wear. And I don't know how I'd feel if this was my last time with Mike. I mean, the one thing I've known for years is that I hated him."

"And you know what they say about love and hate."

"But I always thought it was hate-hate, not love-hate."

"So you were wrong."

"Or not."

Rachel smoothed down her midriff T-shirt and checked for bra bunches. "Am I all smooth?" she asked. "And you were wrong, Lil, whether or not you'll admit it. It's love-hate, with an emphasis on the love. You don't see unsightly lumps on me anywhere, do you? Twisted thong, cellulite?"

"You're perfect, Rach." And too perceptive. And the only unsightly lump in the room was the one Lilly got in the pit of her stomach every time Mike's name intruded into the conversation, or her head.

Rachel wrinkled her nose as she checked out her back view in the mirror. "Think leather makes me look too trashy for a third-grade teacher?"

"Only if you dress like that for your third graders." Lilly stood and tried out her shoes. After a couple of steps, a couple of ungraceful wobbles, she finally stopped and just looked down at them. "Think I could get away with something a little less risky?"

"Just don't bend over and look at them when you walk. Head up, chest out...."

"Easy for you to say," Lilly said, looking down her too-tight top, the top Tannenbaum would be looking down in a manner of minutes. "Did you switch my sizes at the store, by the way?" Lilly tottered on over to the mirror, bumped Rachel away from it and took another look. Not bad, actually. A little closer to the fashion edge than she normally liked. And definitely wasted on the seducee, but overall not a bad bundle for someone who spent her days cloaked in a robe three sizes too big.

"Maybe. But you really should be in a seven—a nine fits too well. You need some underfitting, if you know what I mean. Something to accentuate, instead of merely cover."

"Well, you underfitted me in a five and I can't breathe."
Lilly ran a brush through her hair, deciding to leave it down
and wild.

"And it looks fabulous. Mike will love it."

"Except that I'm going out with the mayor. And it doesn't
matter what Mike likes."

"Well, if Mike likes it, and he's a man who can get women,
I'm sure the mayor will, too, since he's a man who can't."

"You scare me, Rach, with that kind of logic."

"At least my third graders act on it when they fall in love.
They hit each other, throw things…wait, that's you and Mike.
Hello, Lilly. Get a clue."

Lilly tottered back over to her bed and dropped down on it.
"So you're accusing me of third grade love?"

"Just love, girlfriend. Pure and simple." Plopping down
next to Lilly, Rachel put on a pair of stilettos identical to
Lilly's. "I know you mean it when you say you hate him,
sweetie, but you do love the guy, whether or not you'll admit
it, and everything else flies out the window when you two are
together. It's always been that way."

"I don't love him," Lilly snapped.

Rachel stood up, pulled Lilly to her feet, and they both tee-
tered and tottered over to the door, together. "You've never
loved anybody *but* him, Lilly." Both took off their stilettos before they tackled the stairs.

12

And then came Saturday night with the dreaded date

THE DINER ACROSS THE street from the cement factory was everything Lilly expected. Called Dolly's, it was old, worn and cheap—the kind of place where Lilly expected the cracked vinyl seats in the booth to snag her spandex while she slid in across from the dithering, practically salivating Lowell Tannenbaum. He'd edged over to make room for her next to him, but she'd relinquished the chance to hunker in hip to hip, preferring to stay at a cautious arm's length, even if that did mean glancing over at him from time to time.

"Meat loaf tonight," he mumbled, handing her a greasy menu.

She nodded, smiling, not sure if he'd ordered it for her already or if he was merely describing a physical infirmity of some sort. The former was okay, the latter she didn't even want to think about.

Dolly's was practically deserted, except for a couple of people seated at opposite ends of the counter—both eating pie—and a peculiar-looking older woman slumped in the corner booth smoking...was that a cigar? Most of the tables were stacked with dirty dishes in need of bussing by the amply bosomed, platinum-haired waitress who was apparently trying to fix the coffeemaker by pounding on it with her fist. And the air hung heavy with the odor of grease—grease that not only smelled bad, but also left a dull film on pretty much everything in the place.

"Meat loaf," Lilly mumbled.

"I always try to get in here when they have their meat loaf special."

Scintillating conversation, she thought. Well, not scintillating so much as terminally tedious. And she'd been here how many hours now? Eighteen? "Maybe I'll try it." Now, that was a snappy comeback. Much more of this would exhaust her. "What nights—the meat loaf special?" she asked, stifling a yawn. This was way over the top of boring, bordering on death by colorless, flat, insipid, lifeless, monotonous and most of all dull conversation.

Of course, boring and all the rest really excited Tannenbaum, because his face lit up like—and she really didn't want to do the comparison, but she had to—a Christmas tree. "Generally every Saturday, sometimes on Tuesday, also. She's moving to another place pretty soon. Cement factory bought this place out for some expansion, so she's setting up in an old roadhouse down the street. Fixed it up, got her liquor license, and I'm happy to say, with some *friendly persuasion* from a friend, the meat loaf's going with her. She's switching it to every Tuesday, though, since the Saturday night crowd is more into beer and wings." Sniff, hike.

He was already forming, in his wee little mind, a second meat loaf date at Dolly's new roadhouse. Here, there, anywhere, he had plans! "So you make it in here what, two times a week?"

Sniff, hike. "Or more. Salmon croquettes on Fridays are generally pretty good, too. Of course, I don't think those are going with her. Being at your party, I missed Dolly's last croquettes, but I'm betting I can use a little of my *friendly persuasion* on that every now and then." He leaned across the table toward Lilly, trying to strike an intimate pose. "I just can't tell you how much I enjoyed our first date together. Well worth missing the croquettes."

"You missed croquettes for me?" Lilly's mind was racing

through the first-date, second-date, third-date guy protocol, wondering where the missing of croquettes fit in. Since Tannenhorny was considering *this* their second, would that be groping on top of, or under, the blouse? God forbid they got all the way to Dolly's meat loaf Tuesday!

"Well, I heard they were a little strong last night, so it's just as well." His nose turned up in abject disgust. "And if I'd been here at Dolly's, then I wouldn't have scored another date with you."

You only think you scored, she thought.

"And I've got to tell you I've really been looking forward to this all day." Lowell grabbed hold of a plastic glass of water to keep his hands from shaking. "Called Dolly ahead of time, had her reserve my favorite booth." Sniff, hike. "The one with a view." And to prove it he grabbed the ketchup-spotted card marked Reserved from its tuck-away between the greasy menu and the photocopied specials-of-the-day sheet.

Another eighteen hours later, at least it seemed like another eighteen, Lilly glanced outside and sure enough, there was a view of a small park area for the cement factory employees. A half-dozen scrub trees in a small green patch about the size of the diner, two picnic tables and a fifty-five-gallon trash barrel—all highlighted by several yellow floodlights, and that was the view. Unless Lowell was referring to Dolly's gravel parking lot, the only other thing visible from the diner window except for the hulking cement factory itself.

"Used to be an *assistant* assistant foreman over there," he said, his voice swelling with pride. "Night shift. Took complete charge on the weekends."

A cement *assistant* assistant turned mayor. Big jump in career, bigger jump in logic. How did that happen? she wondered. Maybe there was something useful in this tidbit. She hoped so, since they were entering their third set of eighteen hours and so far the only thing she knew without a doubt was Dolly's Friday and Saturday night specials. "So, Lowell, since you were so high up the corporate ladder, what made you switch to politics?" Lilly asked, grabbing the opening he'd handed her.

"Just doing my civic duty." He laid his hand across the table, atop Lilly's, and gave her a knowing wink. "Some people are just meant to be leaders, I suppose, and one day one of the foremen mentioned that I might be good at being mayor. Can't say I'd ever given it any thought before. But they were real nice to me—made up the posters I used, let me off work for campaigning—with pay."

"With pay?" she mumbled. "Wow." So what did the cement factory and Dolly's meat loaf have in common other than the mayor? In a roundabout way, this was beginning to sound like the conversation she'd gussied herself up to get out of him. Gritting her teeth, Lilly smiled as if she'd been waiting all evening for his advance. "So, Lowell," she fairly purred through the grimace. "Your company just did that for you out of the blue? I mean, I'm sure it was easy for you, with your background and all—" the words were getting gummy and repulsive, sticking to the back of her throat "—but it seems so amazing to me." Then she did the unthinkable. She twisted her hand over in his and stroked his palm with her thumb. A single stroke, and not even the full length of his palm. More like an inch, a scant inch. And it wasn't stroking so much as dragging, but she did make deliberate physical contact with the man. Her thumb to his palm, and that elicited an honest to goodness moan from him.

Heaven forbid she should look under the table to see what else she was eliciting.

"I guess you could say I was just a man with a vision for my city, and they recognized it." Sniff, hike.

She snatched her hand back. "And that vision would be?"

Dolly ambled over to the table with her green pad, taking great care to avoid all Tannenbaum eye contact, Lilly noted. "What'll it be tonight," she said, her voice flat.

"The usual," he said, giving her a quick glance, then looking over at Lilly. "I'd recommend it."

"Separate checks?" Dolly asked, writing down Lilly's meat loaf special and coffee order even before Lilly ordered it.

Lilly started to shake her head, since this was, after all, a quasi date. But she was blindsided by a speedy Tannenbaum trump. "Yep. We sure don't want to be accused of doing anything illegal, do we?"

Dolly snorted. "Mashed or baked potato? Corn or green beans?"

"Oh, what the heck. Let's go for all of it," Lowell pronounced, loudly enough that even the cigar-smoking lady in the corner looked over at him. "That way Lilly and I can share."

Share? *Not a chance,* Lilly thought, trying hard to look absorbed in all the Tannenbabble. "Could I have water instead of the coffee?" she murmured.

"Anything else?" Lowell asked Lilly, to which she numbly shook her head and blinked the glaze out of her eyes.

Dolly shuffled over to the kitchen and yelled to the cook, "Two specials, mashed and corn, beans and baked." And somehow, Lilly was betting one of those specials wasn't coming with a check, and that *wouldn't* be hers.

"Hope you don't mind," Lowell said, moving his hand back across the table toward Lilly's. "But if someone saw me buying you a meal they might think I was bribing you, or something. Can't have that, can we?"

She watched his hand inch closer and closer, like a hairless tarantula. One finger at a time crawling slowly across its turf, ready to pounce on its prey. She thought about swatting it, or stabbing it with her fork, but instead she backtracked to her original question, hoping it would suffice as a finger-creeping misdirection. "So tell me, Lowell, what kind of vision do you have for Whittier? I keep hearing about the fiscal responsibility platform and I'm curious." Then she gracefully dropped her hand in her lap, while Lowell's unforeseen need to dredge up an awe-inspiring answer forced him to focus elsewhere.

"Fiscal responsibility," he repeated, nodding. "Put more in than we spend. That's what I'm doing, and that's what will get me reelected."

"You have opposition?" First she'd heard of it, but then, she really hadn't been paying attention.

"My old foreman."

"The one who said you should run?"

He nodded, slumping down in his seat. "Guess he talked it up so much to me he decided he'd like to take a crack at it."

Tannenbaum was nervous and dejected now, Lilly thought. Probably saw his mayoral demise, since the cement factory seemed to have withdrawn support for *their* man, and were sending in the second string. Hmm... Lightly nudging the toe of her stiletto into his shin, Lilly opted for the above-the-pants route. "So tell me, with the economy sliding these days, aren't most towns in financial trouble? Especially the small towns without big tax bases? Towns like Whittier?"

Sniff, hike. "I haven't been letting that happen here."

Lilly scooted to the edge of her seat, waiting for more. But he went quiet. Suddenly he was locked up tight and even a little toe creeping up his pants wasn't going to unlock him. She expected more, needed more, and this tight-lipped touch from the Tannenbaum fountain of verbal pomposity just didn't seem right. Not right at all. Glancing out the window, trying to figure out what to do next, Lilly focused briefly on a solitary figure sitting across the street in the employee park. He was on top of a picnic table, facing the diner. Motionless...

And so familiar.

Of course he would be there. He hadn't said he would, hadn't even suggested that he might. But she was glad he was. "Mike Collier's been counting parking tickets in Whiter, Lowell. Did you know that?" She paused, scrutinizing he mayor for a reaction. And she got it!

The stiff little man stiffened even more. Then he jiggled and quirmed in his seat, pulling his polyester button-down collar way from his neck. "He's trouble. I thought he'd drop it nce he got his parking place back. But sometimes you just an't tell."

"Drop what?" Lilly watched Tannenbaum watch Dolly arry two meat loaf specials over to the table. "His vendetta gainst you? His investigation?"

"Mine's the mashed potatoes and corn," he said, way too ager to reach out and grab it. His first bite was practically wallowed by the time Dolly had the plate down in front of im. And for the next several minutes he kept his mouth ull—always chewing. Bite after bite, drink after drink, gulping, smacking—there was no time for a word, let alone the explanation Lilly wanted. And as he reached the two-thirds oint in his meal, he actually signaled Dolly back over to the able and ordered himself another special, just like the first ne.

It's all about the money, Lilly decided as she picked her way hrough the meat loaf. The money and the fact that he was no onger the cement factory's favorite son.

Lowell timed the completion of his first meal to coincide recisely with the delivery of his second, and he actually ate t—every last bite of it—with military precision. At the end, vhen his eyes were beginning to bulge, he jumped up and an for the men's room, mumbling an "Excuse me," through a haze of mashed potatoes.

The instant his heels tracked through the rest room door, he cigar-smoker jumped up and ran from her lair in the corner booth straight for Lilly.

"Juanita Lane," she introduced herself as she handed Lilly a cell phone.

Naturally, it was Mike on the other end. "Got anything so far?" he asked.

Lilly looked outside, saw him wave to her.

"Maybe. Did you know he's not being endorsed by the cement factory for this campaign?"

"Good job!"

"And I need some antacids. Ever tried Dolly's meat loaf?"

"I've always thought it was pretty tasty."

"Then you'll be glad to know she'll be featuring it every Tuesday night at the roadhouse."

"Look, Lilly, ask him how he accounts for the increase in last year's parking tickets by only seven percent, and the year before that a decrease of thirteen percent. Then have him explain the three-hundred-percent increase since you've been on the bench."

"He's not talking."

"You've gotta be kidding?"

"Nope. He shut up and I couldn't even use my feminine wiles to get anything out of him."

"So you're not going to eat the rest of that meat loaf?" Juanita asked, already picking up a clean fork from the next booth over.

"Well, do your best," Mike replied as Lilly slid her plate over to Juanita.

"That's it? Do your best? You don't have a plan B for me?" Lilly snapped, slumping down in her seat.

"Cherry pie's great. So's the lemon meringue."

Lilly clicked off, twisting so she didn't have to look outside and see Mike. "Why do people...you...just do things like this for him?" she asked Juanita.

Picking up Lilly's plate, Juanita winked. "Same reason you do, I suppose." Then she scurried back to her corner booth and her cigar.

Lowell returned shortly, looking particularly queasy. Sliding back in, he eyed the two crumbs left on his plate and pushed it away. "I have some city business that just came up," he said, his voice sluggish. "So I'm afraid we won't be able to make the movie tonight."

"That's too bad," Lilly said, shooting him the best sympathetic smile she could muster. His only "city business" was dodging her questions. Being an attorney and a judge, she recognized a look of guilt when she saw it, and she was seeing it. Either guilt or way too much meat loaf. Or both!

"Really?" he asked, trying to smile through a series of tiny belches. "Your going out with me kind of surprises me. When you first got to Whittier I didn't think you even liked me."

"Jitters over the job, but now that I've settled in I like being part of a power couple, Lowell. You promised me we'd do great things together. Remember?" He was looking like a dog suspicious of the hand trying to feed it, not sure whether to snarl or take the food. "I've had some bad breaks in the past. Didn't get to the places I wanted to go and now I'm ready. All I need is a ride."

He nodded, still suspicious.

"Give it some thought," she said. "I have some ideas of what we might—"

He laughed. "No need for *new* ideas, baby. The old ones are getting better all the time." Sniff, hike.

Lilly watched him swagger on out to the parking lot, then chug away in his junkyard car—beat-up, worn down, no muffler. Ezra was right, she realized. If the mayor was taking kickbacks, he'd have something to show for it. That's the kind of man he was—all self-invested in his own trifling image. And his car was by necessity, not by choice. Meaning if there was a parking ticket scam, nothing was trickling down into the Tannenpocket because the Tannenego couldn't resist a little showing for his efforts. And there was definitely no showing here.

Very interesting!

Lilly crossed over to the cash register, trying to balance herself on her heels and at the same time stomp some circulation back into her tingling left foot. She was handing over her $5.95, plus a couple of bucks for the tip, when the pie eater at the end of the counter winked at her. Another of Mike's friends, she guessed, glancing to the pie eater at the other end, who also winked. Fishing another couple of bucks from her purse, she handed them to Dolly. "Take a piece of pie to the woman in the corner—the one with the cigar. Oh, and good luck with your new roadhouse, in case I don't see you again."

"You'll be seeing me again," she said, her voice lifeless. "Next week."

Theoretically, Sunday morning should be a good time to sleep in

"HE WENT AND TURNED IT into a no-parking again," Mike shouted into the phone. It was seven in the morning. Another weekend morning shot all to pieces, and Lilly didn't even bother opening her eyes while Mike ranted and raved. "He did it overnight, Lilly. When I went to bed I was legal there, when I woke up I already had three parking tickets on my windshield. What the hell did you do to me last night?"

"Except hooking myself up as half of Whittier's new power couple, nothing." She did have to hand it to Lowell. He was fast.

"Well, I won't pay them. You know that, don't you?"

"So I'll throw you in jail. Not a biggie, Mike." And it did have a certain appeal to it. Mike behind bars...again. Christmas in August, twice.

"What did you do to get him moving so fast?"

His tone was a little accusing, she thought. Maybe a little possessive, too. Like he had a right to either. "Slept with him under the table."

Nothing from Mike. Not even an exasperated sigh.

"You still there?" she finally asked. "Mike?"

MIKE HEARD THE WORDS and he knew Lilly was just messing with him. But they hit him hard, a punch in the paunch, and he was almost doubled over, trying to regain his wits. No, Lilly would never compromise herself like that. If there was one person in his world who would never compromise under any circumstance, it was Lilly Malloy. And he didn't like hearing her say that she had. Even if she was goading him.

But the thought of Lilly and the mayor—no way in hell!

"You still there? Mike?"

He heard her voice, but couldn't find his own to answer. So he hung up, then stalked over to his kitchen sink, picked up an old, chipped coffee mug and hurled it at the brick wall. It smashed as loud and hard as he wanted, landed in a thousand tiny shards on the floor as he expected, but didn't give him the emotional venting he needed.

"So why don't you just tell her?" Rachel asked, climbing off Jimmy's lap and wandering over to the storage area to find a broom.

"Tell her what?" Mike demanded.

"That you love her, for starters." Handing him the broom, Rachel returned to the recliner and snuggled back into Jimmy's lap. "That you want to marry her and spend the rest of your life with her. Because you do, Mike. And you've only got two more coffee mugs left, so you'd better do it pretty fast."

"It's not that simple," he snapped. And it wasn't. Their history notwithstanding, there was the simple fact that he was flat broke, tapped-out and living in an unrenovated, unkempt, unappealing warehouse hovel. Meaning his kingdom wasn't exactly Lilly-worthy. Then there was the whole background about trust. He trusted her, she didn't trust him. Simple as that. Even though Rachel had spent the better part of the last hour trying to convince him that Lilly did have feelings for him, the only feelings he knew of for sure weren't anything to build a lifetime together.

Their relationship was all about right now and everything that had led up to this moment. There was never anything about what might be ahead. Not a promise, not even the hint of a prospect. So sure, he loved her. Loved her like crazy—all his heart, all his soul, all his worldly goods, if he had any. Nothing could ever come close to those feelings again, even though he was just now beginning to fathom the astounding little particulars of that emotion. But a fat lot of good loving her would do him if she didn't love him back. Or worse, if she did love him, but didn't trust him with that love.

"Like I don't know that it's not simple between you two," Rachel said. She smiled at Jimmy, her eyes so brimming with love that the words didn't matter.

Mike saw the same look from Jimmy and it didn't make him feel any better. He almost cringed when Rachel brushed Jimmy's cheek with a tender kiss. Happy for them, twisted in knots for himself. "Well, simple's not in our cards, never was, never will be."

"But you haven't tried, Mike. Of course, neither has Lilly. But you're the one who keeps burning her, so you wouldn't expect her to, would you? Except that she did throw herself at the mayor last night because you told her to. Which, I think, is your answer."

"To what question?" Jimmy ventured, returning the tender kiss to Rachel's cheek.

"To whether or not she loves Mike. Because she wouldn't have been wearing those stilettos for the mayor if she hadn't." Rachel raised her leg and circled her own stilettoed foot. "They're not comfortable, you know, and Lilly hates them. So get a clue, Mike. And get it quick, because once she figures out what the mayor's up to, and I'm betting she already has a good idea, she'll fix it and that will be that. And the only thing throwing another mug at the wall will do is cost you another mug. With your finances, I'm betting you can't afford to go out and buy a new one."

"Come on, Rachel," Mike sighed. "Don't hold back. Tell me what you really think."

LILLY STEPPED BACK as Lowell Tannenbaum stepped inside. She didn't want to be alone with him, not in the same city, anyway. But here he was in her house, his comb-over carefully designed into its Sunday best swirl—one somewhat resembling a bull's-eye atop his head—and his tooth all polished up and shiny for a right and proper date. The man was actually clutching a fistful of wilting daisies, her formerly favorite flower. To top it off, it wasn't even nine o'clock yet. For sure, the sleep gods were conspiring against her—no weekend sleeping in for Lilly Malloy. She was forever doomed to early morning calls and callers. "This is such a surprise, Lowell." She bet he was more surprised finding her in a dingy pink-chenille-bedspread bathrobe, her hair pulled into a ponytail so high on her head it looked more like a spewing fountain of red frizz than hair, and blobs of cold cream all over her face. A facial in progress, her Sunday morning routine when she got the chance. And since Mike had already ended any possibility of sleeping till noon, this was the chance.

In her limpest defense, though, since even the mayor shouldn't be subjected to what he was now seeing, she'd honestly thought it was the paperboy delivering the Sunday edition. He was thirteen, which meant she was old and he didn't care what she looked like unless she was naked. But it was Tannenbaum and he actually did have the paper with him. Apparently he was under the befuddled notion that this was still their last-night date, part deux. "I wasn't expecting you." Self-consciously, she pulled her bathrobe tighter around her, and realized it was too tight, since his eyes were popping right out of their sockets as the bulky, fuzzy fabric pulled across her breasts. *Give me strength*, she thought, letting the bathrobe go loose again. The only thing worse than a gawking Tannenbaum in the morning would be twin gawking Tannenbaums.

"I had some news. Couldn't wait to share it with you." He thrust the flowers at her, then breezed on into the living room, plopped right down on her rocking chair. Naturally, he checked her out in her bathrobe as she passed by him to put the flowers in an empty vase on the fireplace mantel. She could feel his hot little horny eyes burning right through the fabric.

"Thanks so much for the lovely flowers, Lowell. That's so sweet of you." My, she was getting good at this. That almost sounded like a genuine thank-you. "Maybe I should go upstairs and make myself more presentable before we—"

"You're fine," he said, then giggled. Actually giggled. "And I did you a little favor already. Thought I'd kick this...partnership...off in a big way."

Partnership? One night over meat loaf and they were partners? "I can't wait to hear," she said, although she already had over an hour ago.

"The no-parking is back," he said, beaming. "Last night. Called in a favor and got it taken care of just for you."

"For me?" She clasped her chest in mock surprise.

"I know about your history. Thought this might convince him to get out of Whittier, especially since that old building of his is—how should I put this?" He giggled again. "About to be condemned."

That one stunned her. And it was going to stun Mike, too. Even a few days out of business until the legalities were cleared up would ruin him. God forbid he should find out what Tannenbaum was doing, because Mike would go right out and do something reactionary like a public confrontation, which would send Tannenbaum skittering into the woodwork—Tannenbaum and the executives at the cement factory. No way was she going to let that happen. Not for Whittier's sake, or Mike's, or even hers. "You did that for me?" she asked again.

"For us. Collier's a nuisance to both of us."

"How ever did you manage that?"

He grinned. "In Whittier, we're all real friendly to each other when it comes to certain things. Someone needs a particular favor, so someone in a position to do it does."

Then comes the payback, she guessed. No-parking signs, building condemnations, heaven only knew what else.

Sniff, hike. "And so on. It's just a way to help a neighbor. And everybody wins."

And somehow that favor got back to her court. "So tell me what you want, Lowell."

"To be reelected. To find a respectable place in the community—wife, kids, maybe a dog. To be someone everybody looks up to."

The perfect life, she thought. Except the perfect life was earned, not bought and paid for with favors. "Would you care for some coffee?" she asked, feeling a need to get out of there for a few minutes. Get out and think about what next to do, and what to do about Mike.

"Black, not too strong. Gives me acid indigestion if it's too strong."

The perfect life *and* acid indigestion. *Dear God, please help me!* Pushing through the doors into the kitchen, Lilly stopped abruptly when she saw Mike already making the coffee.

"How long have you been here?" she hissed.

"A couple of minutes. Why?"

Had he heard? "So were you listening at the door?"

"About his acid indigestion?" He grinned, dropping an extra scoop of coffee into the maker. "You bet I was."

If he'd heard about his building, he'd be scooping rat poison in the coffee, but he wasn't, meaning he didn't know—yet. And she was going to have to keep it that way. "You can't be here, Mike. What if he comes out and finds you?"

"Then he'd be jealous." Spinning around, Mike took Lilly in his arms, his lips meeting hers with a ferocity she'd never felt from him before. The kiss was passionate and blistering and so unrestrained that all she could do was claim even more of it, and she kissed him back with the same demand. In all his moods, she knew the kisses, knew how to interpret them, how to respond to them. But not this one. And it was short, with so much passion condensed into its brevity that it made her dizzy when he finally pulled away from her. She would have gone back for more, lingered there for a second course, but from the other room she heard the faint, fatuous call, "Lilly?" and knew there was to be no more.

"I've got to go," she whispered to Mike, then shouted, "Just a minute."

Mike grabbed her by the wrist before she could scramble away. She thought he was going to pull her back for another kiss, and she wouldn't have resisted. God help her, she couldn't. Not Mike, not anything. But he didn't. He merely looked at her for a moment, his eyes fixed on hers. When he was finished, he gently shoved her in the direction of the door.

"I love you...."

That's what she heard, anyway, real or not.

That's what he heard, too, real or not.

13

Fingernails on the Sunday morning chalkboard

TANNENBAUM TURNED UP HIS nose at the coffee. "Maybe you should try making another pot," he said. "I can wait...got all day to plan things between us. Make plans on what we're going to do with his building once we—"

"Excuse me," Lilly interrupted. The last thing she wanted to do was let Mike overhear that conversation. "I have to go call my mother *right now* and see if she got Daddy's oatmeal right this morning. He's picky about it."

"And he should be," Tannenbaum agreed, giving her the nod to go. "A man has his needs and it's up to *the wife* to take care of them."

"Kill me," she said to Mike, stumbling into the kitchen.

"I'd rather kiss you, if I get a choice." Mike scooped Lilly into his arms, but instead of kissing her, he merely held her—a simple gesture she liked, one she never expected from him. Kindness, support, commiseration, the feel of his arms around her—knowing this was where his embrace began and ended—it was so perfect and so much what she would have loved from him all those years ago.

"We really did mess up, didn't we?" she said, shutting her eyes to enjoy the sensation.

"The follies of youth," he chuckled, pulling her even tighter—so tight she could hear his heart beating. "And the hormones. For us, I think *especially* the hormones."

"So what would happen if we'd only just met? Right now?

Hello, my name is Lilly Malloy and you are…?" There, she'd asked. It wasn't so tough, but it scared her nonetheless, because it hinted at starting over. And this was such shaky new ground for her—falling in love with someone who'd been such a huge part of her life in good and bad ways for so long. Falling in love with the last person she thought she *could* love. Falling in love with the only person she'd always known she would ever love. "What would happen if we didn't have a history, Mike?" Tough question, but the funny thing was, she wanted to know his answer. Up until this moment she hadn't because she wasn't ready to admit that it was important to her, that she needed it. But she did, desperately.

Of course, she already knew her answer if he asked the same of her. She'd tell him that had they just met, they'd be doing what they were doing right now—getting to know all the details, the ones that had never been important before. This would be their beginning, where they'd talk more, trust more. Most of all, they'd put each other first, no matter what. All the tough lessons they'd had to learn in the past would shape their relationship from this day forward. If he answered her question.

But he didn't, at least not in the seconds that escaped before Tannenbaum tuned up his vocal cords and screeched, "Lilly, make sure the coffee's piping hot this time."

As Lilly pulled away from Mike, full of all kinds of emotions that hadn't yet been defined, he kissed her lightly on the forehead and pulled her back to him. "If we'd only just met, Lilly, I'd have only just fallen in love with you."

"Lilly!" Tannenbaum yelled.

"Mike, I—" she choked out.

"Lilly!" Tannenbaum called again.

"I have to go." And she didn't want to. There had never been anything in her life she wanted to do *less* than leave Mike standing there while she went to anyone else, but she had to because if they couldn't work through this problem, there would be no new beginning. She would leave because that's who *she* was, and Mike would stay because that's who *he* was—the final ending for them.

"Something wrong with the oatmeal?" Lowell asked.

"Um...lumpy," she replied, distracted. Had Mike actually said the words that were making her so wistful now or were they merely figments of that little voice in her head—that steadfast patron saint of all things she truly wanted to hear?

"I don't like mine lumpy, either," he said.

"What?"

"Oatmeal. No lumps. Do you cook?"

"My job keeps me pretty busy, so I don't have a lot of time for cooking."

"Well, that'll change when you find the right man. You'll settle down, quit the job, won't you?"

Those were fighting words to a gal who'd fought so hard for a career, and they snapped her right back into the conversation. "When I find the right man, Lowell, he won't mind that I won't cook or do other domestic chores. But if he wants to cook, do the laundry, scrub the toilets..." Opening her eyes, she tossed out a sweet smile, wrinkled her nose, even batted her lashes at him a time or two. "Well, I'd love a man who would do that for me so I could spend more time at the office. In fact, I'd support him, let him stay home and wear the apron. Have you ever worn an apron, Lowell?"

He stared in bug-eyed astonishment, apparently stunned that Lilly wasn't suitable partnership material for him. Oh well, so much for domestic bliss. Lilly furthered her taunt on that happy note—wrapped it around his neck like a noose and began tightening it. "And you know, Lowell, with the way the parking tickets seem to be coming through lately, I'll be needing that extra time. Three hundred percent more since I took over—that's some pretty hefty illegal parking. And I've noticed some of the same people keep coming back, over and over." She wrinkled her nose at him again. "Interesting, isn't it?"

Lowell squirmed in his chair, began scooting to the edge. "I wouldn't know about your caseload," he muttered, so ill at ease his neck veins started popping.

"Maybe the no-parking zones aren't clearly marked. But then, once you've gotten a ticket in one, you wouldn't park there again, would you? But people do and I can't for the life of me figure out why. Of course, that's good for Whittier, isn't it? All that money coming in, all that fiscal responsibility? Good for your campaign, too, especially since the cement factory has withdrawn its support."

Bingo! That one hit home. He was getting a nervous twitch in his left eye.

"Guess people are just too busy to pay attention," Tannenbaum tittered. Sniff, hike, twitch. Right at the edge of his chair now, he overshot the mark, tipping the chair up on its front legs, causing him to lunge to his feet to keep from falling. Sadly, his comb-over betrayed him at that very moment by sliding sideways from its properly plastered position and replastering its well-greased self into a gob on the side of his head, just above his ear.

"Guess they are." Lilly strangled back a laugh. "You're not leaving, are you, Lowell? Just when our conversation was getting *so* good?"

"Duty calls," he said, running out the door.

Some Sunday mornings it just doesn't pay to get out of bed, and other unhappy tales

"SO WHAT'S HE DOING?" Mike asked from the kitchen doorway. "Have you figured it out?"

"Other than probably trying to cover his butt right now, he's granting favors. Influence peddling. Can't prove it, but that's what it is." Actually, a little bigger than that, since it involved the cement factory placing a mayor in office for one great big favor, which could only be the interstate contract. "And people are paying in parking tickets," Lilly continued. "Because they don't show up on a driving record, and once they're paid, they're forgotten. No harm, no foul. And my court is the most likely suspect, because I have a reputation already. Who's going to look twice if it's found out and it lands in *my* lap? Besides, I need the job and Tannenbaum thinks I can be persuaded *not* to notice what he's doing just so I can keep that job. I mean, I'm an easy mark, and a convenient one for him. New to the job, desperate...."

"I'm so sorry," Mike whispered.

"It's not your fault." She meant that. "Just a whole bunch of lousy circumstances that all added up."

"Almost added up. He wasn't counting on you being honest."

Lilly smiled. "Guess he wasn't counting on you getting so many tickets and making a big deal, was he?"

"Nobody ever accused him of being bright." Mike shook his head. "And I am sorry you're in the middle of this, for whatever it's worth."

"A lot," she said quietly. More than he would ever know.

Clearing his throat, Mike continued, "Anyway, his campaign slogan—Fiscal Responsibility. He'll have lots of bucks in the city coffer come election time...."

"And that's why he's making a big deal about opening the books for everyone to see," Lilly continued. "He'll have lots of surplus money in them, thanks to my court. Makes him look real good to the voters, and he wants to be reelected in a big way."

Frowning, Mike looked over at her. "But the next part is serious, Lilly. Since he's covering his butt as we speak..." He stopped, swallowing hard. "This is where you get off, okay?"

"I think you've got that wrong, Mike. This is where you get off and let the proper authorities take over." They'd investigate, find the real evidence, grab everybody involved. That was the correct way, and the Mike way was to simply blow the whistle and watch the fireworks. "You're going to write the article, aren't you?" Lilly said, even though she knew the answer. "You're going to expose it before we can really catch him because the election is at stake. For the good of Whittier."

"For the good of Whittier." Mike dragged in a deep breath and let it hiss out slowly. "I've got to run the story, Lilly," he said grimly. "When I do I'm betting you'll start seeing a drastic decline in your court load right away. Lowell will pull off his parking offenders, and when that happens, the story is over. I mean, I could still go back and expose whatever evidence we find, but that's not going to have the same result as doing it while it's still going on. So it's time for me to go public. A couple of days, tops, then I have to run with what I have."

"Which is?"

"In legal terms, circumstantial."

"So once a journalist..." Mike was Mike, and let nothing stand in the way of his story. Nothing, including her. "What do I do now, Mike? Just let you take me down again?"

"Not you, Lilly. You've got to understand it's never been about you, and I won't do that to you. You've got to believe me. You won't be connected to this. I won't let it happen."

And she wouldn't let it happen to him, either. This time it had to be her way, and she hoped he had the same trust in her that she had in him.

Some Mondays it doesn't pay to get out of bed, either

"PETE, I'VE GOT THE BENCH warrant ready. Serve it right away and if he doesn't come in voluntarily, arrest him." Lilly signed her name to the piece of paper and handed it to the bailiff.

"I've never done this," Pete Walker said nervously. He

ooked at the warrant, sworn out for the immediate arrest of ne Michael Collier, and his hands began shaking.

"Neither have I, but he's stacked up another dozen parking ickets and I want him in my court this morning. Make sure ou read him his rights. I want everything done by the book."

"Right now?" Pete gulped, clearly more on Mike's train han on hers. "Couldn't I just go talk to him first? Give him ome time to get ready?"

"Right now." Lilly stood, pulled on her robe and went to er desk in the courtroom. Howard McCray, who was happy o fill in for Pete, called the court to order as Lilly looked own at her stack of parking ticket cases. Fifty-four, not in-luding Mike's. Mike's, however, were the only ones she was ooking forward to.

YOU HAVE THE RIGHT to remain silent...." Pete Walker sput-ered.

Mike looked up from his computer. "I'm sorry. What were ou saying?"

"It's in that," Pete said, pointing to the warrant Mike had aid aside without opening. "Sorry, Mike, but you're under rrest. Orders of Judge Malloy. You have the right to re-nain—"

"I know my rights," Mike snapped, grabbing his phone. What the hell was she doing now? he wondered, punching in er private number.

"This is Lilly Malloy," came the automated response. "And this is Mike Collier, I'll see you in a few minutes. Your case s up this morning. If you fail to appear you're in contempt." *eep.*

"This is crazy," he said, hanging up. "Can I at least finish nis article before we go?"

Pete shook his head woefully. "Can't let you do that. She vants you right now and she's not in a very good mood. Said you don't come voluntarily, I'll have to handcuff you." To

emphasize his point, he patted his cuffs. "So don't make m
do that, okay?"

"Fine." Mike hit Save on the list of facts that would add u₁
to the story Roger would write—the facts calling into ques
tion the town policy on parking tickets, along with glarin₁
statistics to prove his point, the one that would not mentio
Lilly's name or implicate her court in any way. He woul
have given up journalism before doing that, and it had take
him all night to spin the angle that wouldn't drag her into i
And he wanted to tell her, to let her know he wasn't doin₁
what he'd done in the past—write first, think later. But h
couldn't, not yet, because she couldn't be involved an
longer. This was his to play out now, his to solve, or take th
fall for. His to keep away from Lilly. And he knew that righ
now she was hurting, feeling betrayed. For the momen
that's how he had to leave it, hoping that when it worked ou
she would understand that he'd done what he had to do—
only because he loved her. Not loving her would have give
him so many easy options, but not loving her wasn't an op
tion. And now, watching Chuck's Wrecker Service towing hi
car out of the no-parking spot directly in front of the *Journal'*
door, he knew Lilly was exercising a few options of her ow
"Wait," Mike yelled, running out into the street, wavin₁
"You can't do this to me. I need my car." Just imagine wha
they could do if they ever got all those options—his an
hers—together!

"Gotta," Chuck called out his window. "Sorry, Mike, bι
the judge called me a little while ago and she said if I want t
keep the city's towing business I have to do this. Nothing pe
sonal, man. Just doing my job. No hard feelings."

"I'll give you a ride over to the courthouse," Pete offered.

"Thanks, but I'll walk," Mike muttered, watching his cε
fade into the distance. And he was still muttering when h
stormed into the court and right on up to Lilly's des₁

crossing over her yellow line. "So I'm here," he said. "What's next?"

"Yellow line," Lilly reminded him, pointing at it with the handle of her gavel.

"You took my car, Lilly. Had it towed, and you know I don't have the money to get it back."

"The only thing you need to get back right now, Mr. Collier, is *you*, behind the yellow line." Lilly nodded to Howard McCray, who was more than happy to hustle Mike back to the defendant's podium.

"Sorry, Mike," Howard said. "But that's the way it is. Got my orders to make sure you keep your distance from the judge." Then he chuckled. "And to keep you from getting another contempt-of-court citation. Guess you already know they can be mighty expensive."

Suddenly, Mike saw the twinkle in Lilly's eyes, even through her jumbo monster glasses. She was enjoying this, enjoying every last humiliating speck of it. And to think that only yesterday he'd almost told her he loved her. He'd thought the words, kind of hinted at them in a roundabout way, and he'd even gone so far as regretting not coming right out and saying, *Lilly Malloy, I love you*. Well, he'd regretted it yesterday, anyway. But today? Lilly was on the verge of throwing him back in jail and there was no way in hell he'd be in love with a woman who'd do that to him, *again*. Or at least *tell* a woman who'd do that to him that he loved her. Which he still did, even though right now he wanted to throttle her. "Don't I have the right to an attorney, Your Honor?" Mike asked.

"RIGHT HERE," Jimmy called from the audience. He stood, gave Rachel a peck on the cheek, then took his place with his client. "James Farrell for the defense, Judge Malloy."

He looked different, Lilly thought. More confident, more official. Happy. She glanced over at Rachel, who was glowing with pride. Amazing what falling in love could do. *Yeah, right. Maybe Mike will have the same love glow after I throw him in jail.*

Why was it so simple for Rachel and Jimmy? she wondered. They met, they fell. Beginning of a beautiful story. But Mike and her—they met, they slugged it out. End of the same ol' story. Nothing simple about that. Nothing even close to simple for them. "You're charged with a dozen parking violations in the past two days, Mr. Collier. After appearing before this court the last time, I would have thought you'd learned your lesson. But it would seem that you have not. So, as a repeat offender, I'm sentencing you to the maximum the law allows—two hundred fifty dollars per ticket." She twisted to address the court. "And for the record, that will be standard for all repeat offenders who come before me with a case I find guilty. The fine and-or sentence will be the same as what Mr. Collier is about to pay or serve. In the event that you're a repeat offender but *don't* come before me, your fine will increase with each parking offense until it reaches the maximum, which is where it will stay until the record is expunged, which, by law, takes two years. So from now on, you'd better be careful where you park in Whittier."

A shock wave erupted from the crowd, and a whole lot of squirming started. "But in the spirit of fairness, Miss Freeman's ready to cross your name off today's court roster if you'd rather go to the cashier and pay your original fine. In other words, I'm offering you a one-time amnesty from the new court procedure I've initiated. After I'm finished with Mr. Collier we'll recess for fifteen minutes in case you choose to exercise that *gift*. Miss Freeman will meet you in the hall and process the paperwork."

Tisha stood, tugged her abbreviated clothes into place and waved, but by the time she got her hand into the air all forty remaining parking violators were stampeding out of the room.

Smiling, Lilly waited until the mass hysteria was quiet before she went back to Mike. "Here's the deal, since I'm feeling really generous." She tossed him a devilish wink. "Twelve tickets at the bargain basement price—three hundred dollars. One time offer. Just like I gave everybody else." He wouldn't pay and she was counting on that.

"And I don't get to defend myself? I don't get to tell the court that my parking place was given back to me, then taken away again?"

"Nope. You don't get to do any of that, Mr. Collier, because I witnessed your car parked in a no-parking zone myself." Then she wrinkled her nose at him. "So will you pay, Mr. Collier, or do we get to welcome you back into the jail?" Juanita was already getting his cell ready.

"I think you already know the answer to that one."

"WELL, MIKE," Cal Gekas said, leading him to the shower. "I guess by now you know what to do." Grinning, he handed Mike a soap-on-a-rope. Grudgingly, Mike turned his back to Cal, dropped his clothes, walked through the foot disinfectant, then on into the shower. *Déjà shower vu, thank you Lilly!*

After the requisite scrub down, Juanita led him to his jail cell, the same one as before. "Can I use your phone for a few minutes?" he asked as she locked him in.

Shrugging a halfhearted apology, she turned away. "No can do, Mike," she called over her shoulder. "Sorry."

"What do you mean, no can do?" Lilly strikes again. "After all we've been through together, you're refusing me?" He tried his grin on her, gave her the flirty little wink—the one that always got him what he wanted, but Juanita just shook her head and walked away. Impervious!

Ego deflated, and bumming out, Mike recognized more of Lilly's handwriting on the wall. It was erasing his touch—the one thing he could always depend on was being commandeered by her, and he was suddenly out there on his own without his basic survival skills. Scary, scary thought, especially while *she* was sitting back there in her courtroom, banging that gavel, exercising his very own maneuvers against him, enjoying every moment of it. "And the blueberry muffins?" he called after Juanita, although he already knew the answer.

"Judge Malloy said no special treatment, Mikey. Sorry, but orders are orders."

Mike spread his bedroll on the metal frame and dropped down onto it. One pillow. One lousy pillow. And no television! Last time it was a matter of principle. This time it was a matter of...Lilly. And he had to hand it to her. She was playing his game, and not doing a bad job of it. For the first time in her life she was protecting herself, striking out offensively instead of being put on the defensive. Big gavel, big bite. Sexy as hell and he liked that. No, he loved that. But then, he loved everything about the Honorable Judge Lilly Malloy, except for the part where she had him cooling his heels in lockup one more time. Hate the deed, love the judge.

So when would she make an appearance? Mike wondered. And she would, he knew, because Lilly didn't have it in her to stay away when there was so much amusement in the form of one jailed journalist awaiting her on the other side of the bars. "Juanita, sweetie, could you manage just one extra pillow for me?"

She managed two, which made Mike feel a little better. Maybe he wasn't losing his touch, after all, or at least not all of it, since Lilly had clearly confiscated her fair share. "Good for you, Lilly," he said, lying back, anticipating her visit.

There's something about throwing him in jail every Monday

"COMFORTABLE?" Lilly asked Mike through the bars.

"We've got to quit meeting like this," he muttered.

"You know why I did it, don't you?"

"For my own good?" Mike stood and walked over to the bars. Her hands were clenching them as he wrapped his fingers around hers. "Or yours?"

"Tannenbaum's going to condemn your building."

"What?" he shrieked. "I'll get that no-good son of a—"

"Which is why you're here. Because you *would* get him. You'd start a riot, Mike. People here love you. They follow you." He looked like a caged tiger, a look that told her she'd made the right choice. "I couldn't let that happen."

"So you're just going to let him take my building. I can't even afford the three hundred lousy bucks to get out of jail, and there's no way in hell I can keep the paper going if he..." Mike stopped, then a sly grin crossed his lips. "You set me up, didn't you?"

"I locked you up to keep you from doing something stupid, like blowing this thing wide open before we had solid proof. You react, Mike. Always have, always will. And this time I just decided to stop you. Jail's a pretty good touch, if I do say so myself." He slipped his hands through the bars, took her hands in his and his fingers were fire on hers, a fire that was already spreading through the rest of her—all from such a slight touch. But with Mike Collier, there was nothing slight. Not her reactions, not her feelings. And yes, she did love him. Heart, soul and everything else. Just the way he was. "I knew you were protecting me, and I'm doing the same for you, because it's bigger than parking tickets and your no-parking zone, Mike. Remember when you told me about the impact the new interstate will have on Whittier?"

He nodded.

"There was one thing you forgot to mention—the cement factory."

"Damn," he muttered, nodding. "Interstate contracts for cement. Right?"

This time she nodded. "That's why the factory backed Tannenbaum's last election, to have one of their own in office to help the process. Someone they could control. But he got greedy. Liked all the little favors and influences that came with the office, so he went out on his own with them, something I'm guessing scared the factory bosses, since he's dumb and had the potential of drawing lots of attention from, say, someone like you. They couldn't afford that so they put up another mayoral candidate, leaving him out in the cold, and he had to invent a way to make his record look real good if he stood a shot at reelection."

"Parking tickets," Mike stated.

Lilly smiled. "Favors for parking tickets, to be precise. He'd do the favors, in turn whoever got the favors also got the tickets that buffed up the city's revenues."

"So you'll let me out now?"

"In a little while. After we trap a Tannenrat."

"A little bit of get-even-with-Mike, a whole lot of strategy. So if it draws Tannenbaum out, what the heck. I mean, what's another few hours? That's right, isn't it? You're not going to make me serve the full thirty?" He pulled her closer to the bars until her face was pressed to them, then bent to place a tender kiss on her lips. "'Cause there are better things we can do in the next thirty days if we don't have to do them through bars."

"A lesson from the Mike Collier primer—sometimes we do what we have to do."

"Yeah, well, I'll accept what you have to do." He grinned. "Maybe even something I might have done. But next time could I come up with the plan? And could it involve you wearing those black spandex pants and stilettos—and me taking them off you?"

Lilly blinked, not sure if he actually did say that. But she really hoped he had.

14

"LOOK, DOLLY, IT'S SIMPLE." Mike paced his jail cell. This was the part where Lilly couldn't be involved, wasn't involved, agreed not to be involved—the part that would definitely get her kicked off the bench, probably out of law altogether. And coercing a potential witness, well, he was going to have to tread very carefully to pull it off. "You tell me about your deal with Tannenbaum and I'll do everything I can to help you keep your new roadhouse. Understand?" He wondered how deep the Tannenhooks were. Dolly was a decent woman with a lot on the line right now, and if anyone would roll over on Tannenbaum, she'd be the one to do it—he hoped. "Dolly?"

Dolly merely shrugged.

"Okay, well, he did have some influence on your getting a liquor license, didn't he? The fact that you got an expedited hearing is in the records." The ones Jimmy and Edith had dug up for him. And sure, this was shooting in the dark, but Dolly's name had turned up in traffic court three times in the past month and it was on Lilly's docket for five more times in the next few weeks. Plus, she'd gone from owning a dowdy little diner to a big-time roadhouse without the proper red tape. As if anybody ever got that lucky without a little help. Consequently, Dolly was wearing a great big Tannenbaum brand on her forehead. That's what Mike's journalistic nose was telling him, anyway. "It was one of the mayor's favors, wasn't it?"

"Maybe."

He really didn't want to hurt Dolly. She was a fixture in the town, the workingman's friend, in a culinary way. Always ready with a piece of pie, cup of coffee and some friendly chitchat. In fact, he'd even been her delivery boy back when he was a kid, at a time she couldn't afford to pay for help, but had hired him anyway because he'd begged for work. "Just tell me the truth, Dolly, and I'll do what I can to take care of you."

She shook her head, clearly exasperated with herself. "That new judge...is she in a lot of trouble, Mikey? Have I done something that could hurt her?"

"A lot of trouble, Dolly. He's running the scam through her court and, even though she's not involved, the publicity will ruin her."

"She's the one you almost did in before, isn't she?"

Mike nodded. "And if I'd known she was in the middle of what Tannenbaum's doing, I wouldn't have...."

"Don't kid yourself, Mikey. You're a straight arrow. You'd have done it just like you're doing now, trying to take care of her...and me. Although I don't deserve it. But she does, doesn't she? Where there's smoke, huh?" Dolly chuckled. "I figured the other night, the way you were watching her through the diner window when she was with him, that something was going on. But it isn't smoke, is it, Mikey? It's fire, and it's about time! So does she know what she's getting with you, other than a whole lot of trouble?"

Mike laughed. "If there's anyone who knows, it's Lilly."

"Okay, but only because it's you. And let me say something first—I never did like him, Mikey. Tannenbaum. Back when he used to come in from the cement factory he always stiffed me on the tip. That wouldn't have been so bad, but he demanded so much service from me. Then he'd leave me fifty cents when it should have been a buck and a half." She paused, drawing in a deep, discouraged breath. "When I went after the liquor license, thinking I could get it right away, like it's a driver's license or maybe a marriage license, where you have to wait a few days... Well, I just didn't know what it would take, and I was ready to open, Mikey. Everything set up and ready to go, then the county commission tells me it could take six months or longer to get a liquor license, that they issue only so many and I'd have to get on a waiting list. They said I could go ahead and open up my roadhouse, but no booze, and that would have killed my business. I would have lost everything, without anything to fall back on since the cement factory bought the land the diner's on for some expansion that'll come on once the new interstate comes through. But Tannenbaum said he could help me move things along faster, and I was desperate. Real desperate. I didn't know what to do, so I let him."

"So he told you what?"

"He told me all I'd have to do is serve meat loaf every Tuesday and get a few parking tickets." She paused, looking down at her shaking hands. "The license is legal and everything. I just got moved up on the list to get it. Anyway, the mayor said he wanted me to do it—get parking tickets—about fifteen times over the next couple of months. It would be easier on me financially to spread it out that way. And he wanted me to go to court on some of them and pay the extra court costs." She looked up at Mike, her eyes full of tears. "He said Whittier needed some extra revenue, what with the shaky economy, and this would be my chance to contribute and still keep everything legal. He said donations get complicated, and it would look like I was bribing someone, but no one would question a few parking tickets. And for that, he'd get things wrapped up for me faster."

Mike sat down on his cot, thinking about all the possibilities of favors for parking tickets in Whittier. Apparently hundreds of them, big and small, all for a little extra cash in the kitty. The new interstate coming through was the first thing that came to mind. That was a big one. The next was revoking his parking space—small, but in the end, Tannenbaum's biggest mistake.

The Monday afternoon someone will never forget

"WHAT DO YOU MEAN, I shouldn't have done that?" Lilly asked, tugging on her robe for the afternoon session. Thankfully, the docket was full of real cases, not Tannenbaum favors.

"For starters, you threw him in jail again. I know we both have a problem with Collier, but throwing him back in jail over parking tickets will draw all kinds of publicity Whittier doesn't need right now. *Publicity I don't need right now.* We're a quiet town, Lilly. We don't want outsiders looking into our business, especially with the new interstate coming through. Do you know what that's going to do for us?"

"They jumped down your back, did they, Lowell? Your bosses at the cement factory. Are they getting a little worried over all the attention you're drawing to yourself...your office?"

"And just what do you mean by that?" he snapped.

"It's illegal, Lowell. Coercion, influence peddling, whatever you want to call it. Really illegal, like in going to prison."

"My word against yours, and yours isn't very good, is it? So I'd suggest that if you want to keep your job, you take care of Collier. Let him out, shut him up any way you can." He grinned. "If you don't, your reputation will be long gone before anybody figures out who did what. Your reputation, your legal career..." Sniff, hike.

"I would, except court's about to go into session, so I can't leave. And Mike's writing the story right now," she continued, not even trying to look contrite. "For a special afternoon edition. Stop the presses for a huge story and that kind of thing. Guess it's up to you to convince him to stop, but I've got to warn you, he wasn't happy about your plan to condemn his building. He's looking for some revenge, Lowell, and you're his target. You weren't smart, Lowell. You were afraid of what Mike would write about you, as well as the fact he wasn't endorsing you, so you were harassing him, trying to flex your little bitty political muscle with him, show him who's boss. Didn't work, though. Men like him don't buckle. They fight back."

Without another word, Tannenbaum ran out of the office, his size thirteens clopping over to the jail as fast as they could carry him. Too bad she couldn't be there for the climax, but Juanita was ready with her cuffs. Punching a number on her cell phone, Lilly said, "Okay," when Juanita answered, then hung up. Three minutes later, as Lilly's gavel banged down on her next session, Lowell skidded to a stop in front of Mike's cell, to be confronted by not only Mike, but Jimmy as Dolly's attorney, Ezra as Mike's attorney, and Dolly.

"Hello, sweetie," Dolly said. "Wanna guess who's not going to be eating any more of my meat loaf? And I heard the meat loaf in prison isn't very good."

That's when Lowell Tannenbaum fainted dead away on the cement floor. That's also when Felix, from the *Journal*, popped in to snap a Tannenphoto to be used with tomorrow's headliner—the one Roger Jackson was already writing on the laptop in Mike's cell. "Don't think he'll be wanting any copies of *that* picture for his campaign," Mike laughed.

Sigh—just another Wednesday morning

LILLY DIDN'T LOOK AT THE ring on Rachel's finger. A modest diamond, but pretty, and she'd been wearing it a full hour now, the last thirty minutes in the presence of a best friend who just couldn't bring herself to look at it yet. "So would you look at it already?" Rachel finally said, wiggling her left hand in front of Lilly's face.

When Lilly did, Rachel dissolved into a puddle of tears. "Do you think it's too fast?" she wailed. "I mean, it's what, not even two weeks, and we're already almost married. Is that crazy, Lil? Am I crazy?"

"Do you love him like crazy?" The way she loved Mike, except for her and Mike... Well, she just didn't know. Their slate was so full, but Rachel and Jimmy were getting a brand-new slate to start with—an empty one with so many possibilities. Possibilities Lilly envied and wanted with Mike and didn't know if she'd ever have.

Rachel nodded, sobbed, then threw herself into Lilly arms. "Sweetie, I really wish you and Mike..."

Me and Mike. He'd broken the story two days ago. Tannenbaum was locked up, the cement factory under investigation, all kinds of people turning state's evidence with their Tannenfavors and, through it all, Lilly's name was only a passing reference, not a focal point. Dolly played out as the local hero, hailed as a whistle blower, with her dedicated—and now very busy owing to all of Whittier's favor recipients—attorney, James Farrell, at her side. And as for Lilly, she'd gotten up in the morning, gone to work, business as usual. That was it. "Yeah, well, things just didn't work out the way I thought they would, which means I don't need anybody to watch my back anymore. So Jimmy can have you full-time now." She smiled, trying to sound light for Rachel's sake. This was her big day, one of the biggest in her friend's life. No use, though, because Lilly was feeling so emotionally stiff that she had to get away from Rach before she dragged her down, too. She had to get out of her house, go to work early, try cleaning up some of the paperwork left over from the Tannenbaum mess, try figuring out the next step in her rumpled life—with or without Mike.

With or without Mike—that was the big question, and a big chunk of her heart right along with it.

The Wednesday morning when even caramel macchiato *doesn't make it better*

EZRA AND LILLY MET UP at Starbucks before she trudged on over to city hall. She wanted a caramel *macchiato* and it wasn't even Saturday. Comfort beverage, although it didn't do the trick, didn't snap her out of her glum mood. Didn't comfort her any, either.

"I've bailed him out both times," Ezra confessed over a plain coffee. "And I'll bail him out next time...if there's a next time. It was for your own good, my dear. Not that you could see it, or would even admit to it, but you're meant to be with Mike, and it's difficult to maintain any kind of a real relationship when you keep jailing him. So I got him out for you. But you don't have to thank me." His eyes twinkled with mischief.

Ezra! She should have guessed. "Well, before I yell at you, tell me, did he know it was you?"

Ezra nodded. "But you weren't supposed to. He said you'd call it a conspiracy, get yourself into some kind of snit over it, and he didn't want what I did to affect our relationship. The man loves you, Lilly, and you love him. And somebody had to speed up the relationship, since neither of you seemed to be doing anything about it."

"Speed up *what* relationship? We busted Tannenbaum together, end of story. Mike's back doing what he does and I'm back doing what I do. And he hasn't called."

"Have you called him?"

Lilly shook her head. "I wanted to, but I was afraid that..." She shrugged. "I don't know. I just don't know."

"Yes, you do know, my dear, and it's been six years. Six years with hardly any progress, and I can't wait another six years for grandchildren. And lack of familial blood notwithstanding, they *will* be my grandchildren, provided you two ever get a clue. Which neither of you seem to have, quite frankly."

"Do you like him, Ezra?"

"If you do, I do, and you do, so I must."

Lilly leaned over and kissed him on the cheek. "I want it,

Ezra. I want everything with Mike, but we have such an extenuating history."

"History, my dear, is just that. History. In the past, over with. You and Mike are all about the future—yours will be miserable if you don't have him, his will be miserable if he doesn't have you. Both of yours will be happy when you finally stop all the silliness and get yourselves together. So that's the clue you've apparently been lacking. Now go act on it while I go back to Indianapolis and await the call."

"The call?"

He smiled. *"The call.* And I'm free all day next Saturday, in case you need a witness."

Will the real Wednesday morning please stand up—finally!

MIKE WAS IN HER COURTROOM when she arrived. Sitting in the front row, typing away on his laptop, glasses sliding down his nose, he barely looked up when she walked in. "Important story," he said. "Be with you in a minute."

Her heart jumped at the sight of him. "Nothing about me, I hope?"

He shook his head. "Everything about you, actually." Then he grinned, finally glancing up. "You and me."

"What are we doing in your story—you and me?" She sat down behind her desk and took hold of her gavel, more to steady her shaking hands than anything else.

"Guess that all depends on what you add to the story after I'm finished with my part of it."

"Your part?"

"Yeah, where I tell you that I'm dirt poor and that's not going to change for a while, and I'm not going to change too much, either, except, I hope, to keep my butt out of jail a little more often."

"And a gorgeous butt it is," she said *aloud.* Not the voice!

"I prefer yours, but that's beside the point. No, actually, that *is* the point." He hit Save on the computer, set it down

nd stood. "And if I can manage to keep my butt out of jail,
hen maybe I can manage to keep it…well, anywhere you
want it." Then he crossed over Lilly's yellow line.

"You're way over my line, Mr. Collier," she warned. "And
ou know what that means."

He took another step, then stopped. "Tell me."

"Well, my part of the story starts with me not throwing you
ack in jail, which means that I must love you." She did, too.
Always had, always would. But it had taken her all these
ears to figure it out. And naturally, she was the last one to
now that it really was love and not just the one thing they
id better than the law should allow. True love, deep and
biding. *And sex better than…better than…* She was waiting for
he voice to finish, but it didn't. Not another word, and she
new it would never come back. From that moment on, the
est was up to her. "My story goes on to say we're good to-
ether, you know. Outside the bedroom. I was always afraid
hat once we stepped out that door, over that line, we
wouldn't have anything. End of story. But I was wrong. It's
nly the beginning of the story, and one that has a lot of writ-
ng yet to come."

"I didn't want to be in love with you the first time we got
ogether, Lilly," he said. "Believe me, I wanted anything but
ove. But that's not how it worked out—at least not for me.
Not even when I was messing up your life so badly it would
ave been ruled justifiable homicide had you killed me."

Lilly laughed. "And I wanted to more than once. Even
nore than once these last couple of days, when you didn't
all me."

"You mean when *you* didn't call *me*?" He grinned, and
ow she loved that grin.

"Guess we both needed a little time at the end of that chap-
er before we started a new one, didn't we? Anyway, Ezra
aid something really profound this morning. He said that it's
ll history now, and history is just that—in the past, over
with."

"And that we're all about the future," Mike continued.

"Mine that will be miserable if I don't have you. Yours tha
will be miserable for you if you don't have me. Ours that wi
only be happy when we finally have each other. He gave m
that lecture yesterday."

Good ol' Ezra! Maybe he did deserve those grandkids, afte
all. "Well, since I do love you, Mike Collier, here's the cond:
tion of your release from my jail, and there's only one cond:
tion."

He moved over to her desk, then leaned down. "And wha
if I don't want to be released, Your Honor?" he whispered
"What if I want to be sentenced?"

"You mean you're willing to accept my sentence this time
Accept it without even knowing what it is?"

"Oh, I know what it is. A little voice told me, and I lov
you, too, Lilly. And I want to spend the rest of my life wit
you, so the answer is yes, I'll accept that sentence and marr
you. And that's a life sentence, by the way, because a life ser
tence is the *only* sentence I'll accept. Mike's law."

"How about next Saturday?" she asked, standing an
holding out her hand to him.

He walked around her desk and pulled her into his arm:
"I was thinking in about twenty minutes, your place. Wi
you wear the black robe?"

Reaching up, Lilly snaked her arms around his neck. "I wa
thinking right now, my office, no robe, maybe the gave
Lilly's law."

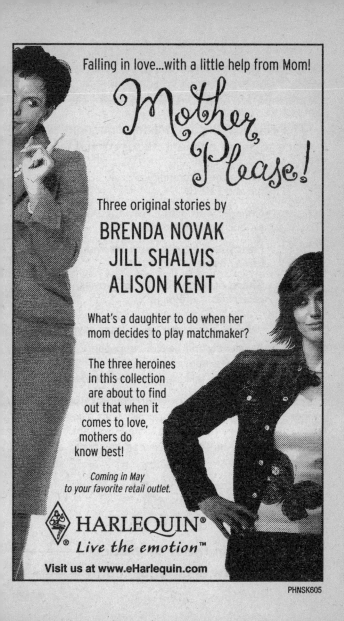

Falling in love...with a little help from Mom!

Mother, Please!

Three original stories by

BRENDA NOVAK

JILL SHALVIS

ALISON KENT

What's a daughter to do when her mom decides to play matchmaker?

The three heroines in this collection are about to find out that when it comes to love, mothers do know best!

Coming in May to your favorite retail outlet.

HARLEQUIN®
Live the emotion™

Visit us at www.eHarlequin.com

PHNSK605

eHARLEQUIN.com

The eHarlequin.com online community is *the* place to share opinions, thoughts and feelings!

- Joining the community is easy, fun and **FREE!**

- Connect with **other romance fans** on our message boards.

- Meet your **favorite authors** without leaving home!

- **Share opinions** on books, movies, celebrities…and *more!*

Here's what our members say:

"I love the friendly and helpful atmosphere filled with support and humor."
—Texanna (eHarlequin.com member)

"Is this the place for me, or what? There is nothing I love more than 'talking' books, especially with fellow readers who are reading the same ones I am."
—Jo Ann (eHarlequin.com member)

Join today by visiting
www.eHarlequin.com!

INTCOMM

**A brand-new story from the _USA TODAY_
bestselling series, The Fortunes of Texas!**

SHOTGUN
Vows

by award-winning author
TERESA SOUTHWICK

After one night of indulgent passion leaves Dawson Prescott and
Matilda Fortune trembling—and married!—they must decide if
their shotgun vows have the promise of true love.

Look for _Shotgun Vows_ in May 2004.

The Fortunes of Texas:
Membership in this family has its privileges…and its price.
But what a fortune can't buy, a true-bred Texas love is sure to bring!

Where love comes alive™

Visit Silhouette at www.eHarlequin.com

PSSV

If you enjoyed what you just read,
then we've got an offer you can't resist!

Take 2 bestselling love stories FREE!

Plus get a FREE surprise gift!

Clip this page and mail it to Harlequin Reader Service®

IN U.S.A.	IN CANADA
3010 Walden Ave.	P.O. Box 609
P.O. Box 1867	Fort Erie, Ontario
Buffalo, N.Y. 14240-1867	L2A 5X3

YES! Please send me 2 free Harlequin Flipside™ novels and my free surprise gift. After receiving them, if I don't wish to receive anymore, I can return the shipping statement marked cancel. If I don't cancel, I will receive 2 brand-new novels every month, before they're available in stores! In the U.S.A., bill me at the bargain price of $4.24 plus 50¢ shipping & handling per book and applicable sales tax, if any*. In Canada, bill me at the bargain price of $4.94 plus 50¢ shipping & handling per book and applicable taxes**. That's the complete price—what a great deal! I understand that accepting the 2 free books and gift places me under no obligation ever to buy any books. I can always return a shipment and cancel at any time. Even if I never buy another book from Harlequin, the 2 free books and gift are mine to keep forever.

151 HDN DU7R
351 HDN DU7S

Name	(PLEASE PRINT)	
Address	Apt.#	
City	State/Prov.	Zip/Postal Code

 * Terms and prices subject to change without notice. Sales tax applicable in N.Y.
** Canadian residents will be charged applicable provincial taxes and GST.
   All orders subject to approval. Offer limited to one per household and not valid to current Harlequin Flipside™ subscribers.
   ® and ™ are registered trademarks of Harlequin Enterprises Limited.   FLIPS03

**Lovemaking this good
should last forever…**

New York Times
bestselling author

VICKI LEWIS
THOMPSON

EVERY
WOMAN'S
FANTASY

Mark O'Grady has a habit of
falling for a woman, proposing…
and then backing out of the
wedding. So this time he's going
to take things slo-o-ow. But
Charlie McPherson is tired of
being every guy's buddy…
and she's determined to prove
to Mark that she's woman
enough to keep him!

*Don't miss this sizzling-hot novel—
look for it in July 2004.*

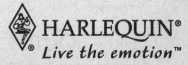

HARLEQUIN®
Live the emotion™

Visit us at www.eHarlequin.com

PHVLT636

**Experience two super-sexy tales
from national bestselling author**

A collector's size volume
of HOT summer reading!

Two extraordinary women explore their deepest romantic desires
in Mallory's famously sensual novels, *Love Game* and *Love Play*.

Catch the sizzle…in May 2004!

"Ms. Rush provides an intense and outrageously sexy tale…"
—*Romantic Times*

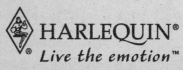

Visit us at www.eHarlequin.com

PHMR635